HOT WATER

HOT WATER

Helen Rothman

D'Oro Press

First published in Great Britain 2001 by
D'Oro Press
19 Mercers Road, London N19 4PH

ISBN 0-9541552-0-3

Origination by
Pre-Press I.T., Weston-super-Mare, Somerset, Great Britain

Printed and bound in Denmark by
Norhaven A/S, Viborg

Acknowledgements

I wish to thank my long-suffering relatives and good friends who gave so generously of their time to read 'Hot Water' and other manuscripts, namely, my husband Tony, Patricia and Marielies, Ted and Joann, Aubrey, Annie and Gidi. Thanks are also due to Edna Fortescue, my chief mentor, Lindsay Maxwell, who took care of the nitty-gritty, Rebecca, who found the title, Luciana Bellasich and Bill Wood, who designed the cover. Special thanks go to my three children, without whose support this enterprise would not have been possible. Everyone named above has been instrumental in helping me fulfil a lifelong ambition – to see my writing in print.

Chapter One

'TEQUILA', as the island was called by its aficionados, lay in a crystal clear triangle of Caribbean Ocean
between Mexico, Cuba and the Dutch Antilles. It was
wooded, wet, and wonderful. Springs abounded and
its patch of rain forest was lush with tropical plants
and fruit. Its beaches were coconut-fringed and the
coral reef, which encircled it almost totally, was still
relatively pristine. There was a distinct Hispanic
influence about the place, which not only manifested
itself in the patois and dress, but also in the cuisine
and the liquor which was distilled on the island. This
potent 'poison' had earned the island its nickname,
and the islanders were proud of it. They had celebrat-
ed their independence day with a Happening which
went down in island history as the happiest, wildest
and most inebriated of all time.

Alas, as the governing body found out almost immediately, governing, like marriage, was not an estate to
be undertaken lightly. While marriage, at least, was
contracted for better or for worse, and divorce an often
lengthy procedure, regimes could be overthrown
without as much as a by-your-leave, and there had
been several sudden changes of government. The
young lions had taken over from the old guard, and
had effectively rewritten the laws which their elders
had laid down. They had decreed that their island
would be a tax-free haven and extradition not a word

found readily in their dictionary. Miraculously, they had been able to curb high rises and pollution. Buildings were restricted to a maximum height of three floors and the importing of cars was not encouraged. Mule-drawn carriages and bicycle-rickshaws were the usual means of locomotion, apart from the somewhat erratic public transport buses which served the island community, the harbour and the airport. The latter had been built with funds generously provided by the big brothers across the ocean, but as part of the funding had mysteriously found its way into the subcontractor's pocket, the runways could not be completed to specification, and remained too short for large jets to land. The subcontractor not only satisfied his cupidity but had also prevented the island from being overrun by eager tourists, looking for cheap holidays.

As Minister for the Environment in his spare time, Juan-Pedro Del Rey was justly proud of his achievement, and went under the nickname of 'Two birds one stone Fellah'. His brother Juan-Pablo had earned the title 'Three birds one stone Fellah' for more ingenious exploits. Juan-Batista, the third brother, was no big stone thrower and was not in the same league.

Big Daddy, however, had got any number of birds with one stone in his prime. Competition was rife between the progeny of the elder statesman. He had fathered a female and three males who were all, in their own way, vying for the heir apparent title. The sons had obliged him to retire to his pink marble-clad villa, from where he watched the proceedings through the somewhat jaundiced eye of an enthusiastic tequila drinker. He was in his eightieth year and needed the warmth of a young body in his bed at night, and sometimes during the day. Age had not impaired his virility, nor his instinct for making a buck or two, and though his sons had managed to put him out to graze, they still consulted him on matters which they felt needed his experience and nous.

Big Daddy, or El Viejo, as he was called by his loyal subjects, had been kicked upstairs and made President with Portfolio of the island republic. It was a title he had created especially for his retirement. He held court however, every Tuesday and Friday, in his residence. It was a custom his children had not been able to make him give up, and as long as El Viejo did not queer their pitch too much, they turned a blind eye to it. They had stripped him of all but representative duties and the old man had smiled at all their efforts to deprive him of his power. The wily old bird continued to dispense favours and receive them in return, during the audiences he granted, ensconced in an oversized rattan armchair which stood on the shady terrace. He was a huge, powerfully built man with tight white curls on his leonine head. His skin was mahogany coloured and his features flat and broad. He prided himself on being directly descended from the Carib Indians, with a smidgin of African and Castillian blood added over the generations. One of his major assets was patience and he listened patiently to visitors who had come for an audience. He also liked to regale them with his own history. He considered himself as a benevolent tyrant, leading his flock to independence and prosperity. It was a tale he never tired of telling to his captive audiences.

It was on such an occasion, on the Tuesday before Holy Week, to be exact, that he received the visit of one Maurizio Capponcini. It was a meeting which had been costly in time and money for Capponcini to set up. He had kicked his heels for over three months waiting for the appointment. The high-powered business man was no stranger to the kind of waiting game

9

he had been subjected to, having dispensed the same sort of treatment himself. He had a certain affinity with the Hispanic mañana mentality, and prided himself on having out-waited if not out-witted better men than El Viejo. The two men eyed each other warily, trying to assess one another. Their reputations had gone before them but they had never personally met.

"You will take a cold drink, a glass of water perhaps?" El Viejo extended his hospitality to the stranger.

"How kind. A glass of ice water would certainly refresh me. The day is warm, Mr. President." El Viejo fanned himself with a brightly coloured Japanese paper fan. He wore a white fine cotton djellaba with embroidery down the front. He looked cool and more comfortable than Maurizio Capponcini who was already starting to sweat underneath his jacket collar and tie.

"Take a seat, Mr. Cappuccino. Amusing, your name. I believe it means coffee with milk, with froth on the top, in your country."

Capponcini smiled thinly. "My name is Capponcini and not Cappuccino. There is often that very confusion about my name."

El Viejo nodded apologetically. "I will try and remember that. You will forgive an old man for his failing memory." His massive body was framed by the Hong Kong style chair, and Maurizio Capponcini, who could not by any means be considered small of stature, felt dwarfed in the presence of El Viejo. The old man clapped his hands and a young woman appeared at the french windows.

"Ice water, Maria Dolores," he barked and waved her away. "She is a handsome girl, isn't she? Her mother was a Spanish lady who came to this island as an entertainer. A lovely woman with flawless creamy skin and luxuriant long black hair. When she danced, her hair swirled about her like a dark cloud and her tiny feet beat out the flamenco furiously. Ah, what temperament! Never a dull moment with her. I married her, you know, and she presented me with Maria Dolores. My wife left me soon after that. Could not stand the climate. Shipped back to Venezuela and left me holding the baby." He nodded his head sorrowfully. "My first wife was of African extraction," he continued. "She gave me three sons and died having our fourth child Maria Beatriz. You have met Juan Pedro, my eldest, the Minister for the Environment. We are very keen on the Environment here and have a special fund for the preservation of the fauna and flora of this island, as no doubt you are aware."

Maurizio Capponcini listened to this almost hypnotic monologue, and had great difficulty in keeping his eyes open as the old man droned on. Then there was a sudden change in tone.

"We have been expecting your contribution for some time now, Mr. Cappuccino. We are disappointed that you, who wish to acquire building land in a prime position on our most beautiful bay, in order to develop a new 'Club Royale', have not shown more interest in our pet project."

Capponcini reared up and protested. "I have contributed generously I think, to that particular fund. I personally handed it to the Minister of the Environment some three months ago. I was given to understand that the sum was acceptable, and that the acquisition of the land and the necessary building permits would be granted forthwith."

"Ah, forthwith. Well put indeed. In our island patois however, it could have several meanings and applications. The dear boy forgot to mention it to me. How much did he stick you for, Capponcini?"

11

Maurizio noticed that this time El Viejo had not the slightest trouble getting the name right.

"$75,000 US, to be repeated three years running," he said coldly.

The old man sat up and slapped his huge thighs. His breath came out in a great sigh. "Not bad for a start. He's a chip off the old block alright." His bloodshot eyes scanned the visitor's inscrutable face. "So that's what you wanted to see me about."

Maurizio nodded and said, "I can't think what is holding up the completion. Maria Beatriz suggested I come and confide in you, and here I am."

"So, it was Maria Beatriz' idea. I did not know that you were acquainted with her. I understood that it was Juan Pedro who was negotiating on her behalf. I suppose you met at the Golf Club."

"Er, yes, exactly."

"She likes to wiggle her bottom on the first tee," the old man chuckled. "Does it rather well too, so I have heard."

"Indeed, she's getting quite good at the game."

"She's better at holding up the bar at the club house," El Viejo growled. "That girl needs a husband, not a glass in her hand." He stared at his visitor. "Are you married?" The inference was unmistakable and Maurizio Capponcini paled under his tan. El Viejo was contemplating a union between his daughter and the Italian.

"I am, Sir, but my wife and I are separated," Capponcini answered hastily.

"Divorce is a long and tedious business in our country and very rarely granted. We are Catholics, of course."

El Viejo shrugged his shoulders. "Pity; it would have solved the other little hitch which is holding up the transaction. You are aware of the law which forbids foreigners to own land on this island."

"Maria Beatriz assured me that there have been exceptions to the rule. Since the land belongs to her, she thought that we could come to a compromise, say, by presidential decree." He hesitated a little before continuing. "I believe your daughter is a little strapped for cash."

El Viejo stared at him and a deep rumble came from his throat. He picked up the silver knobbed cane which lay by his side and thumped it hard on the wooden deck. "That girl's a great worry to me. She's always broke. I've never known anyone spend so much money in so short a time. Is she taking drugs? Is that what she spends it on?" He banged his stick again and bellowed. "I won't have it. I'll have no drugs on this island. I don't mind alcohol, graft, corruption, gambling, prostitution, or white slavery; I'm partial to a bit of white tail myself. What are your views on that? Never mind. I need a drink. I expect you would also rather have a shot of our Tequila than ice water." El Viejo turned his head and shouted. "Maria Dolores – bring some Tequila with the ice water."

The girl arrived carrying the drinks tray. She placed it by her father's side and waited. She kept her eyes down, modestly avoiding the stranger's glance. There was nothing modest however in the way her pareo clung to her shapely body, showing a generous cleavage. Her thick straight auburn hair fell to below her waist and her skin was fair and delicately sprinkled with freckles. El Viejo's large gnarled paw patted her bottom.

"Pour us the drink, my girl, and then go and look to my lunch." He looked after her benignly as she glided back into the house. "She is the balm of my old age. I am everything to her. Both father and first and only lover. You are not shocked?"

Maurizio Capponcini squirmed and cleared his

throat. "As a man of the world of course," he said, "I know that such things are possible, even quite normal among some of the primitive tribes of…" Maurizio Capponcini tried desperately to think of which tribes they were. El Viejo's roars of laughter interrupted him.

"Let me assure you that 'Tequila's' mores are in no way similar to your tribes, whichever they might be. I brought her up, but she's not really my flesh and blood, although my Spanish lady would have had me believe it at the time. That's how she got me to marry her. However, she had been well and truly impregnated by an old pal of mine, a fine-looking Irish tramp steamer captain. He dumped her here after a monumental fight in which she pierced his hand with her stiletto heel. Maria Dolores is the very image of him." He looked at his special diamond studded Mickey Mouse Swatch, then lifted his glass. "A toast to all the beautiful women in this world."

Maurizio lifted his glass as well and they drank.

"Now you'll have to excuse me, my dear fellow. I enjoyed talking to you, but it's time for my lunch. I always lunch at 12.15."

The visitor fidgeted on his seat. "But Mr. President, my request, you know, for the decree. It's just awaiting your signature."

"You will find a box in the hall, Mr. Capponcini. It is for the benefit of widows and orphans of our local fishermen. You haven't forgotten to bring your donation, I trust?"

"Of course not your Excellency, I have it right here." Maurizio patted his bulging breast-pocket. "In small notes, according to the instructions."

"Well now you know what to do with it. I am looking forward to seeing you again next week at the same time. And don't forget to bring me the second

14

instalment for the 'Widows and Orphans' Fund. I will ask them to pray for you next Sunday."

"I'm afraid I was not aware there was to be a further instalment. Maria Beatriz never said anything."

"That child still has a lot to learn." El Viejo smiled. "Maria Beatriz cannot speak for me or the Widows and Orphans. I am the President of that particular charity. She runs her own show, the Arts and Crafts Society. Of course Mr. Cappuccino, you are under no obligation whatsoever to contribute to any of these good works." El Viejo tapped his cane on the boards. "Maria Dolores, show our guest where the Widows and Orphans box is, and see to it that I get my lunch. I'm starved." The audience was as good as over. "Don't forget, my dear fellow, that I never sign a presidential decree after twelve o'clock, so do be punctual next week."

Maurizio Capponcini dropped the envelope into the box on his way out. He was seething both inside and out. His mint green lightweight jeans, his white lawn shirt and his white linen blazer were damp and wrinkled. He wrenched off his polka dotted tie and stuffed it in his pocket. He walked down the path and through the tall, gold finished wrought iron gates to where his hired Suzuki stood baking in the midday sun. There were tiny beads of sweat running through his thick, just barely grey-streaked dark blond hair. The moisture travelled down the back of his neck and back. It was hot on this side of the island and he peeled off his jacket.

He was a handsome man in his mid forties, who had had the good sense to look after his body. He never drank to excess and watched his calories. He ran or swam every day, depending on the seasons, and had a personal trainer for his gymnastics. He had good strong teeth and friendly brown eyes which gave him the ingenuous and benevolent air of an overgrown teddy-bear. It was a mien he put to good use in his business and his private life, both of which ran smoothly and efficiently. He was the head of a multinational company based in Italy, which was an amalgam of leisure wear, sporting goods, and travel clubs. He had successfully copied the Club Med venture, and found equally profitable and attractive venues, with the accent on more comfort and more luxury than his competitors. The clubs were called 'Royale' and accommodation there was very much in demand. They were more often than not only accessible by private jet or yacht, and always had their own harbour or landing strip.

Maurizio had soon understood that most millionaires were looking for exclusivity and remoteness, yet wanted to be among their own kind as well. Aristocrats were also welcome in their circles if their pedigree was impeccable, as were famous artists and sportsmen. The one unforgivable sin was to be poor. Maurizio provided the location, the accommodation, the exclusivity, and sometimes the company.

He was one of the most attractive men in the jet set circuit, played polo with royalty and had plenty of money to spend. Both men and women liked him, and women found him attentive and trustworthy. He had taken any number of them out to lunch and listened to their tales of woe or gossip. They liked to be seen with him, sipping a glass of pink champagne at the bar which happened to be '*à la mode*'. His wife Domitilla had never objected to these noon-time *tête-à-têtes*, and Maurizio had never made a secret of his luncheon dates. He had gleaned many bits of interesting and useful information that way. Domitilla never made jealous scenes or asked him to desist from these

16

meetings. She felt her marriage was secure and their love enduring.

It was the irony of fate that the last of his luncheon dates was to be the cause of their separation. Now he was here, alone, trying to clinch a deal on a tropical island and he desperately missed his wife, whom he had not seen for several months.

Maurizio opened the door of the Suzuki and swore under his breath. He was not going to be pushed around much longer; there were other islands which might serve his purpose just as well. The screech of brakes on the melting asphalt brought the white camper to a standstill behind him. It was a spanking new American vehicle which had been fitted with dark smoked glass and television and phone aerials. The driver jumped out, went to the back of the van and opened the hatch door. She folded down some steps and invited Maurizio in.

"What are you doing here, Maria Beatriz?"

"I could not wait to hear what Pa had to say to you. Come inside and cool down. I've got some champagne on ice." He followed her up the steps and was grateful for the airconditioning which was running full blast. The camper had been decorated with silks and brocade and a crystal chandelier. A Frank Sinatra evergreen was on her compact disc player. Maria Beatriz Del Rey, though not in the very first flush of youth, looked like a strange dark bird of prey lying curled up seductively on the shimmering cloth of gold which she had thrown over her couch. Her large smoky amber eyes glowed in the semi-darkness and the mass of tiny tresses on her head looked like a halo of feathers. She wore a white lace halter over her small firm breasts and the shortest of short white silk shorts. Her long legs were sturdy, bare and smooth, and her feet broad and calloused from walking barefoot. Her toenails were painted a bright crimson, as were her long and sharply pointed fingernails.

She had always been passed over in favour of her brothers by her father. She felt that he blamed her for her mother's death and had never really taken an interest in her. She had been left in the care of nannies and governesses who had been unable to tame their charge. Whilst her brothers had been sent to expensive foreign schools and universities, her education had been more rudimentary, not to say sadly neglected. Nevertheless, Maria Beatriz had a sunny affectionate nature and a generous spirit which she tended to squander on anyone who was kind to her. It was inevitable that she was exploited by all the wrong people, and had few genuine friends on the island. She longed to be loved, romantically, like her idols on the movie screen, and watched old films on her video, but men always wanted to bed her and not romance her. She had started to cultivate a certain raunchiness, assuming that it was the only way to get a man, *her* man.

"Close the hatch, Maurizio, and pour us a drink." He did as he was told and sat down on the couch beside her.

"Well, can we celebrate?" she asked anxiously.

He shook his head. "He wants another instalment before he signs. Perhaps you have all gone too far this time. I think I'll have to reconsider the whole situation."

"Damn the old buzzard, he's just doing it to keep me short, but nothing's too good for that goodie-goodie, mealy-mouthed paleface Maria Dolores. I hate her, so there." She knocked back her drink and picked up a reefer. "Smoke?" she asked, offering it to him.

"No, Maria Beatriz. Put it away." She stared at him.

"Are you angry?"

"Yes, I'm furious. I thought we all had an agreement. This was to be the last contribution to the island charities."

"Oh darling," she pouted and started to undo the buttons of his shirt. "I'm truly sorry. 'Two birds one stone Fellah' assured me that the old man was ready and willing. My, you are hot and sticky. Would you like to have a shower now or afterwards."

"There's not going to be an afterwards, Maria Beatriz. I'm upset and not in the mood."

"You are the only male animal on the island who's ever refused me. Are you a racist or something? Or is it Aids you're afraid of? I've got condoms, see?" She held up a box of rubbers.

"Maria Beatriz, why can't you take no for an answer. I happen to love my wife and don't intend to cheat on her."

She snorted. "You're separated, so don't give me that bull-shit. You just don't like dark skin; I can tell."

"Don't be ridiculous, I have nothing against the colour of your skin. You are a very fine looking woman, very sexy, believe me."

"But you don't find me attractive. You fancy that little yellow bird Mei-Ling who runs 'ye old dive shoppe' ."

"Why can't you just accept the fact that I like diving. Besides, it has always been my policy not to mix business with pleasure." He tried to extricate himself from her arms.

"How odd. My policy has always been exactly the opposite. I love to do business with friends. In fact, I won't do business any other way, capish?"

"I wish you would not use this mafioso jargon."

She laughed, showing her strong white teeth, and shrugged her shoulders.

"Your father worries about your taking drugs. That's why he is keeping you short."

"Why, the sanctimonious old rascal." She sounded outraged. "You should see his collection of opium pipes. All I do is have a drag now and then. I'm much more interested in making love than taking drugs,"

"Why do you hang around with that crowd? Maria Beatriz, they're bad news. Everyone knows that. Why don't you find yourself a good decent man to marry and have children with, before it's too late?"

"Because nice people like you don't want to hang out with me. Besides, Claudio is quite a guy in the sack. He brought me a toy back from Miami." She picked something up off the floor. "He said my education wouldn't be complete without one of these. It's called a vibrator. Would you like to see how it works?" She pushed a switch and a soft whirring noise came from the object. "I was hoping that you would help me in the demonstration of how it works. It's supposed to be more exciting that way. And risk-free for all,' she added virtuously.

"You are incorrigible, Maria Beatriz. Put that thing away."

"You are repeating yourself, Maurizio. Ah well, it seems that I'm out of luck this morning," she said with mock resignation. "No fun and games for poor little Maria Beatriz today. I suppose you had better run along to your dive shoppe. Don't forget to do the buttons up on your shirt."

"How kind of you to let me keep my shirt, at least. That's about all I have got left since you vultures have been at me."

"Oh you poor man, I feel truly sorry for you. Never mind, I promise that you'll have your decree next week. Don't forget the envelope and don't be late. Pa does not like to sign decrees after 12 o'clock. It makes him late for lunch. The old witchdoctor once told him that it also brings *mala suerte*." She helped him button his shirt and handed him his jacket. "I need that money, Maurizio, for the apartment in New York. I can't live in this camper for ever."

"I don't see why not. It suits you. Besides, the island would not be the same without you dashing around in that thing, looking for trouble."

"Some compliment," she muttered and pulled a long pink tongue out at him. "Get out, before I change my mind and rape you, you pig-headed so-and-so."

He laughed good-naturedly. "Let me give you one word of advice before I go. Try and keep away from that roulette table. I've heard that the wheels are, let us say, slightly bent in the casino's favour."

"So that's why I haven't won a thing in the last couple of months," she shrieked. "That he should do this to me, his own sister, damn it. And he the Minister for Religious Affairs."

"Well he's not entirely responsible for it. Your pal Claudio Curria is a major share-holder in the casino. He runs it. Your brother merely gets a percentage of the profits."

She thought for a moment. "So Claudio gives with one hand and takes with the other. At least that's what you are insinuating. Why should I believe you, though?"

"Just think for a moment. You have a little money, you go to the casino hoping to win some more, but you lose. So you have to go to the bank and borrow some at a rather high rate of interest. Then you go back to the casino, and what happens? You lose again. After a couple of heavy losing sessions, you find you have to mortgage your property, and when you find that you cannot keep up with the mortgage payments, the property reverts back to the mortgage company."

She looked startled and glared at him in astonishment.

"That's exactly how it happened to me; that's how they got hold of my town house on the harbour." she cried. "It's outrageous."

"And do I have to tell you who is behind the mortgage company? Yes, you've guessed right. Someone who gives you lots of trashy presents like vibrators and reefers. So stop gambling and at least hold on to your camper."

Her mouth trembled and he was surprised to see a hint of tears in her eyes. "God, I hate this place. You can't trust anyone, anyone at all," she mumbled. "I'm 35 years old." She squinted at him: "OK, 36 and a bit, to be exact, and have done nothing with my life. All my boyfriends have shied away from marrying me because they're scared of Pa. He always used to insult them and kick them out when they came to call. Don't you think that I would like to settle down with a fellow and have babies like everyone else? But I can't find anyone here."

"Even less so in New York. Keep away from that city, you can't trust anyone, anyone at all, there either. You'd be lonely and a nobody there. Here at least, you are the boss' daughter, never forget that."

She sniffed and slammed the hatch down. "I suppose I am, for all the good it does me, though they say that blood is thicker than water."

"Aren't you being a wee bit ungrateful? After all, Big Daddy gave you that splendid piece of property on the bay and you're going to make a packet when we've sealed the deal."

"There won't be that much left over once I've paid my IOU's at the Casino."

"Have a quick dip into the widows and orphans box. I suspect that it's overflowing, now that I've added my humble contribution."

"It's that sodding Maria Dolores who gets everything

out of that particular kitty. I don't know what she needs it for. She hardly ever leaves the villa and never wears anything but those pareos. At least they camouflage her bottom which is quite unfashionably large and drooping."

"El Viejo seems to appreciate it. You'd be surprised at how many men secretly yearn for a little unfashionable extra flesh."

"I suppose that you are one of them," she asked petulantly.

He shook his head emphatically. "No. I like my women lean, with skinny asses and girlish breasts. Just like you, sweetheart."

"Why can't you ever take me seriously?" she snorted in unladylike disgust. "One day, you'll come to me, just you wait and see, Mister." She turned on her heel, tore open the door, jumped up into the camper and settled herself behind the steering wheel. She twisted her long neck towards him and blew him a kiss. She started the engine and drove furiously down the bumpy asphalt road, waving her hand. He breathed a sigh of relief and got into his own car. His patience had been sorely tried this morning and he was gasping for another cold drink. He drove to the harbour and parked the Suzuki under the thatched roof of the small car park which served the boat owners. He jumped into the dinghy, cast off and made for 'Trade Winds'.

The Capponcinis had purchased a house which was perched on a promontory overlooking the ocean. 'Trade Winds' had been built on the ruins of an old fort which had been erected there during the time of the conquistadores. All that remained of that structure was a restored and well maintained watch tower which had served the previous owner as an observatory. The powerful telescope was still in place. There

23

was a small sheltered bay below, where a power boat and a Boston whaler were already tied to a solid looking jetty. There was nothing to obstruct the view from the vast wood-block deck which was an extension to the house and jutted out over the bay. The sea and infinite horizon flowed together in the distance. The deck was flanked by flowering shrubs and exotic palms, and a well stocked wet bar was discreetly hidden behind an exquisite Japanese lacquer screen. Expensive outdoor furniture was dotted about under the sunroof. The property had been featured in several magazines and had justifiably been described as one of the most desirable in the islands. It had an added great advantage, one which would have been considered a handicap by some people. It was only readily accessible from the sea and was an almost inviolable fortress. The steep rocky path from the jetty was totally exposed and afforded no protection to any unwelcome visitors. Indeed, those who were not initiated would set off an alarm when they started to climb the path and the steps towards the house. It was a very private estate indeed. It had been known to be cut off from civilisation during heavy storms and hurricanes. Its owners had been marooned there for several days in succession, without access to the rest of the island. It was not a place where the islanders generally liked to work and the Capponcinis tended to pay higher wages than anyone else to their staff.

Maurizio frowned as he tied up his powerboat next to the one already at the jetty. He was in no mood for visitors, particularly the one who would be sitting on the deck waiting for him. He opened the door of the wooden boathouse and took off his clothes. He would have his swim first, before confronting the visitor. He dived off the jetty into the deep water with hardly a splash and swam to the edge of the frothing reef. The *passe* was just wide enough to let small powerboats through, and no larger vessels ever attempted to enter the bay. Maurizio swam energetically back to the jetty, shook off the water, grabbed the multicoloured towel, and wrapped it around himself as he climbed the steps to the terrace. He kicked off the concealed alarm with the tip of his toe and made his way to the house. At the top of the steps he set the alarm again and went to the bar, ignoring his visitor who was sitting on the rocker, gently swaying to and fro.

"You're late, Capponcini. I've helped myself to a drink as you can see." Maurizio shrugged his shoulders and held out his hands.

"You've helped yourself to almost everything else I have. What do you want now?"

"There is no need to be so aggressive, Capponcini. I merely came to find out if you've finally managed to push your deal through." Maurizio pulled a can of beer from the refrigerator and poured it into a long tumbler. "None of your damned business," he muttered and drank the ice cold lager.

"On the contrary, I have a vested interest in the successful denouement of your venture. Once you've signed and paid for the property, Maria Beatriz will be able to repay her debts. The sum she owes me is quite substantial and my patience is running out."

"So what are you going to do about it? Slash her face or break her fingers? Or choke her with the vibrator?"

Claudio Curria stretched his arms and laughed. "So she showed it to you, did she? I suppose she waylaid you to find out about the dough."

"Why can't you leave the girl alone? Stop filling her head with all this business of living it up in New York."

"Why the hell should I give up a potential goldmine?

25

She's going to earn me a fortune in the Big Apple. She just needs a little more experience, a little more polish, and she'll be the hottest lay in town. For a price of course. A very large price. The beauty of it is that she actually likes sex. Can't get enough of it. You know what she's like. Or do you?"

"No, I do not know what she's like, and I can't think what she sees in a little shmuck like you."

"It's the way I use it that counts, my friend," Curria grinned. "But we've gone off at a tangent. Has El Viejo agreed to issue the decree?"

"He'll sign next week."

"That means that he'll squeeze some more out of you. I don't know what you want to do all this club business for. There's much more money in drugs, believe me."

"I believe you alright but I despise drugs and everything to do with them. Including you and your gang." The smile was suddenly wiped off Curria's face.

"I would watch my language if I were you, Capponcini. There's a lot you've done that you can't be very proud of."

"I did no more than any other businessman in Italy," Maurizio said hotly.

"That's no excuse, is it?" Claudio Curria wagged his finger at his host. "Most of the others are either in jail or confined to their homes. You are one of the lucky ones. They have not been able to pin anything on to you yet." He rose from the chair. "We got you out of la bella Italia in the nick of time because we look after our own, you ungrateful bastard. You'd be under house arrest by now, if we had not spirited you out. So stop all this despising."

"I am not one of your own, I never shall be," Maurizio shouted.

"You can yell all you like, but your wife asked us for help and we gave it."

"I know, I know, that's what you say, but she never consulted me, did she? I don't even know whether it's true."

"That's your version, is it?"

"Oh, what's the use." Maurizio said bitterly.

"None that I can see. There is a shipment coming in tonight, by the way."

"But I've invited guests for dinner," Maurizio protested.

"Cancel it. We can't afford to have any hitches."

"You should give me more notice. It could arouse suspicion."

"We expect your full cooperation at all times, so stop arguing and start preparations." Maurizio watched the Sicilian American go nimbly down the path and get into his boat. Curria gunned the engine and brought the boat about in a foaming swathe. He disappeared around the cliffs and all was quiet again. Maurizio padded into the house and had a shower.

The day had started badly and showed no signs of improving. He put on a caftan and went into the kitchen where a pleasant looking woman was busy at the sink. He investigated the contents of the fridge. The cook had left an attractive looking salad platter for him, prior to taking off in the staff boat for the day's shopping. The staff came and went every day with the staff boat. Maurizio kept no living-in staff. It would have interfered too much with the drops that Curria arranged.

Maurizio sat down at the perfectly laid table. A single shocking pink, double petalled hibiscus was floating in a Lalique bowl, and the Vietri dinner service with which the table was laid gave him the same pleasure as when he and Domitilla had first chosen it for their island house. The woman came out of the kitchen carrying a basket of fresh baked bread and a tureen of chilled soup.

"Cook is bringing in some red snapper for dinner tonight. They phoned from the harbour. I thought we might serve some ratatouille with it, and buttered potatoes. The avocados are just ready for eating Cook says, and she'll prepare them with a sharp mustard dressing for first course. There'll be little salmon canapes with drinks." The woman ladled out the soup and continued. "Still ten for dinner tonight, Sir?"

Maurizio shook his head. "No, Clemmie, I'm about to cancel tonight. I don't feel very well. Must have an upset stomach."

"Then perhaps you should not have that soup. There is cream in it." She made a movement towards his plate.

"Hey, I don't feel that bad. Soup is good for one. It's a well known fact."

"Mr. Rosenberg used to say that, but it was always chicken soup, not Vichyssoise. That was before he sold you this house. Mr. Curria used to come here and pester the life out of him too, poor old man. This Curria still comes here as if he owns the place. He's a cheeky one. Mr. Rosenberg used to say that the man was a ganef full of hutzpah. That means a thief full of cheek, Mr. Rosenberg used to tell me. The staff don't like this Curria fellow at all, he makes them nervous. Besides, he's never once given us a decent tip. I wonder how Mr. Rosenberg is keeping. He never once wrote, not even a postcard."

Maurizio remained silent and continued to eat. "Do I still tell Maria Philomena to make up the pink guest room for Miss Mei-Ling?" He ignored the question. Dinner guests often spent the night at 'Trade Winds'. It was foolhardy to try and negotiate the *passe* at night after a few drinks. "Very well, Sir. I don't know what Missus will think of that, but after all a man cannot be left on his own for ever." She smiled broadly and wagged her finger.

"You are so right, Clemmie, I do get lonesome some-times. You can all knock off early today. I'll manage on my own tonight. Cook can prepare the fish and I'll barbecue it." The housekeeper chuckled and left him to finish his lunch. It did no harm to let the staff think that he was having a little extramarital relation with the diving instructor. It would explain the motorboats coming and going out of the cove at night, if there should be any inquisitive eyes abroad. Maurizio often wondered whether the coast-guards deliberately didn't patrol the coast line on the 'Trade Winds' side. The mini sub which regularly reared its head at the side of his dock remained undetected.

Only a handful of people knew that there was an underground passage which had been hewn through rock at the end of a shallow cave on the property, and was the only other way to reach 'Trade Winds'. The passage had been there for a long time, probably as an escape route in case of a hurricane, or an ancient smug-glers route. It terminated in a dense cluster of mango trees a stone's throw away from the asphalt road which led to the township of Sta. Lucia. One of Curria's henchmen had come across it quite by chance when he had seen a pair of nesting gulls disappear into the thickets by the boat house. He had watched them with his binoculars and then searched the thicket for the nest. He not only found a trio of very hungry fledglings, but also the narrow entry to the passage. He had crawled through it, brushing away the spiders' webs and braving the glinting red eyes of a group of rats which had chosen it for their home. Fortunately for the intruder, they were even more frightened at the appear-ance of the stranger in their midst than the stranger who found them when he shone the torch about him. He loathed rodents but steeled himself to continue to the end of the tunnel, disturbing a mongoose which scampered away, leading him to where the faintest glimmer of daylight marked the exit of the passage.

The discovery of this secret passage by Curria's man was old Rosenberg's undoing. This, and the fact that the old man had accidentally seen Curria's motor boat loading some cargo at sea, had sealed his fate. The powerful telescope had let Rosenberg into a most dangerous secret, a secret which constantly endangered his life. Curria as good as took over 'Trade Winds', intimidating the old man ceaselessly, urging him to sell the property to Curria's consortium, if he knew what was good for him. Rosenberg decided to sell, but to Curria's chagrin, managed to get another client. It happened to be Maurizio Capponcini, owner and managing director of the Royale Leisure Co. who moved into 'Trade Winds'.

The Capponcinis had been completely captivated by 'Tequila' and had immediately started to prospect for a suitable venue for a new club. It had not taken them more than a day to find the ideal spot. The stretch of pure white sand and the small reef which rendered a sheltered anchorage in the crook of the bay was perfection. The coconut palms, the cacti, the mango and acacia trees which wooded the hills behind, would afford privacy to the villas, and the scrubland beyond was just crying out to be turned into an easy 9 hole golf course. A spring ran out to the sea bearing pure clear water. There was only one hitch; the exorbitant price demanded by the owner. Negotiations were started, but did not come to fruition. The Capponcinis decided to bide their time, and spent several weeks at 'Trade Winds', getting to know the locals. They threw a number of parties and were honoured by the attendance of the ruling hierarchy, the few white property owners, and the

Diplomatic Corps. Domitilla was a perfect hostess who knew how to set a table, and thought nothing of flying in certain goodies from Paris and New York. The Capponcinis and their parties grew immensely popular, and invitations to their house were coveted.

There was a mixed population on the island. Apart from the indigenous Carib-Africans, and white property owners who came to spend holidays, there was a small Chinese community which was not very gregarious. They tended to remain pretty much isolated from the rest of the islanders. The only supermarket was run by an immigrant Chinese family which had been established over several generations. They also owned a sports and clothes shop and a jewellery boutique which surprisingly enough could muster some good stones and execute special orders. They had never married into the local Carib-African community, but had imported their brides and bridegrooms from the Far East and the west coast of the US. Nevertheless the three communities lived on reasonably friendly terms. The Caribs were not interested in commerce, and the Chinese wanted no part in politics and government. The whites were mostly out for a good time, except for a handful of Italians and Italo-American businessmen.

They had been the very first of the new breed of businessmen to arrive when the island gained independence. They had not had a difficult job in persuading the Minister for Religious Affairs, 'Three birds one stone Fellah' Juan Pablo Del Rey, to grant them a gambling licence. It was renewable every two years at an undisclosed premium. El Viejo Del Rey, President and Prime Minister, loved gambling and loved winning even more. Claudio Curria saw to it that El Viejo was rarely disappointed. Curria always played at the same table as the President and skilfully managed to increase the pile of chips in front of El Viejo. El Viejo's daughter Maria Beatriz, however, did not benefit from the same treatment. The casino staff was under strict instruction to bleed her. She had already lost her town house, pawned her jewellery and was now desperate to sell the rest of her land to the highest bidder. The Royale Leisure Group had secured the property and was now waiting for the presidential decree necessary to finalize the purchase. Had it not been for the dark storm clouds hanging over the Group and its principal shareholder and managing Director, Maurizio Capponcini, there would have been no happier prospect for the Capponcinis.

Maurizio sat in the twilight nursing a Vodka Tonic. He loved the happy hour and sunsets were always spectacular at 'Trade Winds'. When the last ray had disappeared he lit the hurricane lamps on the deck and waited for the telephone to ring. Domitilla Capponcini called every Tuesday from Milan. She never called from their splendid apartment which she had inherited from her mother in the via Paleocapa. They had established that their instrument was tapped so that she was obliged to use public telephones at hotels, restaurants or railway stations. Sometimes she used the phone of friends where she was invited to dinner, or the beauty salon where she spent several hours a week. He looked at the luminous dial on his wristwatch. It was time. He held out his hand towards the phone and it rang as he touched it. It was a game he played every week.

"Ciao amore, what's new?"

"Not a lot."

"You sound depressed. I thought you'd be uncorking the champagne."

"The signing has been postponed again till next

week. The 'Widows and Orphans' Fund had to have their whack. I wonder what they will think of next." He could barely conceal his irritation. "Let's change the subject," he continued. "What's new in Milan?"

"Things are hotting up even more. The big noise of the Banca Magnani has come under investigation. His passport has been confiscated and he's under house arrest. The bank's dealings are being scrutinized. Can this affect us in any way?"

"You can bet our bottom Lira that it can."

"We're not going to be short of money, are we?" She sounded worried.

"*You* are never going to be short of money." There was a hint of bitterness in his voice. "*I'm* the pauper in the family now."

She laughed softly. "That's how it should be. It's the only way to keep you tied to my apron strings."

"How are the children?"

"They'll be coming home from school at Easter. I've booked our flights to Caracas and on to 'Tequila'. When will you be coming to Europe?"

"As soon as Big Daddy puts pen to paper. I expect it will be at the end of next week. I'll be staying at the usual place, so contact me there."

"Will *she* be joining you?"

"Per forza. We can't do without her."

"I like the 'we'. I could have done without her very well, the bitch. And I thought she was my friend."

"Let's not argue about this."

"Promise that you won't sleep with her again. Promise me that."

"Amore, I promise." He crossed his fingers like he used to as small boy when he told a white lie to his mother.

"I miss you."

"I miss you too." It was the end of the conversation.

This time he didn't have to cross his fingers. He really did miss her. Since their official separation they had not seen each other, studiously avoiding any meeting. The Italian scandal sheets had been full of gossip and speculation about their parting. They had been considered one of the few ideal couples in a world heavy with intrigue and moral corruption. She was an offspring of a Sicilian noble house which had been rumoured to have close links to the Mafia. Her dark good looks, almond shaped black eyes, and unexpectedly long slender legs and tiny waist made her a natural for the world of fashion. She overrode the family objections to pursuing a career on the catwalk, and became one of the most sought after models in Paris and New York. It put her into the enviable position of being not only well-born, wealthy, beautiful and young, but also famous. Her wedding to an equally well-known man about town was a fairytale-like event which immobilized Venice for several days. Her wedding dress, her tiara, her vaporous lace veil, her bouquet, were discussed and printed in glossy magazines all over the world. Her husband let her have the limelight with good grace. It was obvious that he doted on his young wife. They skied, rode horseback and flew together. He taught her to fly the small company jet and they often went away alone together on week-ends. Soon she was pregnant and bore him first a son and then a daughter. Nothing seemed to be able to darken their horizon, until the investigations into fraud and corruption in industry and politics began to throw shadows over most of the Italian business community. At first the Capponcinis thought themselves inviolable. It happened to other companies – not to theirs. To friends and acquaintances, not to themselves. As a precaution, Maurizio transferred the bulk of his holdings to Domitilla and rerouted some of the money authorized for the acquisition of a club property in the Maldives to an already well-bolstered numbered Swiss account. He did not intend to be caught napping. Instead he had got caught in a web of adultery and blackmail.

It had happened during one of his cosy *tête-à-têtes* with the wife of Judge Ferrari. Daria had been to school with Domitilla and the Capponcinis often looked after her when the Judge was busy. The judiciary was overburdened and the investigations reached into the uppermost echelons of high finance and officialdom. Daria Ferrari was bored and lonely and fell in love with Maurizio Capponcini, who used to take her out to lunch and mildly flirt with her. She put on a good show of feeling faint during lunch one day and he saw her to her apartment. He took the key from her trembling fingers and let them into the flat. It was deserted. He half carried her into the bedroom and helped her stretch out on the silk coverlet. She clung to him and did not let go. He finally submitted to her hungry mouth and satisfied her writhing body. He was, after all, only a man, not quite impervious to temptation.

He gathered his scattered clothes and found the bathroom. He showered, towelled himself thoroughly and got dressed. He looked at his watch. It was getting on for 5pm. Daria lay spread out on the bed in a daze of continuing pleasure. She sighed and called his name. He smiled and said softly, "Where can I use the phone? I'm late for an appointment."

"Cancel it. Stay with me."

"I'll try," he lied smoothly, "but I promised to meet Domitilla. She wants to do some early Christmas shopping."

"Go into Beppe's study. You know where it is. I don't want to hear you talk to her. It hurts too much."

He walked into the judge's study and turned on the desk lamp. The last of the weak winter sun could not penetrate the famous Milan smog. He pulled the instrument towards him, moving a large file across the blotter. He couldn't help but see that the file was headed 'Royale Leisure Group.' He suddenly felt a touch of sour indigestion, a churning of fermenting wine, pasta and cream in the pit of his stomach and sat down heavily on the leather chair. He started to riffle through the file, trying to take in as much as he could, but he knew that it was a hopeless undertaking. He would have to come back and take his time. He dialled his home number and asked for his wife, fighting off the nausea.

"You're late, Maurizio, where are you? I've been looking for you everywhere." She sounded irritated.

"I'm sorry, Amore. I got held up. Meet you at Martini's in about twenty minutes?"

"Very well. There's not going to be a lot of time for shopping, though. We're going to the Belladonnas for dinner."

"Of course, I had forgotten. Perhaps we'd better put the shopping off for tomorrow. I'll come straight home, Amore. We can have a drink together quietly before we go out. Still angry?"

Domitilla laughed. "No, I've forgiven you, as I always do."

Maurizio returned to the bedroom. Daria Ferrari sat up and draped a silky negligee over her shoulders. She held out her arms to him as he came back into the bedroom.

"Will you stay?"

"I can't, my dear. We don't want Domitilla to become suspicious, do we?"

He sat down beside her and held her. "When can I come back again?" He stroked her breasts lightly. "How long is Beppe going to be away for?"

36

"He'll be gone for three days every week until the Christmas break."

"How lucky for me, my sweet. Shall we say tomorrow at the same time?"

"Oh, Maurizio, so you really do care for me a little ... I'm so in love with you, it's driving me mad."

He kissed her to stem the flow of her words. It was not a punishment strictly speaking, because she was after all a most desirable young woman, but he wished her a thousand miles away. All he wanted was to spend a couple of hours at the judge's desk and read the file.

"So, Beppe won't be home tomorrow?"

"No, no, my love. He only left this morning early. He won't be back until Friday night. So you see, we have another two afternoons for one another without any trouble."

"How wonderful, my little pet; I wouldn't miss them for anything," he said truthfully. "We must be discreet of course. It wouldn't do to hurt Domitilla."

"Of course not, my love. Poor Domitilla, I almost feel sorry for her. You don't love her any more, do you."

"I don't?" He sounded strangely put out.

"Course you don't. You love me. You can't love two people at the same time. I don't love Beppe either. He's become such an old bore and is never here, or too busy to take notice of little old me." She snuggled even closer to him.

"How cruel of him to ignore such a lovely girl," he murmured, and kissed the top of her blond head. "I must run now. Domitilla, you know?" She sighed.

"Run along then, my lover. Are you going to the Belladonnas tonight?"

"I believe we are."

"Oh good, I'll get Tina to seat us next to each other."

"That's not a good idea at all," he protested vehemently and turned his eyes up in despair.

"Why not? I should have thought you'd be delighted to sit by me."

"Naturally I would be delighted, but it'll be too hard, don't you see? I won't be able to control myself sitting next to the most desirable woman in the whole room, especially after this afternoon. Think of Domitilla. She'd be sure to notice something."

"Yes, you're right. A woman always notices these things. We will be most careful. Barely greet each other, behave almost like total strangers," she said seriously.

"That's my sensible girl."

"But I don't want to be a sensible girl," she pouted. "I would like every one to know that Maurizio Capponcini loves me and that I love him."

He suppressed a shudder. "For heavens sake, think of Beppe."

"God, it makes me ill to think of him. He shall never touch me again," she vowed solemnly. "Alright, I'll be sensible, for now. One more kiss, though," she begged and he complied.

That's how Maurizio Capponcini had acquired a mistress for the first time during his marriage. He had never thought he would deceive his wife so often and with so little real desire. He had resisted other elegant beautiful and sensual women. Daria Ferrari, however, had one trump card the others never had had. She was married to the investigating Chief Magistrate who had forgotten to lock away his files before he left that morning. Fate was a strange catalyst, Maurizio mused as he sat having his second rum-punch on the deck, overlooking the Caribbean which was bathed in the light of an almost full moon. It was time for Curria's people to come and disturb his peace.

Chapter Two

He leaned over the railing and saw the mini submarine surface next to the jetty. Curria's men were busy unloading cases and disappearing into the bushes with them. Maurizio knew they were being stored in the cave. The raw material came from Columbia on freighters and was transferred to the mini subs which were launched in the vicinity of the several safe havens in that part of the world. Maurizio clenched his teeth in anger. There was quiet talk and some calls between the men who were ferrying the cases between the sub and the mouth of the cave. They had spotted a coast guard vessel, which in itself, was unusual. The sailors from the sub were urging more speed and Curria's men were grumbling.

It took the team just twelve minutes to stow away the cargo. Maurizio saw the submarine dive in the cove, and hoped fervently that it might sink to the bottom for ever. He always hoped and prayed for that, but his prayers had never been answered. Finally all was quiet again in the cove. The dirty work had been done.

He turned back and decided to start grilling his fish. He was startled by the light and the alarm going on over the steps. It heralded a visitor from the sea. It was that damned Curria again coming to cadge a drink. Without turning around Maurizio growled, "And to what do I owe this unexpected disturbance, Curria?

Don't you think that one unsolicited visit a day is sufficient?"

"I thought that we were to have dinner?" The voice was deep and vibrant for one so small and slender. Maurizio spun around in surprise.

"I left a message on your answering machine that the dinner was cancelled, so what the hell are you doing here, Mei-Ling?"

"I wish you would not call me that, it's so old fashionedly Chinese. My friends call me Shrimp. Only my parents called me Mei-Ling. Sometimes."

"Well, I like it. It's better than Shrimp or Minnesota."

"It's Minnehaha, not Minnesota."

"I'm sorry, I always get confused. What a strange name to give."

"My parents thought that it would make me feel more American."

"They might as well have called your brother Hiawatha."

"It's funny you should say that. They did." Maurizio stared at the diminutive girl standing on the deck in her wet suit. He waved his hands about. "How did you get here anyway, Mei-Ling?" he demanded.

"Just a little night diving. Have you something I could change into? I'm beginning to feel chilly."

"Go to the pink guest-room. You know the way. Clemmie has it all prepared for unexpected guests. Take anything you like out of the cupboard. How do you like your fish, cremated, or just lightly grilled?"

"Cremated sounds great — that is if you really want me to stay."

"I did not mean to be uncivil. In fact, I'd be glad if you would do me the honour to stay and keep me company."

Maurizio wondered whether the girl had seen the goings on in the cove. It would be dangerous

40

knowledge to have. He really liked her and enjoyed diving with her. He would not have wanted anything to happen to her. He admired her diving skills and courage under water and her no-nonsense attitude towards him. They were only good pals, although the islanders thought that there was more to it than that. It suited Maurizio to let the rumour get around. It sort of made him out of bounds for anyone else. He turned up the gas grill and placed the snapper on it. He basted it with olive oil and crumbled some fresh thyme onto it. He turned it over after a few minutes and repeated the procedure. The skin had taken on the pattern of the grill and looked brown and crisp.

"That smells quite delicious," said the girl. She had put on one of his crisply-ironed shirts which reached over her knees. She had wrapped a towel turban-like about her head and had sprayed herself with Domitilla's perfume.

"Would you like to dress the salad while I uncork the wine? White alright for you?"

"Yummy," she said and busied herself with the salt, vinegar and oil. She gave a good twist of pepper and seemed pleased with her effort. He poured the wine and then put the fish on their plates.

"Eat before it gets cold," he said. He watched her squirt the lemon over the fish and tuck in. She looked like a delicate porcelain doll, with her small regular features and full lips. Her skin was smooth without blemish or wrinkles.

"You are beautiful, do you know that?" he said suddenly. She laid down her fork and knife and looked at him with astonishment. "Don't get any ideas, however. I'm not trying to seduce you. Just stating a fact."

"Shame; here I was, thinking that I had made an impression on you at last." She laughed softly.

"I'm telling you this because I don't want anybody

to spoil your looks. Why did you come here tonight?"

"Because you invited me, of course. I don't always listen to my answer-phone and did not realize that the party was off."

"You don't usually come to a dinner dressed in your wet suit."

"True, you have a point there. I actually did not really mean to come up here, but my tank was faulty and I was about to run out of air. I did not have enough left to get back to the boat, so I had to make an emergency landing, as it were."

"I see, unfortunate of course, but I wonder what you were doing around here anyway, as it were." She met his stare with innocent eyes.

"You would not believe me if I told you."

"Try me," he invited her.

"I work for the CIA."

He threw back his head and laughed so hard that he choked on a bone. She jumped up and hit him sharply on the back.

"It's alright," he gasped and spat out the bone. "You mustn't do that to me Mei-Ling, I could have died laughing."

"It's better than ending one's life in a prison cell, Maurizio. That is something that might easily happen to you if you are going to go on like that." She sounded serious and worried. "I've been watching Curria's antics for some time now, and we are getting ready to move in. What I can't understand is why you are involved in this trafficking. I've known you for several months now, and you don't seem to be the type. I really am sticking my neck out for you by telling you all this. I hope you realize that."

"I think I must be dreaming, or having a turn of some kind." He drank down his wine. "I've never heard a more ridiculous story in all my life. CIA

42

indeed." He squinted at her. "Where is your legit-imization? Go on, show me your proof, like they do in the movies." He sounded mocking.

"I know that you find it hard to believe, but it's true."

"I wonder what Longfellow would think of this Chinese Minnehaha CIA agent?"

"That is what is known as a rhetorical question, since the gentleman in question is too dead to answer it."

"And if all this were true, what can I do about it?"

"You could help us and, by doing so, help yourself. There is not much we don't know about you, Maurizio. We know all about your business, how much money you make, more or less what you've got in your black bank accounts in Switzerland and the Bahamas, and that, compared to some others, you have been reasonably clean. We understand that it is quite usual for Europeans to keep mistresses and that in the past you've resisted the temptation of a lasting adulterous relationship, having had a good marriage over the years. However you've recently acquired a mistress and obtained a separation. Practically an end to the marriage."

"I still have a good marriage, dammit, and you don't understand anything." He smashed his fist onto the table and the wine spilled out of the glasses.

"If you want to talk about it, I would be happy to listen." She mopped up the table with her napkin. "More wine?" she asked. He nodded morosely and got up to get another bottle.

"I suppose you know about the passage?" he called out to her.

She looked startled. "You kidding me? What passage?"

He poured their glasses full again and grinned wickedly. "The secret one of course," he purred.

She shook her head impatiently. "I don't know why I even listen to your fantasies."

He shrugged unconcernedly. "There's no pleasing you, is there? Here I am, volunteering an important piece of information worth at least a recommendation for my pardon, and you don't take the slightest notice."

"So there really is a passage, you say?".

"Yes, just like in an adventure story. I'll show it to you after dinner. I just want to make it quite clear to you, just as I made it to Curria, that I didn't want to know any more. I've got enough troubles of my own without adding drug smuggling to my sins."

"Why are you letting them use you, then?"

"Because they're leaning on me, that's why."

"Are they threatening your family?"

"Not directly, but I owe them." She looked at him sternly. "Yes, I owe them. You can look daggers at me as long and as hard as you like."

"I would not have thought it of you."

"That's so easily said. In Italy every other person owes. Politicians, Clerics, Film Stars. Even little grocers and haberdashers. Everyone has tried to cheat the Tax Authorities. Some more successfully than others. Not so much by cunningly cooking the books, but by simply buying off the tax inspectors. There are a whole lot of interdependent worlds of business, crime, graft and corruption which feed on each other's weaknesses."

"I know enough about corruption. The Chinese are hard to beat at that game – or at any other, for that matter." She eyed him speculatively. "I just had a feeling about you, that you were different, perhaps. That you would rise above your own little intrigues and preoccupations and do something for humanity. I wouldn't have judged you a weak man."

44

"Oh, spare me the flattery. I did things to keep my business going which were against the law. I contravened exchange control regulations, like everyone else did. I greased paws in order to obtain licences. This was considered normal practice and no one paid much attention. Now we all have to have clean hands. Well, I was unable to cleanse my hands. The dirt stuck hard just like the blood did to Lady Macbeth."

"You're not telling me that you've actually murdered someone?" She sounded horrified.

"No of course not, but I'm still to be investigated."

"Supposing I could help you wipe your slate clean, will you help me wipe out Curria and his gang?"

"His people have a long arm. Just doing away with him won't solve the problem. Besides, he has a powerful partner on the island. The Minister for Religious Affairs would object strenuously to any interference with the financing of his churches."

"The United States Government will make him change his tune."

He could not suppress a mocking smile and an ironic comment. "Are you composing a new hymn and preparing the invasion of 'Tequila'?"

"Perhaps." She meticulously scraped her plate clean with a chunk of fresh bread. "One thing is certain, you certainly know how to grill a mean red snapper. Thank you, I enjoyed that. Any dessert?"

"You've got a large appetite for such a small girl."

"That's not an answer to my question. Shall I go and look in the refrigerator?"

"Why don't you do that, and bring the bottle of brandy while you're at it."

"Spoken like a true Italian. They do love to be served on hand and foot."

"I've never had a complaint about my behaviour from a woman before. Besides, you offered." He leant back in his chair and looked out to sea. The wind had risen slightly as it always did in the evening, and pleasantly cooled the deck. He opened the humidor on the side table and picked out a cigar. He sniffed it and rolled it judiciously between his fingers. Mei-Ling came back carrying a tray.

"No smoking before we've finished dinner," she said sternly. "Ice-cream and fruit salad?"

He shook his head. "Nothing for me, thank you. I'll make the coffee. But do help yourself. You can use the calories after your night dive."

After she had cleared the table they sat companionably sipping brandy. The tree frogs were chirping noisily, competing with the cicadas. The smoke from his cigar was wafted away by the breeze. He concealed a yawn behind his palm.

"Are you tired?" she asked.

"No, just bored," he drawled and dodged the cushion which came sailing towards him. He grinned. "I was just kidding, you know that."

"I'm ready, if you are," she said.

"Great, let's nip into bed."

She did not rise to the provocation, but got up and said. "Can I borrow some sneakers? Oh – and we need a second torch."

He sighed. "You really want to go and see the passage now? I was just getting into a romantic mood," he teased. "Come along then. Try a pair of Miranda's sneakers. Domitilla's will be too big for you." He looked at her pityingly. "And do tie a scarf over your head."

"It can't be that cold in the passage," she protested.

"It's not because of the cold, silly. It's the bats," he murmured. She shuddered with disgust and stared at him angrily.

"Now don't tell me that a fully fledged CIA agent is nervous about several thousand bats. They are

46

particularly partial to Asian hair, especially when it's long, lovely and thick like yours." She remained stonily silent. "The real Minnihaha would not have been scared of bats."

She drew herself up to her full height. "I don't believe a word of it. You're just trying to put me off."

"I really should not have told you about this passage. Curria and his gang are not going to like it if they find out that I've blabbed about it to a CIA agent. Think of what happened to old Rosenberg. They threatened him constantly, until he was forced to sell this place and leave the island. Just because he knew about the passage."

"Probably half the population knows about the passage," she said tartly.

He shook his head. "That's where you're wrong. It's a very closely guarded secret. Not even the Minister for Religious Affairs knows about it."

"That's not surprising. He hates the water and the beach. He's allergic to sand-flies as well. What about Maria Beatriz? I hear that she and Curia are thick as thieves. Do you think that he's told her?"

"Not a chance. A man like Curria would never trust a woman with anything."

They walked down the steps to the water. The small bay was brightly lit and the water relatively calm. He shone the powerful torch around them, lingering over the silver shimmering surface of the water which lapped gently against the jetty. The boats were bumping against the protective buoys making little squeaky sounds. Maurizio kicked off the stair lights and motioned her towards the dense bushes. He picked up a machete and elbowed his way through to the rock side. He displaced a piece of trellis which had been ingeniously threaded with greenery and gave the mouth of the cave simple but effective camouflage. He led the way in, lighting the way with his powerful flashlight.

"There it is. Aladdin's cave."

"I don't see any treasure though," she whispered. "It's not very inviting, is it? You say you've never been down it before and don't know where it finishes?

"Right. I haven't the slightest idea, nor do I wish to be enlightened."

"Lead the way then," she urged him.

"Oh no, my dear, this is as far as I go."

She looked at him contemptuously and marched forward. She had no sooner ventured a few steps when she yelled and darted back again. She flung herself against his chest and shuddered.

"Rats, you never mentioned the rats!"

"How could I, I've never been inside before. Besides, that would not have stopped you either." He held her lightly until her shudders subsided. "I shall never understand the Americans. How could they send a delicate flower like yourself to do such a nasty job. You're not fit to do that kind of work."

"Oh yes I am. I'm fully trained and they needed a diver. I also have a cousin on the island which gave me the best cover."

"They taught you to do deal with sharks, but didn't teach you to deal with rats. A grave shortcoming, believe me."

"Stop pontificating and help me," she pleaded now and he chuckled and took her hand.

"Let's go then, but don't blame me for any more wildlife we may encounter, because I truly don't know what's in store for us."

She kept close behind him and he thrust out the machete in one hand and the flashlight in the other. The passage was narrow and not very high. Maurizio had to keep his head down so as not to scrape the rough ceiling. There were little alcoves which had been hewn into the rock face and there were oil-lamps placed in them. The smell of burning oil was still noticeable although the lamps were not alight anymore. Maurizio and Mei-Ling came to a largish chamber which led off to the right. Maurizio shone his torch into the recess and beckoned to her. There was a tarpaulin thrown over a row of neatly stacked metal boxes in the chamber, waiting to be taken to their next destination. Mei-Ling motioned him to continue towards the end of the tunnel and followed him. It seemed an endless journey and she caught her breath several times when rats scurried across their path.

"How much longer do you think it could be?" she murmured. He shrugged his shoulders. The passage took a sudden turn to the left and they were confronted with the grinning face of a man. Limbo Limone, Curria's henchman, held up his torch and waved a pistol about.

"Well, if it ain't Mr. Capponcini himself come to pay me a visit. And who is the little lady with him? Your little China chick?" He levelled his weapon at them. "That was one dumb move, Mr Capponcini, coming here and bringing your chick along. Drop the machete and tie her up," he growled. "And don't waste time — I've a job to do." He threw Maurizio a rope.

"What are you going to do with her? She knows nothing. We were just exploring the passage for a lark."

"I suppose you wanted to impress your little lady friend," Limbo Limone snorted and spat out a stream of phlegm. "I'll have to ask the boss what to do about her. He won't want her running around loose, babbling about this passage. Can never trust a woman to button up her lip. We'll most likely have to dispose of her, somehow or other. Tie her up and gag her. The rats don't like noise around here – they become quite agitated."

"Oh darling, you can't let this happen to me," Mei-Ling cried pitieously. "You know how I feel about rats." She winked surreptitiously at Maurizio. "Tell this nice man that I won't say a word about anything I saw, like the submarine and the boxes stashed down the passage."

Limbo Limone let out a growl. "I don't like to rub out dames, but I've no option now. She knows too much." He pushed Maurizio aside roughly and faced the girl. The sound of the shot was deafening and echoed down the narrow corridor.

"Mei-Ling!" Maurizio cried and fell onto his back, knocked over by the man who crumpled heavily against his chest. Limbo Limone was a dead weight in Maurizio's arms.

"It's alright, I got in first. The bastard didn't stand a chance."

"You shot him? And I thought he was going to get you."

"I suppose you would have been overcome with grief?" she said sarcastically.

"To be honest, I'd rather have you in my arms than this fellow. Is he dead?"

The girl shone the torch attentively over the body and searched for a pulse in the neck. She sighed.

"Quite dead, I'm glad to say. You can safely get up now." Maurizio moved and rolled the man to one side. He got up and looked at the large blood stain which had spread over his own white shirt.

"Are you sure that I'm not hit as well?" He gulped for air. "I think I'm going to be sick. I've never seen a dead, bloody body before."

50

"Neither have I." Her voice shook. "Here, have a tot of rum."

"What else have you got up that sleeve of yours, a coffin perhaps?" Maurizio took the miniature bottle and drained it. "What the hell are we going to do now with him?"

"Why don't we just leave him here?"

"Oh no, my girl, I'm the only other person who knows about the passage. Curria won't take long to point an accusing finger at me."

"You' ll have to get rid of him then."

"I...I've got to get rid of him.? Don't you believe it, Minnehaha. This was your idea and I'll have no more to do with it." He glared at the diminutive figure in front of him who looked at him with great pleading eyes.

"Oh, very well; get on with it then. You pick up his feet and I'll take the shoulders. Let's get him out of this passage and dump him in the sea."

She shook her head. "Not the sea, he could be washed ashore."

"Maybe not, if we dumped him far enough. We could cut him into little pieces and feed him to the fish."

She ignored this piece of gory advice. "I wonder what he was doing here? Probably waiting for someone to pick up the boxes. We must be quite near the end of the passage. Let's take him there and see where it gets us."

"To an early grave," he whispered lugubriously. "I thought I heard a rumbling noise, some kind of engine." She held up her hand to her lips and they listened. They started walking, she leading the way, holding her revolver, he bringing up the rear brandishing his machete. There was a short steep climb to the end of the passage which had been predictably close, but a heavy steel door now sealed it off from the outside world. Maurizio pushed back the well-oiled bolts and cautiously swung the door open. They looked out onto a disused old factory site, and parked directly in front of them was a white camper. Maurizio went up to it and knocked on the window.

"Come on out, Maria Beatriz," he bellowed, "and switch off that Frank Sinatra CD. It's time for a '*marche funèbre*', not for pop music."

Maria Beatriz caught them both in her headlights and screamed. She got out of the camper hurriedly. She had changed her halter and shorts for a clinging white silk jersey dress and her stiletto heels dug into the dirt. She swayed back and forth, moaning.

"What have they done to you Maurizio? Look at all that blood. We must find a doctor, or get him to the clinic before he bleeds to death, Miss Chang."

"There's nothing wrong with me, Maria Beatriz, but what the devil are you doing here, at this hour?"

"Claudio's van has broken down again, and he asked me to pick up some booze for the casino. His van's always breaking down. Limbo Limone's supposed to meet me here, but never mind that. Let's get you to the hospital."

"Thank you for your concern, which has nothing to do with my eventual demise and you not getting your money, I presume?"

"I didn't quite get that joke, but I'm sure it was something unkind. You are always unkind or teasing me. I should really stop worrying about you."

"It's really sweet of you to worry about me, Maria Beatriz, but I'm perfectly fine. It's the fellow back in the passage who needs a little attention."

"What passage are you talking about? There's only this hut here. A disused transformer thingy. See the skull and crossed bones and the 'keep out, danger' sign on the front? Claudio says it keeps the curious folk away and it's safe to store the bootleg liquor here when he ships it in."

"How could you be a party to illegal liquor?" Mei-Ling said sternly. "You are defrauding your own country of badly needed funds."

"My country hardly ever sees those badly needed funds. I have it on good authority that the Director of Customs and Excise helps himself to most of it. Besides, Claudio gives me a little something, which always comes in useful, now that Pa has seen fit to cut my allowance to a bare minimum."

"I told you to steer clear of Curria this morning, and you agreed," Maurizio said reproachfully.

"I'm going to try, really; this is the last time, I told him. He must get himself a new van, cos I'm not going to be used as an errand girl any longer. What are you two doing here? Trying to heist a case of liquor?" she laughed delightedly. "Better hurry before Claudio's man gets here. I won't say a word, I promise."

"Very generous of you," Maurizio said. "You're a real pal." He looked at Mei-Ling. "Isn't she, Mei-Ling?" The Chinese girl nodded solemnly. "And because you're such a good real pal, you'll help us with this little problem that has cropped up..."

"Natch, be glad to Maurizio."

"It's to do with Curria's man, the one you're waiting for. He's had a bad accident behind the shed. We should take him to the morgue right away."

"Morgue? Is he dead?" A note of panic had crept into Maria Beatriz' voice.

"He will be by the time we get him there. We tried to help but it's no use."

"Claudio sure will get mad." Maria Beatriz wrung her hands.

"You must never tell him. All our lives are in terrible danger because of this accident. If we can get this

53

Limone to the morgue, we can perhaps get rid of him for good and no one will be any the wiser."

Maria Beatriz' eyes grew round with horror. She seemed undecided as to what attitude to take. "Did you kill him, Maurizio?" she asked finally.

"No, I swear I didn't, my dear, but Curria won't believe me and will have me rubbed out. You wouldn't want that to happen, would you?"

"No, no, Maurizio," she bit her scarlet finger nail. "OK, I'll take you to the morgue at the hospital, but I don't want blood all over my new camper. You've got to take your shirt off if you want to ride with me, Maurizio."

"Don't worry, I'll take everything off that could cause any damage, and we'll wrap Limone up well before we put him in the camper. I'll go and get him. Mei-Ling, you stay here with Maria Beatriz, to protect her."

"Protect me? ... from what?" Maria Beatriz wanted to know.

"From the urge to hop into the camper and beat it while our backs are turned."

"I would never do such a thing to a friend," Maria Beatriz protested. "One day you'll get to know me, Maurizio. I too have my code of honour, same as you."

"Honour between thieves, my dear girl."

"There you go again, denigrating me," she said huffily. "Friends ... phhh. I've never stolen anything in my life ... except for Maria Dolores' silk stockings, but they didn't fit me anyway, and I put them back even though I had laddered them in several places. So it doesn't count, does it?"

"You're a good girl, Maria Beatriz, I know that. I was only teasing," he pacified her, before going back into the passage.

Maria Beatriz didn't drive over the potholed tarmac with her usual aplomb. The fact that a body wrapped in a tarpaulin was lying on her brand new white shaggy fur carpet somewhat cramped her style. She swung into the dimly-lit driveway of the hospital and stopped with a lurch.

"Oh shit, I hope that that didn't spill any blood," she complained. "Here you are, Maurizio, just as I promised. Now you get him out of my camper."

"We must find the attendant and you can distract his attention, while we organize Limbo the lemon."

"You won't find anyone here at this time of night," Maria Beatriz said. "There's just the night nurse for the patients, and he's usually fast asleep."

"There's no doorman, no admissions nurse?"

"Nah, this is 'Tequila', not New York. Admissions are only admitted after eight o'clock in the morning."

"That's a bit of luck. We can just take him and shove him in a drawer and no one will be any the wiser." Maurizio spoke with more confidence than he felt. "You be the look-out, Maria Beatriz, while Mei-Ling and I do the rest. Don't forget we're allies now."

They found the cold storage and an empty slab for the man. They undressed him completely, took off the gold link chain which was around his neck, his solid gold Rolex Oyster with the diamond hands, the signet ring set with a good size diamond, and the gold hoop from his left ear. Mei-Ling discovered a tag and dotted down 'John Smith' on it. She had tied it to his toe and pushed the slab back into place. She rummaged around and found a black plastic garbage bag into which they stuffed his belongings. No one had disturbed them and they hurried back to the camper. Maria Beatriz drove off as soon as they were seated beside her.

"Where are we going?" Mei-Ling asked.

"I dunno, just away from here," Maria Beatriz muttered. "What shall I tell Claudio about the liquor?"

"She has a point there," Maurizio said. "What can she tell him?"

Mei-Ling thought for a moment. "Where were you going to take it, Maria Beatriz? To the Casino?"

"Nah, he stores it in the new chemical factory, in Devil's Valley. Why they wanted to build a factory down there is a mystery to me. The valley's taboo, brings *mala suerte*. The voodoo man said so, and his father before him. They have been having awful trouble getting our local lads to work there. 'Three birds one stone Fellah' has had to import foreign labour from Venezuela and other places." She stopped the camper and turned to them. "So what am I to tell Claudio? He's waiting at the chemical factory and pretty soon he'll be sending someone out to look for me."

Maurizio put his hand on her knee comfortingly. "There's no need to panic," he said soothingly. "You'll drive to the factory and tell him that you've waited all this time and that no one showed up. Get angry...tell him he's ruined your evening and that he should find someone else to run his errands for him. Get into a real rage...that's sounds reasonable doesn't it, Mei-Ling?"

"Oh, eminently so," she answered confidently and continued in a whisper. "I only hope that he won't pull out her fingernails and knock her teeth out."

"What are you whispering about? It's very bad manners."

"Oh it's Mei-Ling, worrying about her car. Perhaps you can drop us off where you found us before you drive to Devil's Valley. We must not been seen together by Curria, or any member of his gang."

"I suppose your car's parked there somewhere? I still can't understand what you were both doing there, and how Claudio's man came to be dead."

"Don't worry your pretty little head about that, we'll let you into the secret one day, but for now, forget you ever saw us; forget Limbo Limone, forget the hospital. Just do as we tell you and everything will be fine. After all, Claudio's still got his liquor. That's all he's really interested in. Limbo Limones are a dime a dozen and he'll soon hire a new man." They watched her drive away recklessly as usual.

They entered the passage, leaving the steel door unbolted. They carried the bloodstained tarpaulin and the garbage bag with them and hurried along the tunnel. Mei-Ling breathed an audible sigh of relief when they were out in the open again, and Maurizio had pushed back the trellis against the mouth of the cave. They swung the tarpaulin back and forth in the sea until the blood had been washed off it. When it was reasonably clean they folded it and put it in the locker of his boat under a pile of old oilskins and coiled rope. They climbed up the steps again, carrying the black bag and sat down on the deck. There was a heavy silence between them which neither broke for some time.

"You look exhausted," Maurizio said finally. "Go and have a good shower and I'll prepare a nightcap." She nodded obediently and got up. He noticed that she was crying and put an arm around her slender heaving shoulders.

"What's up, my little CIA agent, never killed a man before?"

"There's no need to be so smug and ironic," she stammered.

"Sorry, Minnehaha, I'm just trying to make light of what happened tonight, because, to tell you the truth, I was shit scared and still am. Curria won't let the matter of his vanishing henchman drop just like that.

We've got rid of him for tonight, but what about tomorrow when they find him, as they are bound to, eventually?"

"They won't know who it is, will they?"

"Exactly. Then they will call the police and the Chief is likely to recognize him. We've got to think of a way of getting him out and off the island." He spoke soberly as he took off the coverlet of the guest bed and laid out one of his daughter Miranda's oversize T-shirts. Mei-Ling nodded silently and disappeared into the bathroom. Maurizio went into his bathroom and rummaged around in the medicine chest. He found a small jar of sleeping pills, took one out and placed it on the dressing table in the guest room. He knocked on the bathroom door and said loudly:

"I'm going to lie on the deck for a while after my shower, so if you want to talk, come and join me. If not, take the pill I've put on your dressing table next to the glass of water. It should assure you of a dreamless sleep for at least 4 to 5 hours."

He undressed and took a shower. After he had dried himself and put on a bathrobe, he threw all the clothes he had been wearing into the rubbish bin. He had noticed that there were specks of blood on his jeans. Everything would have to be destroyed. The breeze had risen and it was cool on the deck. Tiny clouds were being chased across the sky, sometimes obscuring the brilliant galaxies of stars for an instant. He poured himself a stiff whisky and lay down on the deck-bed. He gazed at the sky and marvelled at the clarity of it. He thought that he had found paradise when he had first set foot on the island. When he and Domitilla had decided to buy 'Trade Winds' and forge ahead with the plans for a new 'Club Royale', they were riding high on the tide of success. Every avenue had seemed open to them, no ambition too high to be realized. The sky had been as clear, the stars as brilliant, and the breeze as cool and refreshing after a warm tropical day as it was tonight. Yet in a few short months, most of it had been washed away in a flood of dangerous happenings, which he had found difficult to forestall or control. The incidents of this night had just brought it all to a head. He wished he could confide in someone, dissect the problems, share the burden of his plight.

"So talk, that's what you want to do, don't you?" Mei-Ling had come out so quietly that he had not heard her. She lay down on a deck-bed beside him.

"Oh Lord, yes, Minnehaha, I definitely need to talk," he groaned. Very slowly he began to tell her about his involvement with Daria Ferrari and the repercussions it had had on his life. The story began to spill out and she listened, nodding occasionally, occasionally asking a question. So it was that he finally came face to face honestly, without holding back, with all the demons which had beset him for months.

"You know, Mei-Ling, I never intended to cheat on my wife. We had, and possibly will have again, a decent marriage."

The Chinese girl smiled in the dark and thought how just like a man it was to fall into the trap of an adulterous relationship and then say that he never meant to do it. She bit back an acid remark and let him continue.

"It was quite usual for me to take a woman friend out to lunch, and Domitilla didn't mind; in fact it rather amused her to hear all the gossip I brought home." The Chinese girl grimaced, and thought Domitilla must have been mad or very sure of herself to let her good-looking husband off the leash, even for the length of a lunch.

"I suppose I made the mistake of being convinced that I was inured against temptation. I never expected it all to fall apart because of this young woman."

"Daria Ferrari, the judge's wife," she murmured.

He looked surprised. "I can't recall mentioning her name...be that as it may, she's a very good-looking young woman, a Jean Harlow type. Platinum hair and brilliant blue eyes, full lips and an impudent nose. She has a fine petite figure, nice and firm up-tilted bosom and enormous enthusiasm. She manoeuvred me into going to bed with her with a simple little ruse." He chuckled ruefully. "Don't get me wrong, she didn't have to rape me. It was pleasurable and I never thought that it would have any consequences. I thought she wanted a one off and I gave it to her." Again the Chinese girl hid her smile in the dark. How like a man to do what he wanted, convinced that it was really the woman's desire which drove him to it.

"It was sheer coincidence or providence if you will, that I spent part of the afternoon with Daria Ferrari in her apartment, and found out about the file. I had occasion to go into her husband's study to use the telephone, and discovered some fascinating documents on his desk. So fascinating they were, that I thanked my lucky stars for having guided me to her bed that afternoon. I couldn't wait to repeat the tryst and was delighted to hear that her husband would be away for three days every week until Christmas, sowing terror among the captains of industry up and down the country."

"They certainly started a real witch-hunt in your country. McCarthy was almost an amateur, compared."

"You're right about that. Mind you, I'm not saying that there wasn't a lot of garbage going on, and that a good clean out was necessary. I made the mistake of thinking myself above the law. My few unlawful operations were really insignificant compared to some other businessmen's blatant disregard of the law." He stopped and was silent for a while.

"So you found that the judge was about to put your company under investigation?" Mei-Ling prompted him.

"The file was on his desk, right on the very top. It would surely be the next thing he would look at. I had to have time to look through it and see which accusations, if any, were listed. It was not difficult. Daria was only too happy to accommodate me in every way. She is completely besotted with me."

"Did it ever occur to you that she deliberately put your file on the top of the pile, anticipating exactly what would happen?" Mei-Ling said quietly.

"Impossible; Daria is much too bird-brained for such devious machinations," Maurizio contended. "Confucius is not on her reading list."

"Never underestimate what a woman in love is capable of," Mei-Ling replied. Again he was silent, mulling over her words.

"Do you mean to say that she deliberately put the file on the top," he said then, "in the expectation that I would accompany her to her flat that afternoon, and somehow go to the study and find it lying there?" He said in disbelief. "Why would she do such a thing?"

"Need I really answer that question? Think of the result she achieved."

"To get me to return again and again…Sometimes there were no files there at all, and she seldom gave me enough time to really go through them properly. I was constantly on tenterhooks…No…no…". He shook his head decisively. "Daria is completely guileless, she could never have…"

Mei-Ling could not contain an undignified snort. "From just having an innocent lunch with you, this guileless creature managed to separate you from your wife and family, ruin your marriage, and exile you to this godforsaken paradise, and make you beholden to the Mafia. I would beware of the guile of the guileless." Mei-Ling waited for him to proceed with his story. He poured himself another scotch and swished it around on the ice cubes.

"She swore she would commit suicide if I broke off the relationship. She demanded that I leave my wife, although she had not intention of separating from the Judge. In order to protect me she said. She had discovered after a short while that I was examining her husband's files."

"How did that happen?"

"Quite accidentally. At least, I thought so at the time. I went to call Domitilla from the study as usual and Daria followed me because she was so jealous and wanted to overhear my conversation."

Mei-Ling cast him a sideways glance and saw him peering at her in the dark.

"You might be right after all, Minnehaha," he shouted. "She caught me out and I was obliged to tell her what was going on. She started to cry and was extremely concerned. She promised to hide the file in a safe place, so that the Judge wouldn't set eyes on it for a long time. That's how it was; so what do you think?" Mei-Ling remained diplomatically silent. "Well, go on, say it; say what a poor idiotic gullible sap I am, that I never suspected anything at all."

"What a poor idiotic gullible sap you are ... but then it is a far-fetched theory and difficult to prove."

"It is? You made me think it quite plausible. You see, after that she had me completely at her mercy. I never heard anything about my company being investigated, but I had to toe her line. I finally confessed the whole thing to Domitilla and we tried to sort ourselves out. We entered into a legal separation and I shifted most of my holdings into her name. Daria demanded that Domitilla and I should sever all relations, which we ostensibly did. Then I discovered the problem with my passport and hurriedly left the country. It was normal for me to travel a great deal because of the nature of the business, so I came out here to settle the purchase of the land for our new 'Club Royale' and generally organize things like planning permission and financing."

"What was in the file which would been so terrible for the judge to see?"

"I had special exemptions from the exchange control regulations in order to acquire the sites and build the clubs. I had on several occasions failed to use all the allowances for the business, and syphoned off some into a private Swiss bank account. There were some pretty accurate dates of these transactions which, I might add, were made by a friendly bank manager, who is now under house arrest for various other exchange control offences."

"What else was in the file?"

"A recommendation from the financial police that my passport should be confiscated until further notice. To pre-empt that, Domitilla procured a set of false documents for me, so as to enable me to leave the country."

"How did she do that? Surely a little unusual for a lady?" Mei-Ling wanted to know. He didn't answer immediately and Mei-Ling gave him a little time before she proffered her own explanation.

"Her family connections? It is rumoured that her Grandpa, the old Duke, was a big Mafia boss in Sicily."

"I don't really know about that," he said hastily. He gulped a few times. "She never told me how she went about it, and I was cowardly enough not to ask. All I wanted was to get out. The thought of even one day in an Italian jail was too much to bear," he sighed. "I didn't fully realize that it would nail me down here for any length of time."

"What happened to your Italian passport? Did they really confiscate it?"

"Curiously enough, they never did."

"So you never had to use your false papers?"

He shook his head. "I've not returned to Italy since all this happened, but I have travelled in Europe and the USA with my Italian passport and there doesn't appear to be an Interpol warrant out for me," he said wryly.

"There will soon be one," she said sharply. "This drug running business which you tolerate on your property, under your very nose, has put you into a very dicey position. I shouldn't be telling you this, but we are almost ready to pounce. In one way or another. I suppose Curria's crowd provided you with the papers which you probably won't ever need to use. That's how they got their hooks into you, my dear Maurizio."

"Oh my wise Chinese owl, that's exactly how it happened." They remained silently side by side, lost in thought.

"Do you want to hear my views?" she asked finally.

"Mmmm...," he said, and stifled a yawn.

"Do you or don't you want to listen?" She waited for a reply and receiving none, bent over him. His eyes were closed and he breathed evenly and quietly like a child. He had fallen asleep for the first time in months, suddenly and deeply, without taking a sleeping pill. Mei-Ling got up and brought a light cotton blanket from his room. It wouldn't harm him to spend the night on the deck. She covered him and went to lie down in the guestroom. She was bone-tired and ready to go to sleep. After all, according to Scarlett O'Hara, tomorrow was another day, and who was Mei-ling to argue with that.

Chapter Three

Maurizio Capponcini's dream crept over him pleasurably. He sighed in his sleep and stretched his limbs. He was floating several inches over the ground on the meadow of the family estate in Umbria. He felt free and light as a feather, borne along by the breeze. He loved this place better than any other of their properties, except perhaps for 'Trade Winds' before it had become more of a nightmare than a pleasant dream.

He had inherited the estate from an uncle who had been a recluse and died childless. Maurizio and Domitilla had restored the old neglected patrician house lovingly. There was nothing ostentatious about it, but the large rooms, high ceilings, polished furniture and waxed floors gave it a feeling of solidly founded wealth. Some diligent ancestress had embroidered the *gros-point* which covered the twelve straight-backed chairs around the massive refectory table in the dining-hall, and the old love-seat which stood in front of the antique fireplace in the grand Sala. The original wooden floors had been polished by generations of felt slipper clad feet, shuffling over them. The old kitchen had been modernized to take all the latest machines and the old terra-cotta tiles polished and oiled afresh. The bathrooms had been re-plumbed and partly refurbished, although the old free-standing tubs on large spreading claw-feet had been kept wherever possible.

Maurizio flew across the meadow and clear through the oak entrance door into the hall. The candles had been lit in the wall sconces. The candles in the great five branch candelabras which were placed on the sculpted marble-topped consoles flickered brightly. A silver rose-bowl was massed with tea-roses. The scent was almost overpowering. He glanced up at the wide staircase leading to the upper floors. He held out his arms to the figure which floated gracefully down to him. Her black hair fanned out towards him as he took hold of her arms. It was a familiar face but not the one he had expected, nor was the voice the one he had hoped to hear.

"Let go, Maurizio, you're hurting me," she said. "Wake up, please. It's late and I have to go and get my boat in the crabhole, besides all the other things we have to do, like getting rid of Limone's stuff."

Maurizio groaned and dropped his hands from her arms. He squinted at the small girl who was bending over him.

"I don't want to wake up yet; go away and let me finish my dream."

"I've got the coffee going. What do you want for breakfast?" He turned his back on her and was asleep again. She shook him gently.

"Oh alright, alright, stop this Chinese torture. I never eat breakfast, only coffee, strong black and sweet." He got up from the deck-bed and started to shuffle towards his room. "Don't come and see whether I've fallen asleep under the shower. I need my privacy for the next ten minutes."

He returned freshly shaven and showered to the breakfast table, and sat down to drink the steaming cup of coffee. Mei-Ling had a plate of eggs and crispy fried bacon in front of her with buttered rye toast on the side.

"Sure you don't want some? We have a long day to

get through and there's nothing like a good bit of nourishment to help one cope." He looked at her plate dubiously and then opened his mouth.

"I'll have a taste if you twist my arm." She laughed and gave him a fork full. He chewed pensively and then nodded. "Not bad; you've talked me into it." She lifted the silver-plate cloche off the plate which stood ready on the side table and set it before him with a flourish.

"You, my girl, are a true magician. Been taking lessons from Old Crone?" he said amiably and heaped the egg and bacon onto the toast. "I've had the most marvellous night's sleep. Beautiful dreams, which you had the audacity to interrupt, but I forgive you. Now this sumptuous breakfast." He bit into the toast. "What have you got to say to that?"

"That you shouldn't speak with your mouth full. You've got egg all over your face, not to mention crumbs."

"Don't be so darned cute, it's too early in the morning." He rubbed his chin with the paper napkin. "That better?"

"All gone. I've borrowed some more of Miranda's clothes. I hope you don't mind." She wore another outsize T-shirt and tiny shorts and looked fresh and alert.

"What are we going to do about all this stuff?" She pointed to the black garbage bag which they had brought from the morgue.

"Perhaps your cousin Young Chang could get rid of the jewellery for you. Melt it down or something. He's a jeweller and must have the equipment for that kind of thing. You could keep the diamonds and suggest he make an engagement ring for you,"

"I've no one to get engaged to at the moment. Seriously, I don't want to go to Chang, he might start asking awkward questions."

"Good; why not let him? Shake him up a bit, make him jealous, make him take notice, show him that there are other candidates waiting for your favours. You care for him, don't you?"

She nodded. "Oh he takes notice alright, although he tries not to show it. He believes that I've already squandered my favours." A delicate blush showed on her skin. "He doesn't approve of the way I live, that I'm earning my living and am independent. I expect I'm not docile enough to make a good wife according to his lights." She looked down at her folded hands sadly. "He's got the girl from the tourist office who accommodates him very well."

"It's not like you to admit defeat."

"Good God, I'll never do that. Old Mrs. Chang would dearly like to have me as a daughter-in-law and will never accept the girl from the tourist office. That's half the battle." She picked up the jewellery and slipped it into a carrier bag. "I'll think about how to dispose of these. What about the rest of the stuff? Our soiled clothes and his gear? The belt?"

"I thought we might burn them and scatter the ashes on the ocean."

"Very romantic... burial at sea... but I don't think he deserves that we should go to all that trouble. Have you got more logs?" Maurizio nodded. He went to the outhouse and brought a basket full of firewood. He stacked the wood in the open hearth, doused it with lighter fuel and started a small inferno. He splashed fuel over the blood soaked clothes and added them to the fire. An unappetizing cloud of smoke gathered on the deck and slowly drifted away. Finally there were only the shoes left. Mei-Ling held the trainers in her hand and looked at Maurizio. He shook his head and held his fingers to his nose.

"What shall we do with them, then?" she asked.

"If the shoe fits, wear it."

She shook herself in disgust. "They never would fit my Cinderella foot. Why don't you try them on?"

"I'm too good-looking to be one of the ugly sisters." He took the trainers from her and examined them closely. "They actually could have been mine," he said. They were as good as new and in pristine condition. They were one of his own Club Royale trademark sports items. "I'll just put them in the hall cupboard and forget about them for the time being."

The smoke oozing out of the fireplace suddenly became darker and more evil smelling. Mei-Ling stirred the burning heap with a poker and turned up the fancy leather belt which was origin of the stench. They both looked startled when they heard a boat being gunned in the bay below.

"It's the staff," Maurizio said. "At least I hope it's Clemmie and the cook."

"Who else could it be?," she asked nervously.

"Curria looking for his henchman, or the Police. Or someone worrying about what happened to you."

"I've no one to worry about where I spend my nights, as I've told you before."

"What! Not even a contact at the Consulate, old Jason Reed for example? Doesn't sound very CIA-ish to me. Come, let's investigate." He went to the side of the deck and looked down to see who was tying-up at the jetty. He waved rather more enthusiastically than he normally did, as Clemmie and the cook came up the steps carrying shopping baskets and drinks cartons.

"Good-morning, Mr. Maurizio, you cooking up a storm of something powerful bad. I could smell it right down the coast. Why don't you wait for Cook or me to prepare your breakfast?" She looked disapprovingly at Mei-Ling. Clemmie didn't mind house guests, as long as they didn't interfere and mess up the kitchen.

"I suppose you doin' some kind of heathen Chinese special instead of a decent Christian breakfast." She and Cook looked knowingly at one another and trudged into the kitchen with the shopping. "No telling what these foreign folks cook up," she muttered under her breath.

"I don't think your staff likes me very much," Mei-Ling whispered.

"I wouldn't worry about it. They just think that you're a depraved woman."

"Then I will add insult to injury and spend tonight here as well. We have to talk some more and make plans."

"We do?"

"Ah ha. I won't let you chicken out."

They waited until every scrap of clothing had been turned into embers and ashes. The smoke had lifted and the breeze had dissipated the odours. Clemmie walked back and forth, sniffing disapprovingly at the last vestiges of the burnt leather. Mei-Ling went to fetch her wet-suit from the outhouse where she had left it to dry. Maurizio told Clemmie that there would be two for dinner and that the guest-room should be tidied up for Miss Chang. They were planning to do a night dive and it wouldn't be safe for Miss Chang to return to Sta. Lucia after dark. Clemmie rolled her eyes but refrained from comments. She saved these for Cook's ears which were flapping to hear the newest piece of gossip. Maurizio grinned wickedly at Mei-Ling.

"Your reputation is ruined, my dear," he said and took her arm and guided her to the steps. "And you couldn't have chosen a better man to ruin it with."

"Modesty must be your middle name."

"How did you guess?" he sounded genuinely startled. "My full name is Maurizio Archimboldo Modesto Capponcini."

"Quite a mouthful," she said tartly.

Down in the cove they changed into their wetsuits and Maurizio loaded the cylinders, BC's, regulators and fins into the Boston whaler. He added a large can of petrol and a pair of sturdy garden shears. He filled the cooler with soft drinks from the refrigerator in the boat-house. He looked for something to nibble on and added some packets of potato crisps and cheese-straws which were always kept in a well sealed provisions cupboard. He skilfully brought the boat out into the open sea which was a little choppy on that side of the island. The keel slapped into the water as he increased speed and took it around the spit. They had been at sea for about five minutes when Maurizio veered into a little inlet. The water was intensely blue, quite still and deep. Mei-Ling's outboard was tied to a diving buoy, gently rocking in the sunlight. Sheer limestone cliffs encircled the cove. They were up to ten metres high in most places and cactus-fringed. Some sea swallows nested between the cracks in the rock-face during the breeding season and they flew around in some agitation at the unexpected intrusion. Armies of crabs scattered over the lower rocks, disappearing into the water with incredible speed. The little cove had justifiably acquired its name, 'Crabhole', and was a favourite with divers taking their first open water test. Everything became quiet again as the intruders tied up their boat to the buoy and cut the engine.

"You fell asleep last night just as I was going to tell you what my views were," she said reproachfully.

"Very bad manners, I apologize."

"Are you willing to listen now?" she asked. He nodded resignedly.

"I have a proposition to make. If you help me nail Curria and Co., I will recommend you for a full pardon from the Italian Government. I can almost guarantee that it will be granted."

"I really can't buy that. How could you possibly guarantee such a thing? By whose authority?"

"The United States Government," she said firmly.

He looked incredulous. "I'll believe it when I see it. In writing."

"Come to Washington with me and talk to my boss. You'll be satisfied."

"The whole thing doesn't make sense, Mei-Ling. Why doesn't your Government just nail those drug-pushers? They have all kinds of resources which we don't have."

"True, but the US Government can't operate openly in a sovereign foreign country. Especially if a minister is involved, who also happens to be the President's son. Think about it, Maurizio."

"All I can think of is that you've embroiled me in a killing and that we are more or less at Curria's mercy. What are we going to do about Limbo?"

"There is no Limbo. The name is John Smith."

"What's in a name, as the Bard said? Perhaps it would have been simpler to dump him in the sea." Regret tinged Maurizio's comment.

"Perhaps so, but then we would never have found out about Maria-Beatriz and the chemical factory."

"You don't really think that Maria-Beatriz is seriously involved in this matter? She's just being used by Curria."

"Just like you are," she glanced at him. "We don't know how naive and innocent she really is. I suspect that she's a little in love with you, Maurizio, and therefore we are safe for the time-being. It won't be long though, before for one reason or another, she will let the cat out of the bag. You'll have to jolly her along a bit, at least until we've cleaned up here."

"Jolly her along?"

"I wouldn't have thought that it was a fate worse than death," Mei-Ling said drily.

"I like the woman and don't want to hurt her," he said.

"Oh how chivalrous of you, but it's got to be done."

"At least it won't be for long," he said. "I've decided to return to Europe as soon as El Viejo signs the decree for the sale of the property, which will be next Tuesday."

She looked at him pityingly. "You still believe that fairy story? I've heard that he will do that only if Maria Beatriz is thrown in as a wife."

Maurizio could not conceal a real thrust of alarm. He laughed nervously.

"It's too early in the morning for such jokes. I think I need a drink." He took the lid off the ice-chest and took out a coke. "Want one?" She shook her head.

"Don't change the subject and don't panic. All you have to do is show willing for a short time. Why don't you get the tarpaulin out? We've got to get rid of it as soon as possible." He bent over the locker and hauled out the tarpaulin. It was still damp.

"Shall we cut it up and divide the spoils? You get rid of your share and I'll dump mine." Silently she picked up the shears and cut it into strips. She gathered half of them and threw them into her outboard. She gathered her mask, BC, snorkel and fins.

"Where are you going?" he asked.

"Home, and then to the consulate. They'll have to help me out with John Smith. I'm also going to book our flights to Caracas and Washington."

"Aren't you taking a lot for granted?" he said abruptly.

She smiled at him sweetly. "I think you truly have no choice. Furthermore, you should ask Maria Beatriz to come along for the ride. Keep her out of mischief." She transferred nimbly into her dinghy. "Please hand me my cylinder." He did as he was bid. She started her engine and made for the *passe*. "See you for dinner this evening," she called and waved to Maurizio who remained nailed to his seat as if paralyzed. Suddenly he let out a long yell which resounded around the crabhole. He did it again and again until the anxious knot in his chest untied itself. The sea-swallows strafed his boat frantically, fearing for their brood. He gunned the motor and swerved out to sea. As soon as he was out far enough, he threw the strips into the ocean, then turned the boat back toward 'Trade Winds.'

Mei-Ling Chang was a fighter. She had learned from an early age that nothing would come easy for her. Her diminutive height, her alien appearance, even her given name Minnehaha always elicited unkind snickers and sideway glances. From nursery school onwards, she had had to stand her ground against bigger and stronger children and had often come home with a number of scratch-marks and bruises. She would not take any abuse without putting up a fight.

As she grew older she had increased her physical strength by taking up karate, judo and body building. As an adult, she had developed a perfectly proportioned body which only hinted at the actual power that had been trained into it. Her facial bone structure was beautiful, her skin flawless and her almond shaped eyes velvety black. In her adolescence she had wanted to become an acrobat in a circus, to her parents' great consternation. She loved acrobatics and gymnastics and had become a member of the gymnast team in high school. There had been talk of her being trained for the National team, but an injury to her back closed that chapter of her ambition. She decided to go to law school, a decision which her parents wholeheartedly approved of. They owned a small chain of grocery stores and were more than happy to finance her education. They loved the idea of having an attorney in the family. Her brother Hiawatha was to carry on the family business and was set to major in economics at college.

During her last year at law school, Mei-Ling was tutored by a discerning academic who recognized how versatile she was. She was both logical and intuitive, a combination which was to be invaluable for her future sphere in life. It was he who suggested she enter government service after graduation. She duly got her law degree with honours and applied for a job with the agency, sponsored by her tutor. There was something in the work offered that gave her a satisfaction she had not known before. She was trained and honed into an extremely efficient agent and, after a couple of years spent on home ground, was sent off to her first foreign assignment. There was nothing fortuitous in it being 'Tequila' which was getting an unsavoury reputation for drugs. The agency had discovered that Mei-Ling had a cousin of sorts living there, who dealt in gems and jewellery. That, together with the fact that she was a scuba instructor and could ostensibly earn her living, gave her a good enough cover to move to the island, without arousing undue suspicion.

Cousin Chang was not too pleased at the prospect of

this new family member descending on the island, who would undoubtedly make demands on him. However, his mother, Old Crone Chang, as she was known, was happy to welcome her cousin's daughter. Young Chang would finally have the opportunity to meet a suitable girl with a view to marriage. There was no girl in the Chinese community on the island who fitted the bill. Young Chang knew all about his mother's scheme and wanted none of it. Up to now he had enjoyed his bachelor life and his arrangement with the girl who was in charge of the tourist office was quite satisfactory on most counts. Not only did she send him clients, but also took care of his physical needs when they overcame him. She was reasonably undemanding and content to please him. He had taken over the decoration of her apartment, installed air-conditioning, a Jacuzzi, and an outsize double-bed which mirrored itself on the ceiling. He could be generous and sometimes gave her a trinket from his stock or bought her imported sexy lingerie from the States. Occasionally he took her to the club for a meal. Young Chang had a good veneer of western civilization and mixed with the In crowd at the yacht club. He sponsored a yearly race for which he had provided a handsome trophy in the shape of a silver galleon in full sail, mounted on a rouge marble base. He and his mother, Old Crone, were about the only ethnic Chinese who moved outside their tightknit community.

Old Crone Chang had been born in the old country but raised in San Francisco. She had never fully mastered the English language and had – outwardly at least – remained thoroughly Chinese in her ways and customs. Her marriage had been arranged with a suitable young man who was a goldsmith by profession. He was a gentle man, a skilful artisan who loved his work. He made fine pieces of jewellery in his father's workshop. He was paid a minimal wage and lived with his family. Old Crone Chang moved in with them after the wedding and was kept well under their thumb. She bore a son who was named Deng, and was called Young Chang by the family. After her confinement she was made to drudge even harder than before by her in-laws. She started a silent rebellion; she would not share her husband's bed again until he had promised that they would move to their own home. Chang was fond of his wife and missed his conjugal rights. He agreed to think about such a bold undertaking. When a distant cousin suggested they join them in the islands and start a business of their own there she urged him to accept. They packed up their few belongings, took their son and left the paternal home accompanied by frowns and murmurs of disapproval.

It was hard at first and Old Crone was wary of the native population. She kept herself to herself, minding her son, and working as hard as before. The little shop prospered however, and Chang's work was admired by all the communities on 'Tequila'. He reset old jewellery and even designed some new pieces, borrowing money from a cousin to buy gold and precious stones. Soon they moved into a fine stone house and she had a native to help her in the kitchen and in the vegetable and flower garden. Old Crone herself tended the herb garden and grew all sorts of esoteric medicinal plants which she dried, pounded and brewed into healing potions and salves. She had brought along an ancient Chinese herb manual which supplied her with many recipes. She began to acquire quite a reputation with the local population, dispensing her medicines for small sums of money. This brought her into direct conflict with the local witchdoctor who did not take kindly to this foreigner poaching on his territory. He found it difficult enough to follow in his father's footsteps without this old Chinese crone's interference. Of course it was undeniable that she had some good magic and understandable that he should lose some of his clients to her. It was very galling nevertheless, and it was rumoured that he would begin a powerful *mala suerte* incantation against her, like his father before him would have done.

Old Crone Chang was, amongst other things, quite a clever diplomat. She took herself off to visit the disgruntled witchdoctor in his hut and they came to an agreement which was to prove profitable to them both. They pooled all their knowledge and used all their wiles to good account. Sometimes they arranged happenings and held consultations together, putting on a good show of their very own brand of Voodoo-Sino-Carib magic. They prescribed potions against the evil eye, *mala suerte*, fever and diarrhoea, loss of hair and rotting teeth. They predicted the future to some of their more exalted clients, always being careful not to predict anything too positive or too negative.

Old Crone didn't really approve of sticking needles into wax and rag dolls, but it was obviously part of the ritual and the witchdoctor and his followers enjoyed it. They began to be so busy that they had to give consultations by appointment and employed a young girl, who sat outside the hut on a stool in front of a rickety table under a striped umbrella, to enter the appointments into a grubby exercise book which also carried the tariffs for the various services rendered. These were expressed in terms of cash and kind, according to the client's possibilities. The witchdoctor favoured chickens, which he used in his rituals first and then threw in to the stewing-pot afterwards. Old Crone

Chang was more oriented towards cash, but was not adverse to sharing a suckling pig with her partner. The witchdoctor admired and revered Old Crone now; he respected her wisdom and knowledge and the partnership flourished to their mutual satisfaction.

The witchdoctor was sitting cross-legged on his woven mat and Old Crone was boiling up water for a herbal tea which they drank together every morning before receiving their first client. He was a strapping fellow in his mid thirties, with strong white teeth and an abundant mane. His twisted locks of hair were tied together on the top of his head with a glittering coil of Christmas festoons. He was a good advertisement for their hair-loss lotion and their gum tincture. He had further decorated his head with three shimmering green cock's-tail feathers.

"Let us talk, Old Crone," he said. Old Crone nodded and poured tea into the fine china cups.

"My mother wants a new house. A stone house, like yours, Old Crone. We have enough money now to build one."

Old Crone sat still and looked inscrutably into the distance. She took a delicate sip from the steaming cup. "I can understand that your mother wants a stone house. Every woman does. Tell her to be patient a little while longer. It's not wise to show one's wealth. People will think that they are paying you too much if you go out and build a smart house now. Think about your calling, practise your magic, show the people that you too can walk on hot coals, like your father and grand-father before you. You must earn their total respect. Soon you will have to prove yourself and dance on fire."

"Ah'm shit scared, Old Crone. Must Ah really do that at the Happening?"

"Sorciero, you must do it … you will do it … I'm sure you have the gift."

The witchdoctor hung his head. "Ah's never yet made real magic, not like my ole man did. Suppose my feet gets burned?"

"I have concocted this marvellous healing salve which will take care of your feet, so stop worrying. I'll smear it all over the soles before you start, and I'll give you a special potion to drink. It'll make you think you're dancing on ice, not on fire. When you've proven yourself at the Happening, you'll be able to choose a bride even from the most eligible circles."

Sorciero started up, panic written all over his face. "Ah don't want no bride, not me, Old Crone; Ah jes wanna fuck. Yes Ma'am, that's good enough for me." Old Crone pursed her lips disapprovingly.

"You'll have to start minding your manners, young man, and your language, because I have plans for you. You could have a grand future, with a little help of course, from me."

"That's always what me Mammi says. 'Sam' she says 'You've got to make somethin of yousself. Now that you's earning good money, we need a stone house, so folks will respect us, like before your Pa died.'"

Old Crone poured more tea and said patiently, "It's not the stone house which will bring you respect, but good magic, so concentrate on that. Practice, practice and more practice. You must have faith in yourself, Sorciero, and it will all come naturally."

"Ain't nothin natural about dancin on hot coals."

"Perhaps there isn't, but it's part of the business." She crossed her tiny black-shod feet. "Now I want you to do me a small favour," she went on. "You know my son, Young Chang? It is a great source of sadness to me that he has not taken a wife yet. I long for a grandchild to hold in my arms before I die. I would have the perfect wife for him, Mei-Ling Chang, my second cousin's daughter, but he is entangled with this woman from the tourist office, Maria Clara. I want you to put a spell on the girl, so that she will give up my son. Then he will take more notice of Mei-Ling. What do you say Sorciero? Have you some small magic for that?"

The witchdoctor picked his healthy teeth with a filed down orange twig and pondered. When he had finished with his teeth, he turned his attention to his fingernails. It seemed that the dirt collected under them gave him an inspiration.

"Ah's got an idea," he answered and picked up one of the small wax effigies which were in a basket beside him. It was a female figurine. "Ah's goin to stick pins into the head and leave it outside her front door. She'll be runnin to see me, and when she come Ah's going to tell her to stop all this fucking with Young Chang, or all her hair'll fall out. A fair warning. She'll stop seeing your son and will buy the hair-loss potion. Everyone is content." He smiled delightedly.

Old Crone nodded her approval. She uncrossed her feet, took the empty cups, rinsed them under the cold tap and put them back in the basket she brought with her every day. She clapped her hands and the young girl outside beckoned to the first client of the day to enter the hut.

Mei-Ling unlocked the door to her cottage and went to the telephone. She had one of the few answering-machines on the island. She turned it on and listened to the messages. There was only one. Jason Reed's drawl asked her to come to the consulate to pick him up for their luncheon date. She switched the machine off and spent some little time in her bathroom, washing her hair and manicuring her nails. She oiled her skin with a fragrant salve produced by Old Crone, and then coiled her hair into a shiny smooth twist on

81

the nape of her neck. She put on a chungsam made out of starched cream linen. It was slashed practically to the hip on one side, and had tiny pearl buttons on the bias across the shoulder. She looked at herself in the mirror and applied a faint layer of lipstick, a pearlized olive green shadow on her eyelids and black mascara on her thick lashes. She screwed single pearls into her small lobes and was satisfied with her appearance at last. She slipped on high heeled patent sling-backs and threw a black patent shoulder purse over her shoulder. She put the gun, the gold Rolex and the gold jewellery into the inside zipper pocket. She picked up a cream, wide-brimmed fine straw hat with a cream and black satin ribbon trim and was ready to start her day all over again.

Her first errand took her to Young Chang's shop. She saw Old Crone looking at her through the slits of the louvres which enclosed the terrace of the stone house. The shop had been built as an extension of the house and Young Chang had enlarged it further. He still lived in his mother's house, having been able to escape the Chinese colony's relentless matchmaking efforts. He was without doubt the best catch of the colony but was not about to give up his bachelorhood. It was only with the advent of Mei-Ling's arrival that he had been tempted to think of giving up the comfort of his mother's home. He was very attracted to Mei-Ling, but at the same time could not reconcile himself to what he considered her loose morals.

It hadn't taken Mei-Ling long to guess, when she first arrived on the island, what was on the Old Lady's mind. Her welcome had been dignified and warm and Mei-Ling had accepted the offer of making her home with her cousins until such time as she would find her own accommodation. Young Chang had been polite but distant. He was not often at home. Mei-Ling had immediately picked up her contact at the consulate, and was often seen out with the consul, Jason Reed. The old lady's hope that her son and Mei-Ling would take to each other seemed vain. Yet she felt that there was always a strange undercurrent between them, that they were not entirely indifferent to each other. Mei-Ling spent several evenings a week with the old lady, keeping her company at dinner, listening to her stories about the island. When Mei-Ling moved to her cottage, Old Crone missed her. She had got used to having the attractive young woman around, who had shown her the respect due to an older relative, and had real aptitude for playing Mah-jong. Young Chang had also found her presence pleasing, although he totally disapproved of her way of life, her free and easy relations with the men who took her out and her diving pupils. He was not entirely insensible to her attractions, but he was not going to have her pushed down his throat by his aged parent. He treated her politely and gentlemanly without a hint of any ulterior design upon her virtue.

She found him stuffy and straightlaced, but handsome and intelligent. He was indeed good-looking, tall as the Chinese from the North were, with good features, and a full, well shaped mouth, which could break into a charming smile. She often was tempted to think of what it would be like to be kissed by that mouth, but had quickly been discouraged by his attitude. They became pals, cautiously treading the path of friendship. She guessed all about his affair with the girl from the tourist office and he covertly watched the progress of her budding romance with the consul. Now rumour had it that she was also having an affair with the Italian businessman Capponcini who was about to build a fabulous club on the island. Young Chang couldn't deny that he felt a twinge of jealousy when he heard people talk about it. Island gossip was the main source of amusement before the arrival of television sets, and there were few of those about. The programmes were sparse and the frequent and sudden failure of electricity made broadcasting quite erratic.

Young Chang came out of his back room when he heard the carillon chime. He couldn't help but admire his cousin's neatness of appearance as she came into the shop. He came forward and pecked her cheek.

"You are looking elegant, dear cousin. What brings you here? Are you going to take tea with the old lady?"

"I will presently, but actually, I've come to see you."

"Then come into the back room. I've just installed a new air-conditioner and we'll be more comfortable."

She followed him obediently and they sat down at his mahogany desk. A large safe stood in the corner and an antique vitrine stood against the wall. Ornate silver objects were displayed in it. The floor was laid with expensive Italian marble tiles. There was no doubt that the business was prosperous.

"I had thought of selling some jewellery; can you help me?"

He looked startled. "Are you short of cash Mei-Ling? You know the old lady and I are always ready to help you out. We're family after all. You shouldn't have to sell your family jewels."

"Dear Deng, how generous of you, but I'm not selling family jewellery. They are just a couple of baubles that were given to me," she smiled sweetly. "You know, by a friend. It's all over between us now and he's left the island and I just want to get rid of the stuff. Perhaps I'll just throw it in the sea…" She saw him frown and his mouth twitch. She loved to needle him. She raised her eyes to him and said. "That's what

84

I'll do, throw them to the fish and maybe one day someone will pull out a Marlin with a gold and diamond Rolex in its gut." His mouth twitched again, but he decided to ignore the pain and asked whether she would have lunch with him at the Yacht Club. "There's a special member's buffet today," he offered.

"Oh Deng, what a shame," he could hear the genuine regret in her voice. "I've already accepted to go with Jason Reed." Young Chang looked disappointed and it pleased her. She stood up and pecked him on the cheek. "Thank you, Deng, all the same. You should give me a little more notice, I have a rather full schedule these days, what with my diving pupils and well, other commitments. I'll just run in and say good morning to your mother before I go to the consulate."

An hour later Mei-Ling was immediately shown into Jason Reed's office. He rose and came to greet her. He was a young man of average height, slightly overweight, sandy haired, shortsighted and unobtrusive. He had an open, frank face and wore small round granny glasses which were always slipping down his short nose. He was the very image of an inexperienced young diplomat working on his first assignment. He greeted her pleasantly and they sat down. He called the receptionist and asked her not to put through any calls. The receptionist winked at the marine who was standing guard. It was common knowledge that Mr. Reed had a yen for Miss Chang. Their orders were to let her in any time of day or night.

"So what's new?" he asked. "Did you get Capponcini to play ball?"

"Some, but not enough yet." She put down her hat and purse on the desk.

"There was an unforseen accident. I shot Curria's man Limone last night. Capponcini and I parked him in the morgue."

"Am I hearing right?" he asked. She nodded, opened her purse, and took out the dead man's jewellery. She placed it on the desk in front of Jason.

"These are Limone's belongings."

He handled the Rolex a little enviously. His own Swatch was rather low-key compared.

"Better tell me all about it, and don't miss out any of the juicy bits." He set up a recording machine and then snapped his fingers. "Now."

She spoke evenly and clearly for about twenty minutes. He raised his eyebrows a few times but didn't interrupt her. He knew her reports to be accurate and concise. When she had finished, he turned off the recorder and sat back in his chair. He played the tape through again and they both listened to it carefully. Then he asked her whether she had anything to add or change. She shook her head.

"Have you brought in the gun?" She took it out of the purse and gave it to him. He dropped it into a drawer of his desk. "I don't like Maria Beatriz's involvement. She's not a bad girl but Curria's got her in a corner because of her gambling debts. Do you think she's going to keep her mouth shut about Limbo Limone?"

"I think so, at least for a little while. After all Curria's got his shipment, all intact."

"He'll wonder about what in hell has happened to Limone though. What are we going to do about him? Any ideas?"

"How about you claim him as a US citizen who's met with an accident and ship him out of here? The bereaved family could arrive on a charter flight and take their late lamented with them for burial at home."

"You make it sound to simple, Mei-Ling, but there are such minor details as death certificates, personal effects, documents and coffins."

She frowned, creating a charming effect of criss-cross lines on her otherwise smooth brow. She looked like a young kitten and Jason was tempted to stroke her face. "They are minor details, Jason. All you have to do is slip the doctor on duty a fist full of dollars for the death certificate, and I'm sure you've got a passport or two lying around which could be used for John Smith. The important thing is to get yourself over there and claim him before they start inquiries as to who this boyo is."

"Why didn't you just throw him overboard, like the tarpaulin?"

"It didn't seem the right thing to do at the time. Besides, we wouldn't have bumped into Maria Beatriz and found out about the true purpose of the new pharmaceutical company in Devil's Valley."

Jason tried to curb her. "You don't know about the true purpose until you actually see it. Facts, my dear girl, and not feminine intuition is what we are aiming for. Are you positive those cases contained drugs and not alcohol?"

"That's a ridiculous question; what else could they contain? They've been using Capponcini's bay for several months, if not longer. I saw the mini sub come and go regularly."

Jason Reed thought for a moment, drumming the desktop with all ten fingers.

"Stop playing the piano, Jason, and hit the road."

"OK, I'll go to the morgue and deal with John Smith. You, *you*," he pointed a finger at her, "you find out what goes on in the pharmaceutical factory and what they are brewing there. Get Capponcini to help you."

"Can I really deliver the immunity bit?"

"Washington would have to formally approve it; why don't you just string him along a bit, you're quite good at that."

"Thank you for the compliment, but Maurizio wants it in writing. I suggested we flew to Washington together and spoke to Mr. P. Can you fix us up with an appointment?" Jason looked doubtful and got up from behind the desk. "I'll try, but you've promised a deal more than we had agreed on."

He took his jacket off a hanger in the closet and slipped it on. "You should never stick your neck out like that, Baby,"

"I tried to get him to help and he has. Now he wants to safeguard himself and his family. It's only natural."

"What family? I thought he was separated, getting a divorce," Jason said.

"Yea, well anyhow, do the best you can. What time lunch?"

"One p.m. punctually."

The Yacht Club was festively decorated for the special members' luncheon. The tables were laid with emerald-green tablecloths and starched napkins to match. Tall white and green cut glass wine goblets, fine silver-plated cutlery and a spray of orchid blooms graced every table. The tables were set out on the vast covered veranda which overlooked the yachting harbour.

At least a dozen ocean-going motor yachts were moored at the quay-side, as well as some sleek sailing vessels which had been racing round the oceans of the world before taking a well deserved break in 'Tequila's' sheltered natural harbour. Youngsters of all nations crewed on these boats, but the majority were young American, Australian, British and Scandinavian men and women. They were always suntanned, pony-tailed, slim and wiry. They had an unmistakable air of the sea about them; their eyes were almost always light and dreamy, their hair bleached by the sun. They were welcome guests at the Yacht Club because the locals lusted for new blood. New blood which wouldn't be too demanding; new blood also looking for some transient comfort after long weeks in cramped quarters at sea. Looking for a bathtub, unlimited fresh food and gin, a good bed with or without an attractive occupant to share it with. The Yacht Club was hosting a table for twenty of these young crew members and they were standing at the bar, socializing with the locals before attacking their outsize American broiled steaks.

Maurizio Capponcini sat at his table and sipped his wine thoughtfully. He was alone and enjoyed the scene which was unfurling before him. He was watching the bar and the people crowding around it. Curria, standing near Maria Beatriz, was urbanely discussing the best route to take around Cape Horn with one of the racing vessels crew, for all the world as if he had done nothing else from babyhood. At the same time he was eyeing the sun-bleached pigtailed girl in cut off jeans and a tight and faded T-shirt who had accompanied the young man. He already imagined her after a going over at the beauty parlour, her feet pedicured, her broken nails repaired, her young skin oiled and massaged to a silky finish, and her hair fragrant with a frivolous scent. She caught his stare with her slightly vacant sea-green eyes and blinked. He raised his glass and toasted her gallantly. The fact that they had both arrived with other escorts didn't deter Curria from moving closer to the boat-girl's bar stool and starting a mild flirtation with her. The conversation progressed slowly because her English was halting. It wasn't her mother tongue. She was Norwegian, she explained, from Oslo. Yes, they would be staying the week, resting and loading supplies. He stroked her tanned bare arm and smiled wolfishly. Maria Beatriz tugged at his sleeve, but he brushed her off like an annoying insect. She looked around for a friendly face and hit upon Maurizio sitting on his own. She marched up to his table and stood by the empty chair. He rose and pulled it back.

"Good morning, Maria Beatriz, would you care to join me?"

"You are a real gentleman, Maurizio, not like some other people I know." She sat down and he poured her some wine. "Tell me, Maurizio, don't I look great today? Do you like my outfit?" She was seeking approval like a child. He looked at her intently, studying her appearance. She wore a lemon silk two piece, consisting of a halter and palazzo pyjama. She had tied her head up in a multi-coloured gauze silk turban, the ends of which trailed over her shoulder and down her back. She had on a necklace of gold and large pearl beads and hoop earrings. She looked like an exotic cockatoo, with her coloured headdress, her slightly aquiline nose and piercing black eyes.

"I think you look extraordinary," he said and meant it. There was nothing wishy washy about Maria Beatriz's looks. She always made a statement when she dressed. It didn't always come off, but it was always worth a second look.

"Will you join me in some lunch?" he asked courteously.

"That louse Claudio insisted I come with him, and now look what's happening. He's chatting up that crew cow and hasn't even noticed that I've come to sit with you." She tossed her turbaned head.

"Forget Claudio, he's not worth even a glance of yours. I'm glad you've come to sit with me. We were worrying, Mei-Ling and I, about how you got on last night."

She bent her head to his conspiratorially. "He was

hopping mad because I arrived late without the liquor and Limone. I explained it all to him just like you said. I also got hopping mad just as you said for me to get. Boy, you should have seen and heard me ... He wanted me to drive him back to the hut, so I did, for the last time, I said. He spent a few minutes there and then started to bring out the crates, cursing and yelling for Limbo Limone, that's what his nickname is. Limbo. No need to tell you that Limbo never showed." She smirked knowingly. "I drove Claudio and the crates back to the factory and some boyo helped him unload."

"He didn't raise any questions or seem suspicious?"

"Why should he? I was being as helpful as I could be, but I also swore it was the last time, that I had better things to do than to drive to the morgue in the middle of the night". She saw him start and clapped her hand over her mouth in dismay.

"Did you really let that slip? You do realize how dangerous our situation is?" he said gravely.

She nodded vigorously. "He was so angry, he didn't even take it in, about the morgue, so stop worrying. Your secret, whatever it is, is safe with me. I would never harm you, Maurizio." She glanced over at Curria who was still busy with the crew girl. "He'll have her in the sack in no time, you just wait and see."

"Do you really mind?" he asked gently.

"Naw, I never did like him much, but at least he paid me some attention, which is more than some other folk do," she said meaningfully. He took her hand and kissed it lightly.

"Shall we go and help ourselves? The *hors d'oeuvres* table looks very tempting, don't you think?" he said as he pulled back her chair.

Mei-Ling and Jason Reed came to their reserved table and Jason had ordered champagne. It was standing by the side of his chair in a frosted wine cooler. He poured the sparkling pink liquid into the chilled flutes.

"What are we celebrating?" she said smilingly as they clinked glasses.

"Not much, but the show must go on."

"How was the morgue?"

"Fine, as morgues go. Elegant Carrara marble everywhere."

She sipped some more champagne and simpered at him.

"Were you able to claim the body?" He laughed delightedly and nodded.

"Oh yes, indeed. He's all sealed up in his pine box, ready to be delivered to the grieving family."

"Any trouble with the death certificate?"

"None at all. The doctor didn't even want to look at him. The doctor had had rather a carousing night aboard one of the boats, and it was about all he could do to keep his Alka Seltzer down. Took my word about the fellow having had a heart attack. More champagne?"

"Why not? Waste not want not, especially pink champagne." She looked around and waved to Maurizio and Maria Beatriz. "We'll take a peek at the pharmaceutical factory tonight, Maurizio and I. Look at Maria Beatriz, doesn't she look like a colourful jungle bird? She really is attractive, don't you think?"

"I'll settle for a Chinese nightingale, or even an ordinary home grown sparrow." Jason Reed had never been an adventurous type when it came to his sexual preferences. It astonished him therefore, that he found Mei-Ling extraordinarily pleasing.

"Shall we go and help ourselves to the buffet? The locusts are already on the march." He guided her to the buffet tables and handed her a plate. "Isn't that Young Chang with his tourist attraction? Yes I thought so." Mei-Ling smiled and nodded at them. "Would you like me to ask them to join us?" Jason continued.

"Please don't," Mei-Ling said firmly and concentrated on the food. "That cold salmon looks good, and how about that lovely bouquet of crayfish?" She held out her plate and Jason heaped it with her favourites. When he had helped himself they returned to their table and tasted the salmon in the chef's special *sauce verte*.

"We've chosen well, I think." Jason said and looked at her curiously. "It's not really in my interest to say this, Mei-Ling, seeing how I feel about you, but Young Chang is very personable. I can't understand why he does not appeal to you."

She spooned some more *sauce verte* on to her fish before she answered. "I never said he didn't appeal to me. Furthermore, I don't think that he's entirely indifferent to me. It's just that he's obviously tied up with this girl and Old Crone is trying so hard to matchmake that it's almost put him off, but I can wait. It won't be long now." She forked up the salmon and chewed on it happily. Jason Reed burst out laughing.

"So you're really out to get him, you little minx."

"I love living here, I love diving, and I love emeralds." She held out her glass for more champagne. "I could even grow to love Young Chang. Did you know that Young Chang is one of the best and most knowledgeable emerald dealers in the world?"

Jason shook his head. "I only know that his mother makes powerful magic, so folks tell me."

"Have you ever participated in one of the island carib voodoo Happenings? Old Crone and Sorciero, the local magic man, are setting up the Easter one during the *Semana Santa*, much to the distress of the Catholic Church. It always draws a much bigger crowd than their Sunday service in the Cathedral. I'll take you if you want to come with along me and be bewitched."

"I'm bewitched by you already, so I'm not sure." Jason said. "I'm not into all this ethnic tribal ritualism. Do they sacrifice young virgins and all that stuff?"

"They would if there were any left," she assured him. "It's a very rare commodity these days, I'm told. Alas, they are reduced to using cockerels for their ritual nowadays."

Maria Beatriz was picking at the food on her plate. She still felt affronted by Curria's behaviour. By now he had his arm around the boat girl and was escorting her to the buffet, oblivious of Maria Beatriz's furious glances.

"Why are you so angry, my dear?" Maurizio asked. "I thought you might enjoy having lunch with me."

"Oh I do, Maurizio, but you're a married man, even though you are separated, and that louse Curria's made me lose face by dumping me for that crew cow."

"You've still got all of your face left, and you look mighty attractive, so stop thinking about it," Maurizio reasoned with her.

"Thanks, you're really good to me, not like that ass-hole Claudio, who's cheated me out of my property. Oh how I wish could find an honest, unattached fellow who would be there only for me. I would make him so happy," she said yearningly. Maurizio patted her hand sympathetically.

"I'll get even with him," she growled then. "I'll go and have a small conference with Sorciero, he should put a bad hex on him."

"That's a fine idea," Maurizio agreed wholeheartedly. "The badder, the better. That's my motto."

"Do you believe in our Island magic?" she demanded.

"Haven't tried it yet."

"Then come to the *Semana Santa* Happening with me and you'll be amazed. Sorciero has announced that he will dance on fire for the first time like his father and grandfather before him." She rolled her eyes in awe and anticipation.

Young Chang and Maria Clara of the tourist office brought their plates back to the table. He pulled her chair out politely which pleased her. She liked the gallant attentions of Young Chang, especially when they were performed in public. It gave her a certain standing in the eyes of her modest clan. Young Chang, after all, was a wealthy pillar of the business community and was seen at all the important functions. She basked vicariously in his sunshine. She was a tall girl with a magnificent russet silky mane and smooth dark complexion. That, and her ample, rather top-heavy bosom were her best points. If only he would marry her, then her happiness would be complete. Normally she would have gone to consult Sorciero on how to achieve her objective. However, since his alliance with Old Crone, she was not quite at ease with the witchdoctor. Old Crone was always punctiliously polite to Maria Clara, but never invited her to the house. Disapproval fairly oozed out of Old Crone's pores.

"This is a delicious meal, Deng," Maria Clara gushed. She leaned forward and displayed two dusky breasts resting in the cups of her black brassiere. They only momentarily caught his attention. It roved quickly round the veranda again until it settled on Mei-Ling who was flirting with Jason Reed. Jealousy welled up in Maria Clara, spreading a light sweat over her neck and face. "It's not very nice to stare at another girl when you're with me," she complained.

"She's not another girl, she's family," Young Chang answered drily. Mei-Ling seemed to sense his glance and slightly turned her long slender neck. She smiled at him brilliantly and gave him a little sign. He acknowledged the greeting by a small bow. He regretted having brought Maria-Clara to the luncheon. Her physical charms no longer held him totally in thrall and her conversation even less.

"Will you come to the Happening with me on Palm Sunday, Deng?"

"I don't know whether I approve of all that nonsense."

"But Old Crone...I mean Mrs. Chang, your mother, will be present, so there can't be much wrong in going, can there?"

"My mother is a law unto herself." Young Chang managed to avoid the decision.

"What about the bullfight? Will you take me to that? I have a splendid white silk mantilla which my grandmother wore at her wedding," she said wistfully. "I've never been invited to the bullfight." Young Chang looked doubtful. An invitation to the annual *Semana Santa* bullfight was tantamount to an official betrothal. It was a custom they were both aware of, having grown up on the island. He usually took his mother, or went with some male acquaintances. It was the most prestigious event on the island, after the President's New Year's Eve Ball. It was also a good deal more exciting, taking precedence over Carnival.

Carnival had been imported from the South American Continent, while bullfighting had come over with the first *conquistadores*. It was usual for a *torero* of some renown to be flown in especially for the occasion. There were also a number of homegrown aspirants who were tolerated in the ring. Mostly the bulls were reared on the island, but El Viejo always imported a couple of awesome ones from Sevilla. The horses were trained throughout the year by the *picadores*. It was a well orchestrated production which attracted all of 'Tequila'. Those who could not afford to buy a ticket or were not invited, climbed the surrounding trees, walls and telegraph poles. They participated noisily from the top of their precarious perches and it was not uncommon for one or two to take a nasty fall and break some bones. The ambulance stood by, not only for the bullfighters but also for the otherwise injured.

Traditionally the bullfight started at three o'clock in the afternoon on Palm Sunday. The Catholic Church thought it was immoral and sinful to enter into such festivities practically on the eve of the Lord's Crucifixion. The Church thought it more fitting and reasonable to celebrate the resurrection of the Lord, rather than his death. The missionaries had not been able to eradicate this heathen custom even after two hundred years of relentless effort. The bullfight remained a fixture on Palm Sunday, as did the witchdoctor's Happening. Old Crone Chang's advent had given more lustre to Sorciero's big magic moment. She had added that little bit of extra pizzaz from the mysterious East. She would sit regally dressed in a scarlet mandarin's gown, which was richly embroidered with gold thread, surrounded by burning joss sticks. She would occasionally stir the bubbling brew in the cauldron in front of her. She concocted a different mixture every year. It was however always liberally laced with hash and alcohol, which explained the popularity of the brew amongst the participants who were invited to partake. This year would be Sorciero's true initiation, and he would perform his dance on hot coals for the first time. It was going to be his best performance yet and he could hardly wait to show off his new trick. It worried him a bit that there would be no dress rehearsal for the dance, but he had great faith in Old Crone's painkilling salve and she reassured him that it would alright on the night.

The whole island was gradually beginning to throb with the approach of the *Semana Santa*. The Roman Catholic clerics were dusting down the black Madonna for the procession around the island's scattered churches. Choir boys were practising their hymns, and their mothers were busy soaking the surplices in bleach to give them that extra brightness for the Holy days. Fresh sand had been carted to and spread in the bullring; the horse-brasses were being polished, the saddles waxed, and the new costumes sewn. All the hotel beds had been booked months in advance and the harbour was going to be chock-a-block with yachts large and small. The airport was logging charter flights from other islands from dawn to dusk. It was going to be 'Tequila's' greatest and busiest *Semana Santa* ever.

Chapter Four

Mei-Ling accompanied Jason Reed back to the Consulate after they had finished luncheon. It was only a short walk, but the heat was intense after the comfort of the fan-cooled, shady veranda of the Yacht Club. She felt sweat soaking into her hat band and knew that her starched ivory linen was beginning to wilt. She usually coped very well with the climate, but she was weary and could have done with an afternoon siesta after the exertions and traumas of the last twenty-four hours. She must prepare for another almost sleepless night in the company of Maurizio. She had noted with satisfaction that he was doing his bit with Maria Beatriz and that Curria had not seemed the least put out by the disappearance of Limbo Limone. She wondered how long that would last.

At the Consulate a sheaf of messages was awaiting Jason. He and Mei-Ling settled down side by side at his desk and chewed through them. Hiding behind Jason's deceptively bland facade was a sharp and tough brain. He had a good grasp of the drug scene in South and Central America. He had been watching the Caribbean involvement for some time and had been teamed up with Mei-Ling. They worked well in tandem and trusted each other's abilities. Washington had replied to Mei-Ling's request for an appointment with the boss. It was not convenient, or useful it seemed, to receive her and Capponcini before Easter.

She frowned and handed the message to Jason. He cursed, pulled the telephone towards him and started to dial. When he got his party on the line, there was nothing easygoing or indolent in Jason's tone as he confirmed the urgency of the matter in hand. He listened to the answer and scribbled on his notepad. He pushed it down the desk and made a thumbs down sign. 'Go on feeding him promises' she read. She slammed her hat on to her head in a fury and stormed out of the office, past the yawning marine, who had the temerity to wink at her. She hopped into her small pick-up truck and made for home, stopping at the market for some groceries and fresh vegetables on the way. She would ask Maurizio to come to town for dinner instead of her going to "Trade Winds". She would have to string him along and hope that he would agree to investigate the plant in Devil's Valley during the night. He could sleep in her guest room for a change. She smiled wickedly, knowing that Young Chang could see anyone who came and went from her cottage through his field glasses, and that he watched frequently.

Maurizio tied the boat up to the dock. He had been to the bank and come back later than he had thought. He felt a bout of indigestion coming on. He wasn't sure whether the cause was the opulent buffet luncheon he had eaten or the fact that Curria's speedboat was also tied up there, and that his boatman was in the process of emptying a bucket of swill into the pristine cove.

"Stop that immediately, or I'll report you to the harbour police," he yelled at the boatman, who looked at him with some defiance.

"My Boss say it's OK..." he grunted

"I'm Boss here, so stop now," Maurizio said

threateningly and sprinted up the steps to the deck, where he found Curria lying on a deck-bed, smoking the usual thick Havana. On the deck-bed next to him lay the crew girl he had picked up at the Yacht Club. She had cleaned up nicely and was wearing one of Domitilla's expensive silk caftans. She was fast asleep, breathing peacefully.

"What the devil do you think you're doing, Curria? You can't just bring any Tom, Dick or Harry here, and dress them up in my wife's clothes," Maurizio shouted.

"I should think not; her name is Christelle, not Tom, Dick or Harry. I'm not a pervert, you know. And don't yell, you'll wake her up and I want to talk to you."

"I'll yell as much as I like. This is my house and my wife's caftan."

"Shurrup, Capponcini and listen good." Curria had lost all his urban charm. He spoke in Italian with a strong Sicilian accent. "Limbo Limone has disappeared. What do you know about that?"

"Best news I've heard in years, *Mi congratulo con te.*"

"This is no time for feeble jokes, Capponcini. What happened last night after we left the cove?"

"I grilled a delicious red snapper. Do you want to know what I had for dessert?"

"Chinese fortune cookies I guess." Curria snarled. "You don't know when to stop, do you? Did you or didn't you see Limbo last night?"

"Sure, I saw him. He was unloading the sub. Everyone must have seen him."

"Don't play the fool. You know very well I mean after they had unloaded, later. Did you hear or see anything?"

Maurizio shook his head. "Can't say I did. Limbo's probably shacked up with some bimbo." He was the only one to laugh at his little rhyme. "Did you know I was so talented, Curria? A real poet." Curria shook his fist at Maurizio and scowled.

"Tuesday night's the next shipment. Be prepared. I may need you to help me now that Limbo's missing," Curria said.

"You're not going to get any more help from me. I agreed that you could use the jetty and the cave. Other than that, nothing."

"You're in no position to negotiate, my fine gentleman. Next Tuesday as usual." Curria turned to the girl and shook her shoulder unceremoniously. She sat up and yawned, startled at the sudden violence.

"C'mon, we're leaving," Curria said. She acknowledged Maurizio with a nod and said plaintively, "Where are we going?"

"We're going home."

She looked bemused. "I thought this *was* your home."

"*Quella non capisce niente,*" Curria laughed.

"*Vattene al diavolo, bastardo, e porti questa putana con te,*" Maurizio said to Curria with ill-contained violence. He would have liked to slam his fist into that swarthy face. "Go quickly otherwise I'll ram that damned cigar right down your evil throat." He did not wait for Curria's reply but stormed into the house and threw himself on the bed. He clasped his hands behind his head which was throbbing with anger and frustration. The turning point had come. He would help Mei-Ling get the bastard with or without written assurance from Washington that he would receive immunity from the Italian Government if he returned. Probably it was better to be under house arrest in Italy, than be under house arrest under Curria's law. He turned on his answer-phone and listened to Mei-Ling's message. It was a non-committal invitation to

102

dinner, and she would be waiting for his reply. It was just as well she had not mentioned anything else. Maurizio wouldn't have been surprised if Curria had just listened to the messages. He had as good as taken over 'Trade Winds'. Maurizio checked his watch and set his alarm for two hours later. That would give him an hour to rest and get ready for the evenings work before he had to take the dinghy back to Sta. Lucia and his dinner date. He spoke briefly to Mei-Ling and then closed his eyes. He swallowed the sudden surge of half-digested food which bubbled up into his throat. He got up, went to the bathroom, stirred a spoonful of bicarbonate of soda into a glass of water and downed the frothing mixture with a shudder. Then he lay down and dozed off. Again he dreamed of home and the Tuscan landscape which he so loved. Whenever he thought he had got there, it dissolved in mist. He cried out in misery as dark rain clouds swept over the sunny blue sky and he was drenched by sheets of water. He woke up with a start, covered in abundant sweat, tears pouring down his cheeks. He hadn't wept since his mother's death many years ago. Maurizio Capponcini felt sorry for himself for the first time in his life and he didn't like the feeling.

Sorciero was getting ready for his dress rehearsal. He had unpacked a feathered head-dress which he shook energetically. A cloud of dust burst from it and swirled around the porch. He sneezed and continued shaking it until he was satisfied that it was reasonably clean. He smoothed the feathers down, took it inside, and put it on. It hung all the way down his muscled back when it was in place. It had been in his family for years and had been worn by his father and grand-father at all the Happenings. Family lore had it that it had been brought over from the South American

103

mainland by an ancestor, but the mass of Ostrich feathers which were inter-spaced with parrots and peacock feathers made the origin somewhat doubtful. It was nevertheless a splendid piece of decorative apparel. The art of witchcraft, and indeed the title of witchdoctor, was handed down from father to son, and each generation carefully instructed the next one in the various secret and public rituals. Sorciero however, was going to introduce some of his own magic, aided by Old Crone Chang. His father, the old Sorciero, had noticed that his followers had grown scarcer in the last few years and his purse grown lighter than in the good old days. He had put it down to the white man's arrival and with it the white man's medicines and entertainments. Now he had passed away and his successor, Sorciero Junior, had teamed up with Old Crone and they had turned it around. Things were looking up, he felt sure. Already there were so many more clients who were seeking help, and after a successful Happening there was no telling how many more would be added to their list.

The small wooden house in which Sorciero lived with his mother was situated at the beginning of Devil's Valley. It was no accident that the witch-doctor's residence was there. There was an eerie atmosphere about the densely forested valley. It was also declared taboo by the islanders unless accompanied by the Sorciero. The old Sorciero had established a clandestine Tequila still in the valley which augmented his income. He didn't want anyone poaching on what he considered his patch, so the rumour of evil spirits in the forest was quickly propagated. The chemical factory had at first seemed to be encroaching on his territory, but when Old Crone managed to get dollops of hash and pure cocaine from the nightwatchman of the factory to enhance her brew, Sorciero had made peace with the encroachers.

The windows and doors of the house were wide open so that the breeze would cool the air in the rooms for the night. Sorciero stood in front of his most prized piece of furniture, an antique mahogany cheval mirror which a grateful client had bestowed on him. He was applying streaks of white and red war paint to his face, neck and forearms. He riffled through his trinket basket and tried several nose rings carved out of whalebone and tortoiseshell. He finally settled for an alligator-shaped one made out of shell. He pinned a long safety pin threaded with black and red coral beads through his lower lip and grinned into the mirror, baring his teeth. He turned from side to side, checking his headdress with critical eyes. He wore only a fake leopard skin loincloth over his not inconsiderable genitals. He rippled his muscles like a professional body builder and fancied himself fierce-looking enough. He slipped a walkman around his neck, put on the earphones and turned on the music. He started to prance around, stamping his feet in time to the rhythm, gesticulating with his arms and hands. It was quite a slow dance at first, which then increased in speed and movement as he listened to the music. He watched his reflection in the mirror and made horrible grimaces, shouting unintelligible guttural words, which ended in a bloodcurdling scream at the end of the dance. As it was only a dress rehearsal he had decided not to try the actual hot coals, as he continued to dread the whole procedure.

"Ahr ugh, ahr ugh," he grunted and started his dance all over again, improving it as he went along. He made the feathers of his headdress swing down his back by shaking his head rhythmically to the music. He thrust out his pelvis and did a Mick Jagger grind, a movement he had copied perfectly from a Rolling Stones video.

Maurizio and Mei-Ling had left their vehicle behind some clumps of cacti at the top of the road leading into Devil's Valley. It was a dark night because the moon was obscured by rain clouds. They had dark clothing on and wore black hose over their heads. Mei-Ling had reluctantly cut up a pair of her best St. Laurent glossy black tights in order to fashion their protective covering. They were armed with a diver knife and a flashlight each, while Mei-Ling had a wire-cutter tucked into her belt. They walked silently in single file behind the rays of Maurizio's powerful torch. They saw the lights on in Sorciero's cabin and Maurizio quickly clicked the torch off. Mei-Ling suddenly pulled Maurizio back as they heard the frightening sounds and they listened to the awful shouts which emanated from the cabin. They crept to the open window and peered in. Sorciero was on the last bit of his ritual dance and his eyeballs were whirling around in their sockets. He stopped dead in his tracks, eyes rivetted now on the window and the two black figures staring at him. He pulled his tongue out and gurgled alarmingly, thrusting out his arms, palms outward towards the window, in a defensive gesture.

"Ah ugh, Ah ugh, Mother, help me, help me, the two black devils are after me," he bellowed and fell backwards onto his faded, patterned carpet in a dead faint.

Maurizio and Mei-Ling hurried away into the forest and took cover. They saw Sorciero's mother pulling the blinds to, and heard her screaming at her son, begging him to wake up. When all was quiet again, they walked forwards, keeping to the edge of the road. It was at least a two mile walk to the chemical factory.

The sky became even darker and a sheet of rain fell violently, drenching them. Mei-Ling cursed and they took cover under the trees. The storm was soon over and the stars and the moon were bright again. They heard a car engine and pushed further into the trees to avoid being seen. They came into a small clearing.

"D'you see what I see?" Maurizio murmured and pointed to the one storey structure which stood in the middle. "That couldn't be the factory, could it?"

"Rhetorical question?" she murmured back.

"How do you say 'yes' in Chinese?"

"I don't give language lessons for free."

"So, what is this place, if you're so clever and knowledgeable?"

"It's Sorciero's clandestine still," Mei-Ling said. "Care for a drink?" She waved him towards the building. It was dimly lit inside and there was a distinctly pungent smell of alcohol in the air.

"How do you know that he has a still?"

"Old Crone was telling Young Chang about it; that was before they realized that I understood the lingo. It is quite lucrative it seems. Old Crone uses the stuff for her potions, for free of course."

"Fine family you have," Maurizio whispered sarcastically.

"Ever heard about people living in glass houses throwing stones?" she answered.

"Yea, yea, yea," he said with some impatience. He took her arm and edged her away from the building. "The coast is clear now, car's gone. Shall we move it along?"

"In the dark you sound like an English aristocrat," she teased him. "Totally Establishment."

"Don't I look like one as well?" He sounded hurt. "All that money spent on an English education, and I still look like an Italian peasant."

107

"No, no — you look like a well preserved South American playboy, a little bit decadent, but not unattractive for all that."

They were back at the edge of the road. They walked briskly for a moment, observing silence and listening to the sounds of the rainforest. Strange chirps, squawks and rustling came from its depth. Water dripped off the leaves and splashed into the little pools formed by the intense downpour. There was no .sight or sound of another vehicle and they proceeded rapidly down the road. It took them fully twenty minutes of forced marching to reach what they assumed were the wires which fenced in the chemical factory. There were flood lights placed at regular intervals around the perimeter and a solitary figure was ambling along carrying a shotgun. He stopped to light a cigarette and then continued to walk, gun slung over his shoulder.

"Who's that?" Maurizio whispered.

"Nightwatchman," Mei-Ling answered.

"Only one?"

"One only, I checked; presumably they never expect any trouble. Do you want the wire-cutters now? This looks like a good spot."

"Supposing an alarm goes off, or something, when we cut?"

"That's a risk we'll have to take, but I don't think they'll have wasted their money on that. The locals never come here because it's taboo, *mala suerte*, and government property. The others don't want any encounters with the Mafia, so go for it, cut."

They were inside the perimeter and sheltering against a wall of an outbuilding when the nightwatchman came by again. He didn't notice the neat aperture cut into the fence. He drew in the smoke of the cigarette and blew smoke rings into the moonlit night. The odour of marijuna travelled towards them.

"What if he sees us the next time round? Will I have to thump him, or have you got another neat little handgun hidden up your breeches?" Maurizio stifled a yelp of pain as she kicked him on the ankle.

"Sorry," she breathed, "the urge was irresistible. Does it hurt?"

"You're damned right it does. You could at least kiss it better."

"You deserve another one for that remark. Come on, let's move."

They darted across the yard towards the two storey, squat, modern building. There were a couple of cars parked by the entrance. She pointed to the Range Rover, and mouthed "Curria". The shadow the vehicles cast provided the only shelter around the factory. They crouched beside them and waited again until the nightwatchman had started on his new round. Maurizio pointed at the windows. There was a light showing in some of them.

"There must be a night shift," he whispered. "I thought you said there was only the nightwatchman."

"I never said that. I only said that there was only *one* nightwatchman."

"Funny, I get a distinct feeling of '*deja entendu*'. What did you say about the nightwatchman?" She giggled.

"And stop that noise, they can hear you all the way to Sta. Lucia."

They ran the few paces to the entrance and tried the handle of the massive doors. They stayed firmly closed.

"I suppose you'll pick the lock now," he muttered ironically. She ignored him and took out something which looked like a steel nail file from the miniature knapsack she was carrying. She inserted it into the lock and twiddled it about. The expected click announcing that she had succeeded eluded her however. The doors stayed shut.

"We could try a key," he suggested and pulled out a bunch from his knapsack.

"Don't be ridiculous," she spat out and redoubled her efforts.

"The man's going to come around the corner any moment. Just let me try," he argued and pushed her gently aside. The third key he tried released the door and they quickly moved inside. There was no movement in the dimly lit hall. She grabbed his arm and drew him into the first doorway.

"Where did you get the keys?" she demanded fiercely. "You've had them all along, I suppose. You're really part of the organization after all, not just an almost innocent bystander as you tried to make out. What a damned fool I was to trust you."

"Why can't you ever give me the benefit of the doubt? You pronounce me guilty before I've even stood trial." He grinned at her. "Do you want me to tell you about the keys?" She shrugged her shoulders contemptuously. "It doesn't matter any more."

"I know this isn't the best place to start a long explanation, but I'll do so nevertheless. Curria was at 'Trade Winds' with the yacht girl when I got back from the town. We had a great argument and he stormed off with his bird, leaving his keys behind. They were wedged between the mattress and headboard of my bed. The bastard had evidently made good use of all the facilities. I thought the keys might come in handy, so I brought them along. Does that earn me abuse and another kick on the ankle, or unequivocal praise?"

"It earns you an A for a good fairy story, speedily improvised and well told."

A door suddenly opened, throwing more light into the hall. Maurizio and Mei-Ling flattened themselves against the wall and held their breaths. Two white coated figures crossed the hall chatting to one another. They were extolling the merits of aspirin and the drug with which they had improved and refined it. They spoke Spanish and were probably from the South American continent. They entered another room and Maurizio had a glimpse of stainless steel counters, test tubes and microscopes before the door closed behind them.

"D'you think that it's a legit chemical factory, and that we're wrong about the whole thing? Aspirin is legal everywhere."

"Not a chance. They have to have a good front, for the sake of the government. Let's try and get down into the basement; that's where the real drugs are being cooked up, I'll bet."

They tiptoed down the stairs and came to another locked door. Maurizio produced the bunch of keys and within seconds they were in the basement. The basement was quite large and extended under the yard. Some doors were open and they could see some bunk beds crowded into a windowless dormitory. Noisy extractor fans were operating, but the air was heavy and fetid. In another room there were some shower stalls, urinals and toilets. Mei-Ling wrinkled her nose in disgust at the odours which wafted through the hall. They walked silently to the end of the area and stopped in front of a solid looking steel door which was well furnished with locks and bolts. On the left of it there was another largish hall in which the kitchen and a food-stained long refectory-like table and benches had been placed. The smell of stale cabbage and curry hung in the air, disclosing that night's menu.

"Remind me not to book a table here for our next dinner date together," Maurizio mouthed. "There's someone coming," he warned and pulled her down under the table. It was the only place which afforded some cover. A man carrying a shotgun trudged down the stairs and went to the steel door. It was the nightwatchman. He unbolted and unlocked the door and threw it open. Some gaunt pale men shuffled out and were herded towards the stairs. "*Vamos, vamos*," the nightwatchman urged them on. "10 minutes for some fresh air and a smoke before you get your beauty sleep." He handed out the reefers. "And no dawdling or other foolishness. Remember what happened to the last one who tried to get away?" He lifted his gun menacingly. "Boom , boom and he was dead."

As soon as they were alone again, Maurizio and Mei-Ling abandoned their hiding-place and ran to the steel door.

"So these are the so-called imported guest labourers," Maurizio said. "They look more like slave labourers. What can they be doing in there?"

"Refining drugs. Cocaine from the coca leaf which they ship in from South America. Those men looked drugged as well. You saw the nightwatchman hand out the hash. Keeps them docile and happy. Let's have a look at the place." They entered and surveyed the underground laboratory.

"Let's take some samples. I'll get them analysed in town." She pulled some small clear plastic bags which contained some white powder and a tube of pills off the conveyor belt and stuffed them in her knapsack. "Time to get out, there's nothing more we can do here," she said.

They were back on the road hurrying towards their vehicle. They had jogged practically the whole way. Maurizio was totally covered in sweat under his black wet suit. It had been the only suitable thing he had found to wear for the evening. He had an uncontrollable urge to urinate, and veered into the forest, peeled off his suit and relieved himself with a grunt of satisfaction. She waited for him by the side of the road. She laughed silently as he came out from behind the trees dressed only in his undershorts.

"Strip-tease a new career you're practising for? Joining the Chesterfields?" she asked sarcastically.

"One more snide remark from you, missy, and I'll go the whole way," he threatened. The sound of a car made them both dash for cover. She heard him whimper and stretched out her hand to silence him. A Range Rover raced down the road, throwing up gravel and dust.

"That was Curria," she said.

"A pox on him and all the cacti in the world. Hope you have some tweezers at home to pull out the spines which are imbedded in me. I doubt that I shall ever be able to sit down again."

"Poor man," she said consolingly. "Don't worry, they are easier to get out than sea-urchin ones, and I've got an ointment for it. Old Crone's Special." They had reached her pick-up truck and she pulled the door open. "You'd better kneel and keep your head down. There are some mighty bumps coming our way." She swung the truck on to the road and made for home. It had taken a deal longer than she had thought, but she was quite pleased with their night's work.

He lay face down on her bed and she was busily operating on his buttocks with her tweezers. There were angry red pinpricks spread over them and he moaned every time she pulled out a spine.

"There, that's most of them done. Now for an antiseptic and the ointment. You'll be as good as new in the morning."

"Never... I'll never be the same again," he complained. "I feel humiliated beyond words."

"Then stop talking and finish your drink. I think I may have to go out for a little while, but I shall be back to tuck you in." She slapped his buttock playfully.

"Ouch, you little sadist," he cried. "I think you're actually enjoying my discomfort and pain. Completely heartless you are. Leaving me alone with my bottom and pride in tatters." She laughed and kissed him lightly on the back of his neck.

"You've done very well, Mr. Capponcini, for an amateur, that is. So pick up your pride and stitch it together again."

Maurizio felt a little more comfortable after having spent a fitful night in Mei-Ling's guest bedroom. Old Crone's ointment had effectively numbed his buttocks and he sat down without yelping. The smell of good strong coffee had tickled his nostrils and had woken him up. Mei-Ling had prepared a delicate and flavoursome breakfast of tropical fruit and wafer-thin pancakes doused with honey. There was an amicable silence between them as they sat on the deck and concentrated on the food. He held out his cup for more coffee and took another pancake. They had decided on a plan of action and Maurizio had agreed to postpone his return to Europe until they had carried it out successfully.

"D'you really think we can pull it off?" he asked.

"Yes, I really do," she said earnestly, with more confidence than she actually felt, and he seemed to accept her optimistic point of view.

The sea was almost as calm as he had ever seen it, even to windward. It was unusually hot and breezeless. He wondered again at the beauty of the island and the limpidity of the waters around it. His little paradise, almost lost. He tied up the boat and walked up the steps waving to Clemmie who was leaning over the parapet of the deck. As he came nearer he saw that she was in a state of great agitation. She was usually a calm person and he feared some ill news.

"What's the matter, Clemmie?"

"Haven't you heard, Mr. Maurizio? He's dead. He died in the night."

"Who, Curria?"

The tears were running down her plump cheeks. "Il Viejo, our beloved President. It's been on the radio news."

"Oh, I am so sorry to hear that, Clemmie."

"The father of our nation, our big Daddy." She sobbed and her shoulders shook with grief. Maurizio tried to comfort her but cursed the old man inwardly. What business had he to die before signing the decree of the sale of the land for the Club? It was most inconsiderate of him. Now the hand-outs would have to start all over again to the new President, but he, Maurizio Capponcini, wouldn't go along with it. More sobs and wails came from the kitchen quarters. Maurizio knew there was no more work going to be done today and decided to give the staff the day off. They were happy to go back to their families and to the churches to mourn their President. Maurizio waited for them to depart, then flicked on his answerphone and waited for the messages.

The first was from Curria announcing his visit during the course of the morning. The second was from Daria Ferrari, burbling about how she couldn't wait to be with him. The third was from Domitilla confirming hers and the children's flight to 'Tequila' for Easter. Maurizio scrubbed them all and went to his bedroom. He moved the mattress and slipped the key-ring back where he had found it. He pushed the bed back and straightened the bedspread. He caught sight of his face in the mirror. He looked pinched and tired. Maybe another cold shower would help, and a cold beer. He wondered whether he had become a true alcoholic during the last months. He turned on the radio and listened briefly to the funereal music which boomed solemnly out of the loudspeakers. Now and then the music stopped and the speaker's voice, bathed in bathos, reiterated the news of the President's death.

Maurizio stepped out of the shower and tucked a towel around his waist. He wandered out onto the deck, leaving a trail of damp footprints on the polished tile floor. He and Domitilla had chosen the tiles in Tuscany and had had them shipped out to 'Tequila', together with the elegant and well-matched furniture. The tiles were rustic Italian cotto. They covered the deck and the stairs leading to the pool. The pool itself was tiled with Prussian blue mosaics. Sea water was pumped up from the cove into the pool and then spilled over the broadside back into the sea in a glistening waterfall.

He looked over and beyond the pool, across the sea to the horizon. A sensation of pure joy washed over him, as it always did, when he looked at that particular view. He went to the cooler and took out a beer. He squinted down at his stomach, hoping the excesses of the past few months hadn't already left their ugly pockmarks on his body. He could have done with a massage, and when all was said and done, with a woman. He had led a monastic existence for more than three months and had warded off all the attempts of seduction by 'Tequila' females. He had a real desire to hold Domitilla in his arms again and renew acquaintance with her generous and beautiful body. At this very moment however, it looked as if he could

116

even have wrapped himself around Old Crone Chang, or very nearly. He smiled wryly at his untimely erection swelling underneath the towel and let the beer trickle down his throat. It was inevitable that Curria should arrive just at that moment to disturb the peace of a perfect morning.

Curria's head appeared at the parapet. His hair was smooth and black, slicked down with gel. He looked and acted like the typical mobster of the thirties. He was preening like a peacock, pleased with his new multicoloured silk shirt, black silk trousers, black Gucci loafers, and of course, sunglasses. He was followed by a new side-kick who Maurizio hadn't seen before. Curria stared at Maurizio with marked hostility.

"Where've you been? I've been looking for you."

"l had a night in town."

"Is that so... well, well, well, Maurizio Capponcini has finally succumbed to island magic." He pointed to the bar. "I need a drink. Go get me one, Griletti, the fridge is over there." He scowled at Maurizio, who looked him with contempt.

"The manners of a pig. Can't you wait until you're asked?"

"You wouldn't have asked me, you goddamned snob," Curria sneered. He turned to the man who was standing by the icebox, not knowing whether to open the door or not. "Get it now, Grillo, a beer, and have one yourself, I'm sure our Gran Signore here won't mind. Let me introduce you. This is my new man, Griletti. I've had him come from Miami. He was a good friend of Limbo Limone. People don't just disappear like that, without a trace. Grillo is going to try and help me find out what has happened to Limbo." He held out his hand for the bottle of beer which Griletti had opened. "I'm asking you for the last time,

117

Capponcini, Are you sure you know nothing about this mysterious disappearance?"

"I certainly didn't put cement socks on him," Maurizio chuckled. "That's rather more in your line, I think."

"I don't consider this a laughing matter," Curria said icily.

"So don't laugh, nobody's forcing you."

"Let's change the subject, then, Capponcini. I lost something here yesterday. Did you find anything of mine?"

"Depends on what. If it's the crew girl's virtue, you won't find it here, I'll wager."

"You don't mind if I search your bedroom; come with me, Griletti."

"I certainly do mind. You had no business to be in my bedroom."

Curria smiled superciliously and replied. "On the contrary; the business I was engaging in demanded it. *Si, Signore*".

"You'll go too far one day, Curria," Maurizio said mildly and picked up the newspaper which was lying on the table. "By the way, did you know that El Viejo kicked the bucket today?"

Curria shrugged his shoulders. "Yeah, no great loss. The brothers will have to fight it out between them. I'm sitting pretty, no matter which one comes out on top."

Maurizio buried his face in the paper and ignored Curria's presence. Curria went to join Griletti in the bedroom. Maurizio listened to the sounds coming from behind the open door. Griletti was obviously moving furniture around and Curria was cursing him for not discovering the missing object. At last Curria gave a yell of triumph and came back followed by a disgruntled Griletti. Curria jangled a bunch of keys which hung on a heavy gold chain.

"By the way, I've notified the police about the disappearance of Limbo Limone. Chief Pereira will want to ask you a few questions. In fact I can hear his launch coming into the cove now."

"I think you're quite mad. What would Limone have been doing here any way; paying a social call? What have I to do with all this?"

"Nothing, I hope, for your sake. The fact remains, however, that Limbo was around here the night before last and that was the last time anybody ever saw him."

Chief Pereira was accompanied by two constables and a dog. Everyone knew the animal. It was the only sniffer dog on the island and scared the shit out of the local population. The Alsatian was straining at the leash as it bounded up the steps dragging his handler behind him. The boat trip had obviously not agreed with it, and it vomited all over the polished floor.

"Wipe up this here crap," Chief Pereira snarled at the handler.

Maurizio ignored the mishap on the floor and greeted the Chief of Police. "Join the party, Chief. Have a drink. I suppose your men would like one too. To what do I owe the honour of this visit?"

"We shouldn't really, we're on duty. But I'll make an exception in this case. It sure be hot today and what with this great loss our nation has suffered, a beer would be most welcome. My men can search the premises in the meantime."

"Search my house? Whatever for?"

"It's about Mr Curria's man, Limone. He's not to be found on the island."

"I can't understand why my house should be singled out."

"Not only your house, Sah. We are combin' the island – a door to door search, as it were."

119

Maurizio glared at him. "You have a warrant, I suppose?"

"Of course, here it is." Chief Pereira pulled a printed plastic card out of his trouser pocket and waved it Maurizio. Maurizio looked at it and gave it back.

"Is this your idea of a joke? My name isn't even on that dirty piece of plastic."

Chief Pereira smiled happily. "That's all I need on 'Tequila'. We don't hold with personalized search warrants." He tilted the bottle against his mouth and drank noisily. There was a sudden commotion in the house and the dog started yelping in a high-pitched excited crescendo. One of the constables appeared on the deck pulling on a white trainer, the other end of which was firmly gripped between the Alsatian's impressive fangs.

"He won't let go, Chief," the constable complained.

"Well pry it loose, Mon."

"Not me, Sah," the constable shook his head emphatically. "The brute has already drawn blood from his own handler."

Maurizio joined the argument. "I'll send you the bill for a new pair of trainers, Chief," he thundered. "Look at the state my shoe's in, half torn to pieces."

"I'm real sorry, Mr. Capponcini. We'll replace them. The dog's still undergoin' trainin'." The Chief turned to the constable. "They'll come off your wages, Mon."

"Why mine, Sah? It's not ma dog. Juanito's schoolin' him, not me." The constable seemed close to tears. A policeman's wages were notoriously low, and it was understood that they would augment their income by taking bribes.

"Oh, just let him have the damned shoe now; he'll tire of it soon." Curria was looking intently at the disputed trainer and said, "There must be a reason why the dog went for that particular shoe. Come to think of it, Limbo had a pair just like that. Perhaps they're his?"

"Do me a favour, every other person on 'Tequila', not to mention the rest of the world, owns a pair of 'Royale' trainers. They have been our best selling number for a couple of years," Maurizio claimed. "I have several pairs here, but the white ones were almost new."

"Why did the dog go for them then? It doesn't make sense. The dog has picked up Limbo's scent, if you ask me," Curria insisted.

"Listen, Curria. You and Limone go in and out of this place all the time. No wonder the animal has picked up some scent; Limone didn't often have a bath." Maurizio wrinkled his nose in distaste. "If you ask me, Limone's in the local cat house, indulging in a binge."

"No, Sah, he ain't," the constable said. "We took a good look in there. Tried all the rooms. Sah."

"And all the girls too, I'll bet. Any new ones in?" Maurizio asked.

"Yes, Sah, there's one new yeller Jap chick, she can turn a trick you wouldn't believe," the constable blurted out. He could hardly contain his excitement. Chief Pereira's withering look dampened it instantly.

"Bring the other shoe, Mon, and go and get the handler here. He should do his bloody job and handle it. Where is he anyway?"

"Tying up his arm, Sah. The animal took a nice chunk out of it."

"So he's bleeding all over my white carpet," Maurizio yelled and stormed into the house. They could hear him screaming about the bloody mess. The dog let go of the half-chewed trainer and bounded after Maurizio, presumably to protect its master. Barks, growls and yells, sharp protests and accusations grew into a monstrous cacophony. A bundle of man and dog was propelled onto the deck. Maurizio had lost the towel which had been wrapped around his waist. He shook one fist at the dog and the handler, while protecting his manhood from the snarling dog's teeth with the other.

"Off, off, the whole lot of you, before I really forget myself. You've done enough damage for one day," he shouted hoarsely.

The Chief picked up the torn trainer. "I could have you arrested for assaulting a police officer, Mr. Capponcini, but I'll make an exception in your case. You're known to be a generous gentleman, and I'll send you some tickets for the Policeman's Ball. Your contribution will be most welcome. C'mon, guys, get the other shoe and let's go."

In Sta. Lucia the people were mourning their defunct President, each in their own way. There were mourners on street corners and in the churches. Prayers were being offered for his soul everywhere. There was a big gathering outside Sorciero's house, listening to his grieving litany. Every so often the crowd joined in, clapping hands in rhythm to the dirge. The girl sitting outside at the table checked her list and let in people who had appointments. In between laments, it was business as usual at Sorciero's hut.

Young Chang's girl-friend from the tourist office had been waiting her turn for some time. She was finally let in and bowed low before Sorciero. He was crouching above a brazier of glowing coals, chanting now and then in a high piercing falsetto. He stared at Maria Clara for a long time and she waited patiently, sitting cross-legged on the faded carpet. There were perfumed joss sticks burning and she felt quite faint with the smell of them. Sorciero cut an awesome figure with his burning black eyes and naked torso and she squinted at him timidly. She was holding a small waxen doll in her hand, and proffered it to him.

"Look, Sorciero," she said finally. "I found this outside my front door yesterday, what does it mean?"

He took the doll and examined it. It was obviously a female with pronounced breasts and short legs. The head had a few strands of black horsehair glued to it, and was stuck full of rusty pins. He sighed long and sorrowfully and looked at her with pity.

"It is a spell, my girl. No doubt about it. A bad one." He continued to stare at her. "Have you felt anything at all, like a sort of pins and needles on our scalp?" He put his hand on her head and gently passed it over her hair. "Ah, you see?," he showed her a fist full of hair which he had produced by a simple sleight of hand. "It's your hair. The spell will make all your hair fall out. Poor girl." She gasped and pulled at her abundant tresses herself. A few wisps came away.

"Why would any one want to put a spell on me, I have no enemies? Help me, Sorciero," she begged. "What can I do to stop it?" .

"There is only one way, my girl." He tilted his head back and chanted, "Only one way, only one way..." He closed his eyes and said, "Are you willing to sacrifice the dearest thing you have?" She nodded reluctantly.

"And what is it, by the way?"

She blushed in the half-light thinking of Young Chang and the things they did together. She would have to give up Young Chang, if she wanted to save her hair. It was the thing he loved best about her. If she didn't, she would become bald and Young Chang would ditch her. She knew she was in a cleft stick. She remained silent.

"I can't help you if you don't follow my instructions, and you must be truthful. No cheating about the dearest thing you have. What is it?"

"My boy-friend, Young Chang, Sorciero," she admitted finally.

He nodded wisely and said, "You are a good, truthful girl. Give up this stranger and find someone of your own kind. Repeat after me: I solemnly swear never to have anything more to do with Young Chang. I won't speak, write or telephone him, or answer his letters or calls." Her lip started to tremble. "You will say this ten times, and as you say it I will remove the rusty pins from the doll's head. That should break the spell. Remember though, no backsliding. It could be fatal. Not only to your hair, my girl. Death perhaps... Are you ready? Then let us start."

"But I love him, Sorciero, and he as good as promised to take me to the *corrida*, and you know what that means," she protested. "I was going to wear my grandmother's white lace mantilla, which she, sainted woman, God rest her soul in peace, wore at her wedding."

"You would certainly need it, poor child, to cover your baldness, if you don't do as I say. Forget the *corrida*, forget Young Chang. Repeat after me, now, before it's too late." She complied tearfully, chanting the words after him. He removed each of the ten pins and then threw the doll into the hot coals. She grasped her head and cried out in distress. The wax spattered and flared until the doll melted down. She remained with her head bowed until he dismissed her.

"I recommend you buy a small bottle of the hair lotion which I have mixed. It can make powerful magic. It costs only three dollars, but if you want a real bargain you should take the large bottle. It contains double the liquid, but costs only five dollars. It will restore any hair you might already have lost." He said it so earnestly that he almost convinced himself of his magic powers. Sometimes he felt a strange sensation in his body and, if he could only hold on to it, he was sure that he would make real magic, like his father and grandfather before him. The trouble was, that just as everything was about to be revealed to him, he invariably fell into a trance and couldn't recall a thing. He had felt the sudden pain she had experienced in her head as he took out the rusty pins from the effigy. Surely that must mean that he was close, very close to true magic.

Old Crone Chang was satisfied. Young Chang had had lunch with her as he usually did when he was not otherwise engaged. He had also gone into town, as he usually did immediately afterwards, to spend siesta time with Maria Clara. Contrary to his usual custom however, he had returned within fifteen minutes. He had stalked past his mother, who refrained from any comment but hid a smile behind her hand. He had slammed the door of his bedroom shut without a word. Old Crone had nodded her head in approval. Sorciero had been as good as his word and the girl from the tourist office had obeyed his command. She felt a twinge of pity for her son, whose pride, she imagined, had taken a blow; but a little hurt pride could be soothed by a clever girl like Mei-Ling. Old Crone lay back in her chaise-longue and closed her eyes. She would nap for a couple of hours, before starting to prepare the dinner she had planned for Mei-Ling who she had invited a few days ago. She had, however, providentially shopped for three people, knowing that Sorciero would be receiving Maria-Clara's visit today. Young Chang was going to dine at home this evening; of that she was certain, now that Sorciero had instructed Maria Clara on how to fight the curse.

The door of Young Chang's bedroom slammed again and woke her from her afternoon siesta. He stopped in front of her chaise-longue and looked at her questioningly .

"Is anything amiss, my son?"

"Nothing that I can't fix again," He pulled the knot of his tie tighter. "I don't suppose that you know anything about this business of the wax doll?"

She looked at him blankly. "What doll?" she murmured.

"Your pal Sorciero hasn't told you?"

"I have not seen him today. I stayed at home to prepare the dinner for my guest. Has anything happened to Sorciero, or has it anything to do with the President's death?"

"No, no nothing at all. Never mind, forget it," he said impatiently.

"You are out for dinner, my son? I have invited Mei-Ling to keep me company. I'm preparing Peking duck. It's her favourite."

"It's my favourite too…I'm surprised that she has the time to spend the evening with you, what with the American Consul and the Italian, Capponcini, both vying for her attention," he said, annoyance in his voice. He looked at his mother again searchingly.

"You quite sure you've not heard anything about this ridiculous spell?" She shook her head innocently, "I may go to the club for dinner," he said, watching her impassive face. "On the other hand, I might come and have some Peking duck. No one makes it like you do."

"Ah, my son, you flatter me," she sighed. "Please assist me, I have to check my provisions." He held her small delicately boned hand and helped her rise. "I suppose that the shop will stay closed for the rest of the day?" she said.

"Yes, and tomorrow and the day after as well. They will broadcast when the funeral will take place. I hope that the government won't cancel the *Semana Santa* festivities. That would be catastrophic for business. Apart from Christmas, it's always the best time of the year for us."

"Don't worry, my son, nothing will prevent them from having their usual celebrations. There will be even bigger and better ones, like the presidential wake and the swearing in of the new President." She patted his cheek. "Everything is going to be just fine."

Mei-Ling was filing her toenails. Not that they really needed to be pedicured, but she was making an extra effort today to be as neat and appetizing as she knew how. She had washed her hair with almond shampoo and had rolled it up on large curlers. Then she had massaged sweet almond oil into her skin all over her body. The white damask silk chungsam which she was going to wear tonight was hanging up, freshly washed and ironed. It was a bit over the top for a small family dinner, but Old Crone had phoned to say that Young Chang was also dining, so she had decided to wear traditional Chinese garb, knowing it would please Old Crone. She was just painting her toenails with a pale pink pearly varnish when the telephone rang. She picked it up reluctantly.

"Hallo here, what are you doing this evening? I thought we might have dinner at the Yacht club."

"Sorry Jason, I have a date. Did you send the samples away?"

"Not yet. These jokers have closed the airport in mourning for the President. They'll go tomorrow, I hope. Sorry you can't make it, but come into the consulate tomorrow, we have to talk."

She put the phone down and continued her pedicure. She spread her toes and waited for the varnish to dry. This time she picked up the phone and dialled.

"Any news your end?" she asked.

"Lots. The President's died, Curria was here to look for his keys and found them where he had lost them. Chief Pereira came with two constables, a dog and a search-warrant, at Curria's request."

"What were they looking for?"

"Limbo Limone, as if you didn't know. They were doing a house to house search it seems. The dog picked up a pair of my white 'Royale' trainers. You know the ones. It tore one of them to pieces. The police took them away just because Curria maintained that his man Limone had a similar pair."

"Shit," she said fervently.

"You said that as if you really meant it!"

"They can't prove anything, can they?"

"You tell me," he answered. "Want to have dinner tonight? I'm beginning to miss our cosy evenings together."

She laughed. "I have a date, but thank you all the same. Tomorrow perhaps?"

"You're on."

Mei-Ling spread a clean sheet over the seat of her pick-up truck before getting dressed for the evening. The truck really needed a good clean-out, but she never found the time to do it. She put her high-heeled sandals and the white orchid plant on the floor in front of the passenger seat. Back inside her cottage she studied her face in the mirror and applied her make-up. She accentuated her almond shaped velvety dark eyes with eyeliner, mascara and eyeshadow. Her glossy black hair fell down her back in graceful waves. She had on a filmy white lace bra and sheer stockings fastened on to a lacy suspender belt. She had decided not to wear any briefs and felt rather like a hooker as she pirouetted in front of the mirror, but she was pleased with her appearance. Sexy, but not too vulgar.

128

She sprayed perfume behind her ears, on her wrists, and after a slight hesitation on the inside of her thighs. It was time to dress. She slipped on the chungsam and did the buttons up on the shoulder. She screwed in her pearl studs and put on a long string of pale grey shimmering baroque pearls. They were the only fine jewellery she possessed and had been given them by her mother, who had inherited them from her mother. A veil of pearl pink lip salve on her full shapely lips and a dusting of powder on her nose put the finishing touches to her preparations. One last glance in the mirror and she then was out of the door and into her pick-up truck. The Chang house was only a short drive away, but it took her some little time to weave through the crowds on Main Street. The mourning had turned into a kind of folk feast and the bars were doing a bumper business. Groups of inebriated citizens were standing around, loudly discussing the succession to the Presidency. A couple of enterprising youngsters had erected a makeshift BBQ in Harbour Square and were busy selling grilled, spicy chicken wings and legs, pork sausages, sweet corn and bell peppers.

Old Crone sat regally in the carved black lacquer armchair waiting for her guest. She was wearing the traditional black silk gown and her white hair was pinned up in a French pleat. Her once fine complexion had wrinkled like silk tissue paper, but her black eyes were still sparkling and lively. She looked around the living room, checking that all was as it should be. There was a *famille noire* bowl filled with white Bougainvillea standing on an 18th century black lacquer and chest, which was decorated with a design of gilt cranes and spidery trees. An antique Chinese silk carpet in faded daffodil and black motifs lay on the marble floor. A set of authentic Chinese

Chippendale dining chairs was placed around the table in the large dining alcove. A bronze incense burner was emitting a tantalizing odour. Old Crone took pride in her home and had chosen only good pieces to decorate it. The climate was not ideal for her precious antiques, but she hoped they would last her lifetime and that Young Chang and his bride might enjoy them after her death. Old Crone had a natural flair for the beautiful and the authentic, even though she was born into a poor and modest artisan's family in the old country and her childhood had certainly not been surrounded by fine furniture and porcelain.

The chimes tinkled and she sent the servant to open the door. Mei-Ling came in, carrying the white orchid plant. She looked not only cool and very beautiful in her shimmering white chungsam, but also demure and dainty. Old Crone sighed with pleasure. She had discovered a kindred spirit in her young distant cousin, who was the authentic jewel she had destined her son to possess. Mei-Ling came to her and kissed her papery cheek lightly, then placed the orchid on the plant table next to the others. There were four others there already, in full bloom.

"Come and sit next to me, my dear. Thank you for the orchid. White is my favourite as you know. It is good to keep an old woman like me company when you certainly could have had many more interesting engagements."

"I'm delighted to be asked to share your meal, honourable Cousin."

After these preliminary civilities, the two women fell into animated conversation. The main topic was the President's demise and the succession to the office. They both agreed that the sons were a sorry lot, corrupt and greedy. They had inherited all their father's bad traits, without having his charisma and intelligence to cover up for them. El Viejo, at least, had been a leader, fighting for and achieving a trade union for the labour force, some social reforms and, ultimately, independence from a former colonial power.

"Is there a law against a woman becoming president of the island?" Old Crone asked.

"Not that I know of. Should I propose you, honourable Cousin? I could think of some worse candidates."

Old Crone chuckled and patted her hair. "You are a shameless flatterer, Mei-Ling, and I confess, I think I would do a good job, but I was really thinking of Maria Beatriz. She might well be quite capable under the right sort of guidance. She has had an education of sorts and is well liked by the islanders. She's not as greedy as her brothers and has at least done some visible good work with her Arts and Crafts Society."

"Do you honestly think that she could do it?" Mei-Ling sounded dubious, but Old Crone nodded sagely.

"Her brothers would never stand for it. They would rather see her dead," Mei-Ling objected.

"But if it is the will of the people?"

"The people, honourable Cousin, are sheep, and can be led any which way by a clever manipulator. Here like anywhere else."

"Now that is exactly what I thought, my dear. Sorciero could show them 'the any which way' at the Happening."

Mei-Ling smiled affectionately at Old Crone. "You are incorrigible, honourable Cousin. I didn't know that you were interested in politics."

"I'm a feminist disguised as an old Chinese woman. I'm interested in many things, including politics."

Mei-Ling looked at her elderly cousin speculatively and said, "Will you answer me one question, honourable Cousin? How can you work so closely with an individual like Sorciero? He's nothing but an ignorant fraud, hoodwinking an ignorant population."

Old Crone studied her delicate, smooth, small boned hands. She stretched them out towards Mei-Ling and said, "I've worked hard, my dear, very hard. These hands were not always so well cared-for and ladylike as they are now. I swore to myself that some day I would not be exploited any more as I had been. First by my own parents, then by my parents-in-law; even my husband, Old Chang, thought nothing of ordering me about and making me work like a slave. He was successful in his business, but I had little benefit from his success. He was not cruel to me, or anything like that, but I was always some sort of inferior being in his eyes. I was always the first to rise and the last one to go to bed. It was the lot of a Chinese woman, so I had been told by my parents in the old country, to kowtow to the males in the family and to constantly see to their comforts. I was lonely, my dear, when we moved here, although there were some Chinese families on the island, amongst them distant cousins of ours. They tried to be friendly, but the women were no better off than I was. When Old Chang passed away, I decided to change my life. I began to grow herbs and concocted remedies, salves and unguents. I used them for members of the family, as there was only one doctor and the hospital was little more than an infirmary.

One day this man came to see me. He had heard of my remedies and asked for my help. One of his relatives had an unpleasant eczema which no one could cure. The patient was none other than Sorciero, the island's magic man. I went to Sorciero's cabin, and discussed it with him. He reluctantly let me treat him, and success was almost immediate. He told me about himself and his work. It was an hereditary office and his ancestors had practised great magic, he told me. Only he, it seemed, didn't have the gift. He had somehow missed out. Try as he might, he could not get the hang of it. I was sorry for the man; he is sincere in his endeavours. So we put our heads together and sometimes succeeded in making magic. Especially where ointments and healing drafts were concerned. I taught him some showmanship and he was a quick learner. He has a kind heart and a fine physique. You will see him at the Happening, he can be quite impressive."

Mei-Ling couldn't suppress a small giggle, thinking of the exhibition she and Maurizio had witnessed.

"Honourable Cousin, do you really believe in all this mumbo jumbo?"

"I neither believe nor disbelieve; I have an open mind. I have seen him go into a genuine trance and say the strangest things. He could be a real healer, I think. So you see, my dear, now you know how we came to be associates. I have earned a fair amount of money with which I have bought objects which were denied me. I love beautiful things, carpets, jades, and of course books ... manuscripts of old recipes."

"Surely my cousin Deng does not deprive you of anything?"

"No, he is a respectful and dutiful, generous son, but you know yourself, my dear, once you've tasted independence ... the things that give me the most pleasure are the ones I have earned for myself."

Mei-Ling looked at the frail old woman with admiration. "Honourable Cousin, I was happy to accept your invitation because I enjoy your company. There was, however, another reason for my coming here tonight. I wanted to warn you about the brews you dish out to your clients. It would be advisable to modify the recipe of your potions and sever relations with the nightwatchman at the chemical factory. I have heard that the Government is going to crack down on the drug scene."

"My dear, there are always rumours in the air. You should not worry your beautiful little head about it," Old Crone dismissed Mei-Ling's warning. "Rather tell me why you are even prettier tonight than usual. Is there some special occasion, some party you are attending after dinner?"

"Having dinner with you and cousin Deng is always a special occasion," Mei-Ling replied politely. Old Crone nodded her approval. The girl had been properly brought up; brought up to respect and honour her elders.

"Honourable Cousin, please do take my warning seriously. My connections at the American Embassy have been quite specific about the proposed clampdown."

"Alright, my dear, I have heard and thank you. I don't know whether Deng will dine with us. He was in a strange mood today. I believe he may have ended a relationship with the young woman who works in the tourist centre." Old Crone smiled with satisfaction; she was obviously pleased with the turn things had taken. They heard a car pulling up sharply outside the house and both women turned their heads expectantly towards the door.

Young Chang came in and looked at the two women who had been waiting for him. He was moved by the frail dignity of the one and the sheer beauty of the other. He kissed the wrinkled cheek offered by his mother and bowed formally before pecking Mei-Ling's cheek. She smelled clean and spicy, and looked like an immaculate pearl, her skin flawless, her hair shining, her full lips delicately tinted. Her well proportioned small body filled the chungsam in all the right places. She would have made the perfect wife for him, were it not that she was no better than a whore, flaunting herself with Jason Reed and the Italian businessman Capponcini. She spent hours under the water with a series of strange men, and generally behaved like a totally liberated American girl, not at all like the demure docile wife he had been brought up to seek.

The Peking duck was placed on the table, with all trimmings. Mei-Ling picked up her chopsticks and took one of the pancakes. She delicately spread it with the sauce, the shredded duck breast, the crispy skin and the spring onions. She rolled it up and offered it to Old Crone. Then she prepared another one and offered it to Young Chang. He accepted it with a small bow. She smiled at him and he was astonished to notice that there was something like an invitation in her almond eyes.

It triggered an instant response, not only in his eyes, but also in his crotch. He bit into the pancake and it melted in his mouth. The food was superb, as it always was at his mother's table. He wondered whether his cousin could cook in the Chinese way. At the same time he wondered what he would find if he took off all her clothes. Small, pink tipped firm breasts, flat stomach, arched back, tight buttocks. The bulge in his trousers became uncomfortably large.

Of course he had seen her in her bathing suit on a number of occasion at the Yacht Club, but her costumes were relatively modest and she never wore a bikini or a tanga. It made it all the more tantalizing. He moved his foot unobtrusively under the table until he found hers. She didn't move away. Indeed, it seemed to him that she reciprocated and increased the pressure. He was pleasantly surprised. He had always fancied her, but thought she was not attracted to him. She seemed to favour European and American men. Besides, he knew that his mother was trying to marry him off, and he felt he wasn't ready to commit himself. Not to marriage; with anyone; least of all to Maria Clara. She was a good girl, but rather like serviceable earthenware compared to the fine bone china Mei-Ling was made of.

They had finished eating and were sipping perfumed Jasmine tea out of the finest, almost transparent porcelain cups. Mei-Ling complimented Old Crone on the superb dinner as politeness demanded. They conversed about island politics and mores until Old Crone nodded off, her head falling down on her chest.

"I must go," Mei-Ling said softly. "I give a diving class early tomorrow morning."

"I will see you home."

"That's very civil of you, but my car's outside."

"You can hardly call that pick-up of yours a car. I don't know why you can't drive a decent vehicle."

"I need the pick-up for my work, Deng. Furthermore, decent vehicles are very expensive to import."

"A girl like you shouldn't have to work. Certainly not as a professional diver. Your place is in the home."

Mei-Ling bridled visibly. "So you think that's all I'm good for, sweeping rooms and cooking dinners and having babies?"

"You forgot the laundry and the washing up," he said wickedly. "Besides, there's nothing wrong with having babies."

"There is, if you've no father to give them. Anyhow, let's stop arguing. I'll find my own way home."

"You must do what you think best, Miss Independence." He sounded put out.

She walked to the door and let herself out. He heard her pick-up move off.

"Why don't you go after her, my son? You want her, don't you?" he heard his mother say quietly behind him.

"I thought you were asleep."

"I was only dozing. Stop wasting time or you will really lose her. It might be too late already."

"That's where you're wrong, honourable mother, I believe that there's hope for me yet." He smiled faintly and let himself out.

Deng Chang knocked on the door and waited. He knocked again. Perhaps she wouldn't open the door and would let him wait outside like some beggar. Perhaps she hadn't gone home after all but was meeting with one of her lovers. He felt his anger mounting and was about to leave when she opened up.

"I apologize, Cousin, for being less than civil to you this evening. May I come in for a nightcap?"

"I thought you abhorred such American customs?" She stood back and let him enter.

"What will it be, Scotch, or a glass of champagne?" She leaned back against the door and he didn't answer but stood close to her. He touched her hair tentatively, then stroked the curve of her cheek. Her lips parted and she felt breathless. He traced her full mouth with a gentle finger. His hand travelled down her neck and stopped on her breast. He felt her recoil as if in panic. He looked at her questioningly and let his hand drop to his side.

"I've wanted to make love to you from the very first moment I saw you. I thought, tonight, that you felt the same way."

"Oh yes, Cousin, I do," she turned away in embarrassment.

"You suddenly seem frightened and shy. It's not like you."

"Everything is happening so fast, Deng," she said and leaned against him, her head against his chest. He held her gently and caressed her back. They moved into her small sitting-room.

"I want to undress you," he murmured. "I've wanted to do that all evening." She nodded and let him unbutton the shoulder of her chungsam. She shrugged out of it and it fell to the ground. "I want to look at you, Mei-Ling," She hung her head. "You are very beautiful; your skin is so fine, so smooth, so sweet. Let me touch it." He bent to her cleavage and kissed her. He released the hooks of her brassiere, and his mouth fastened on to her nipples which responded instantly to his lips. His tongue wandered over her, licking, sucking, then coming up to her mouth. He brushed her soft full lips and she cried out softly. He picked her up and carried her into the bedroom, exploring her willing mouth. He laid her on the bed and undressed swiftly. She watched him until he was naked, then reached for him, and they found each other in a tangle of intertwined arms and legs.

"I didn't know, Mei-Ling, I never imagined."

"That I could be a virgin?" she smiled at him mischievously.

"You were always so sure of yourself, almost brash, going out with all these men, being wined and dined, accepting presents."

"Well, I waited for you to do something, but you never made a move and I wasn't going to be a wallflower for ever."

"I suppose you have more secrets that I don't know

138

about ... I want to know everything about you. I want to see into the last corner of your soul."

"Why?" she asked simply

"Because I think I've fallen in love with you," he confessed.

"What about Maria Clara?"

"We kept company, but I never loved her, or wanted to marry her. It was just mostly about sex. Besides, the men in our family always marry virgins."

"Then I don't qualify any more, but perhaps Sorciero can remedy that. It's been rumoured that he can conjure up a perfectly satisfactory hymen, for a large consideration of course."

"Stop talking nonsense, my perfect pearl of the Orient," he murmured and lay on his back. She caressed him tentatively and watched his growing erection. He groaned and lifted her onto him. She was light as a feather as she moved above him.

"I didn't even take off my stockings," she murmured.

"Leave them on, I love it ..." Her body took over and broke into frenzied movement, contracting in great spasms, as she rode him, crying out in her first orgasm. She fell against him and moaned.

"Deng, save me, I'm dying, ... I'm drowning."

He held her and smiled knowingly. "Will you come to the *corrida* with me, Mei-Ling?" he said after a little while.

"That's tantamount to announcing our betrothal. I don't think I can come to the *corrida* with you," she said faintly.

He sat up abruptly and looked into her eyes. "Why not?" he asked angrily.

"You've not asked me to marry you, properly, that is."

He tumbled off the bed and kneeled down. He

picked up he hand and kissed it fervently. "Mei-Ling, will you do me the honour of marrying me?"

She looked at him seriously. "I am honoured by your proposal, Deng, and I will marry you and love you. There are certain conditions, however."

"Conditions?" he bridled visibly.

"One very important one, in particular. No one will rob me of my independence and I want to go on working and earning my own living."

"What if you become pregnant? Surely you wouldn't endanger our baby by taking risks while you're diving?"

"I never take risks when I'm diving, Deng. And about the baby, I'll stop diving if I get pregnant."

"Good, that's settled. Let's try for a baby right away," he said and cradled her in his arms.

Chapter Five

There was to be no prolonged lying in state for El Viejo. The climate didn't favour such customs. His progeny was anxious to get him six feet under as quickly as possible, and get the new President elected. This was seen as more of a formality than an election. It was understood that one of the sons would take up the banner and proudly continue to rule the island in the tradition to which it was accustomed. What had to be determined was which one would succeed to the presidency. There was a feverish canvassing for votes and currying for favour among the members of the governing body which was to elect the new Head of State. It was an office which was held for seven years, with a further possible seven. Although it had been stripped of most of its official power, it still carried some clout and afforded the new Leader with a pink marble-clad villa, a stretch limo with uniformed chauffeur, an armed guard at all times, free trips abroad, a large entertainment budget, and a not inconsiderable income which was augmented when needed by a quick dip into the 'Widows and Orphans' piggy bank. El Viejo had managed to hold on to the office for almost two terms. It was rumoured that he had amassed a vast fortune which was now to be divided by the siblings.

The funeral was scheduled for 11 a.m. on Palm Sunday. This would allow the attending dignitaries from other countries to enjoy the *corrida* in the afternoon, after a light luncheon at the Yacht Club. They would then rest up in their hotels before attending Sorciero's Happening, and finish off the night with a sumptuous breakfast wake at Government House.

El Viejo would have enjoyed it all immensely, Maria Beatriz thought as she brushed away a tear. It was sad that he had passed away. She had been quite fond of the old tyrant, and had nursed a sneaking respect for him. He had, after all, pulled himself up without even a boot strap, having possessed no boots at the time. He had fought and won self-rule for the island and created a sort of democracy. That he had fallen into the trap of ruling more like a dictator than an elected Head of State was not surprising. It had happened to great men all over the world during the course of history.

Maria Beatriz felt no respect, however, for her three brothers. She had recognized that they were weak and corrupt. As for Maria Dolores, she was beyond the pale. She had managed to draw the old man into her net and become the favourite. Everybody knew that she was the tramp steamer captain's bastard and that she slept with El Viejo, but she carried the name Del Rey. Old Viejo had not even needed to adopt her. She lorded it over the staff at the marble clad villa and helped herself from the 'Widows and Orphans' box.

Maria Dolores would have to move out of the villa now; it was a government residence. The 'Widows and Orphans' box would pass into the safe keeping of the new President. Maria Beatriz felt a twinge of pure joy at the thought of Maria Dolores' downfall. She wondered which of her brothers would take up residence in the villa and how Old Viejo's private estate was going to be divided. She urgently needed the money and a substantial inheritance would relieve her pecuniary shortfall.

She admired herself in the mirror of the hotel suite she had moved into as soon as the news of her father's death became public. She knew that her credit rating had rocketed overnight. After all, she stood to inherit one fifth of the estate. She licked her lips and applied more lipstick and a dusting of pale violet face powder. She had managed to pull on the tight fitting satin knee breeches over the coral pink hose, and squeezed her broad feet into the buckled pumps. Now she gathered all her little plaits into a pony tail which was held back with a black velvet scrunchy. She slipped into the richly embroidered bolero and put the torero's hat on. She turned this way and that, feeling pleased with herself. This was to be the first time in the history of bullfighting on the island that a woman would descend into the bull ring and fight the ferocious animal. She had practised secretly on the farm where the bulls were being bred, and had shown considerable skill. She was to be the surprise act of the day. The toreador costume had been specially ordered in Spain for her and she felt grand in it. To avoid any untoward accidents during the *corrida*, a sharpshooter had been hired to put the bull down if Maria Beatriz couldn't handle the animal.

Like Sorciero, she practised the poses for her passes and thrusts in front of the large mirror, sticking the bandilleras into a stuffed bull with loud shouts of 'Ole, Ole'. The stuffed bull was mounted on a platform which rocked back and forth. She increased the speed of the machine by turning a dial. The bull almost rocked off the platform. She would show this Maurizio Capponcini that she was worth at least as much if not more than that small Chinese hussy with her proprietary airs. After all, why should diving be more glamorous than bull fighting? The bull was as dangerous as the shark. Maria Beatriz draped the red cape over the sword and plunged the sword into the neck of the bull. She bowed to the mirror, hearing the roar which would pour out of the throats of the public. Yes, she would show them all. The telephone rang shrilly and roused her out of her reverie.

"Yes, yes – what is it?"

"It's the car ma'am, waiting to take you to the church for the funeral service."

"Oh damn, I didn't realize it was so late. Tell him to wait, I won't be a minute."

"Your sister Miss Maria Dolores is waiting in the car. She is getting quite impatient."

"I have no sister, you idiot," she yelled. "Tell them not to wait. I shall find my own way there." She peeled herself out of the costume and slipped on a black linen suit. It was the only garment she possessed which was suitable for the occasion. She wrapped a black chiffon turban around her head, rubbed off the lipstick and slapped a huge pair of sunglasses on her nose. She stuffed a packet of paper handkerchiefs into the black backpack she usually carried. Who knows but that she might shed a tear or two and need to wipe her eyes and blow her nose.

The white camper edged its way through the huge crowds which clogged the narrow streets of the capital. They willingly made room for Maria Beatriz and waved to her. Everyone recognized the camper and knew who the occupant was. They had a soft spot for the dead President's daughter and her flamboyant ways. She was a trifle wild, but then she always was good for some entertaining titbit in the local press.

Maria Beatriz left the camper standing at the cathedral doors and hurried into the house of God. The Cathedral was packed with local and foreign dignitaries. The Diplomatic Corps was there in its entirety. She marched up the aisle to the front pews which had been reserved for the grieving family. She reluctantly took the seat which had been assigned to her by the usher. It was next to Maria Dolores. Maria Beatriz looked at her with contempt. The girl was covered in black lace and the black mantilla, which was held up by a richly jewelled comb, covered not only her head and shoulders, but most of her face as well. She was holding a black silk handkerchief with which she dabbed at her eyes occasionally.

"You look more like a widow than a daughter," Maria Beatriz murmured.

"I am both," was the swift reply.

"Perverse cow," Maria Beatriz hissed. "You'll have to leave your marble palace. Make room for the new President."

"I'll be glad to. El Viejo knew that you were all going to be rotten to me after his death, so he bought me an apartment in New York, in the Carlyle Hotel. Best part of town. He also gave me the whole of the 'Widows and Orphans' fund. He said I deserved it on both counts. It'll be quite a relief to get to a civilized place and be among decent people for a change, not stupid bastards like you."

Maria Dolores smirked behind her black lace veil and squinted sideways at Maria Beatriz. She was delighted to see how her words affected the latter. Maria Beatriz' nostrils started to quiver and her mouth twisted into an angry grimace. What Maria Dolores didn't expect was that Maria Beatriz would lift her hand and slap her soundly across the face, dislodging the comb and mantilla in the process.

Maria Dolores held her cheek and screamed. "That's exactly what one would expect from an ignorant, uncivilized bitch."

The incident didn't pass entirely unnoticed, although the organ was being played at full strength and only the people sitting nearest to the girls had heard the scream. A titter started among the congregation which turned into a full scale '*fou rire*'. Maria Dolores abandoned her attempt at ladylikeness, lustily tore off Maria Beatriz turban and began to shred it into little pieces. The Archbishop, who had been going through the motions in front of the altar, turned round and spread his arms.

"Have you no respect for our departed brother who lies in this coffin? I demand silence," he shouted. Maria Dolores took advantage of the moment, rose and ran to the coffin and threw herself over it, loudly proclaiming her grief. She was promptly joined in her wailing by the professional women mourners, thus drowning out the continuous gales of laughter. Old Viejo's sons rose in unison from their pews and tried to prise Maria Dolores from the coffin. She resisted ferociously, kicking and scratching, screaming, "Daddy, Daddy, why did you have to die? How could you leave me at the mercy of these cruel men? Help me, help me." The laughter died down as quickly as it had begun. The spectacle had become awesome, with the Archbishop, the choir boys and acolytes joining in the tug of war. There was a great fireworks of camera flashes as a hysterical Maria Dolores was carried out of the Cathedral and helped into an ambulance which was parked outside for exactly such an eventuality. There were no further incidents and the service was brought swiftly to its conclusion by the Archbishop, to the unmitigated relief of all the congregation.

The official brass band was joined by the traditional steel band as they led the slow march to the cemetery. The hearse followed on a horse-drawn gun carriage with the chief mourners trudging close behind. There was a lot of surreptitious glancing at wrist watches. After all, nobody wanted to be late for lunch and the *corrida*. When the last shovel of earth was thrown over the coffin and the wreaths placed in the right order, there was a scramble for the waiting official cars and the lowlier means of transportation. The official guests arrived at the Yacht Club and attacked the buffet and the champagne. Maria Beatriz decided to pass up the luncheon and drove back to the hotel. She feared that even a tiny bite would be fatal to the tight fitting breeches. She would drink a bottle of water instead of lunch and have a rest before her performance in the bull-ring. She turned up the air-conditioning to its full strength and threw herself on the bed. Her thoughts were in a turmoil and kept swirling around in her head. The mere idea of Maria Dolores living it up in New York made her blood boil. The treachery of Old Daddy for providing the means, while keeping his own daughter on a short leash, was humiliating. This arrangement of course did have the advantage of getting Maria Dolores out of her hair for good. Maria Beatriz mulled this over for a while and began to enjoy that thought. She remembered Maurizio's advice about being a small fish in a big pond if she ever went to New York herself. 'Tequila', after all, was not such a bad place to be, especially if one had plenty of bread. She would keep her prime property on the beach and build her own marble villa there. She might even run for President. She laughed out loud and picked up the telephone. She dialled the number and left a message on Maurizio's answer phone, before turning onto her side and falling asleep.

At three o'clock sharp the *corrida* started. It was the one time when the mañana mentality of 'Tequila' took a back seat. The aficionados had been queuing ever since the television station had stopped showing the funeral. Grief had given place to a festive mood and bright cottons had usurped the traditional black mourning clothes. There was music in the air and multi-coloured balloons floated in the sky. The smell of frying garlic sausages and grilled shrimp was everywhere. People were holding cardboard plates heaped with food, while they shuffled slowly forward towards the entrances to the arena. There were three entrances, one of which was reserved for the dignitaries and privileged ticket holders who drove up in their cars or hired rickshaws. It was an occasion everyone dressed up for, rich and poor alike. Brightly coloured Spanish style, flounced skirts, white, embroidered, starched tops, and mantillas for the women. Men wore black trousers, tight fitting bolero jackets, and black fedoras.

A fanfare of trumpets announced the start of the procession which preceded the actual bull fight. The arena was totally sold out as usual, and a great yell went up as the first bull was let loose into the ring. It was a fine young animal which trampled around the arena, snorting all the while. It was not long before its wandering attention was drawn to the red cape which was being shaken at it by the matador who had entered the ring. He was a tall, powerfully built black man who waved to the crowd while he was performing his veronicas. The bull suddenly lunged forward and almost caught the fellow off guard. He took to his heels and sought refuge behind a wooden screen. Loud jeers and cat calls filled the air, and shouts of 'come out, you yellow bastard and fight' echoed around the arena.

Maurizio sat with the Italian Consul in the front row reserved for the 'Corps Diplomatique' and members of the Government. Maurizio didn't really enjoy bull fighting but had accepted the Consul's invitation because he intended to pump the man about the situation in Italy. Maurizio wanted the Consul to make certain discreet inquiries as to what would happen to him if he returned to Milan. Maurizio would help Mei-Ling and go along with her plan to nab Claudio Curria, and he had as good as decided to return home, no matter what. He winced as the bull made for the horses which had now entered the ring. The picadors were fending it off with thrusts of their spears, tiring it out. The bull charged the nearest horse and butted it, tearing a nasty gash into its hind quarters. The crowd cheered, urging the bull on. The animal was losing blood and seemed to fall back, waiting. The picadors left the arena and the matador, having regained some of his courage, initiated the planting of the *banderillas* in the bull's neck and shoulders. He then approached for the final *coup de grace*. He darted backwards and forwards in front of the bull which had appeared to lose all interest in the proceedings. Egged on by the crowd, the matador ventured closer and closer until he stood directly before the animal. He held the sword up and lunged at the bull. It was obviously the moment the bull had been waiting for as it leapt forward and lifted the man on its horns. The women shrieked as the bull trotted around the ring with the struggling bullfighter impaled on its head. There were shouts of 'long live the brave bull' and all kinds of missiles were thrown into the ring.

The next two fights were not as dramatic, and the bulls were duly disposed of in the proper manner with the usual 'Oles'. There was a brief interval during which cleaners gathered up the debris and tidied up the ring for the surprise star of the afternoon. Young Chang and Mei-Ling were sitting together. She noticed that Claudio Curria was in the government box, as a guest of the Minister of Religious Affairs, and that Maurizio was sitting with the Italian diplomat. Jason Reed was shepherding an American couple from Caracas. He waved to Mei-Ling, who waved back. Young Chang went rigid with proprietary jealousy.

"Are you sure this fellow doesn't fancy you?" he demanded .

"Everybody fancies me," she teased. "I wonder where Maria Beatriz is? I thought that Maurizio was going to take her, or that she would be attending with her brothers."

"You're right. It's not like her to miss the *corrida*. She's always attended as far back as I can remember," Young Chang agreed.

"I'm not sure that I'm really enjoying this," Mei-Ling said.

"We can leave, if you want, after the next one. We would be lynched if we disturbed the spectators now."

Another fanfare announced the resumption of the *corrida*. The *cuadrillas* took up their respective positions and the bull emerged, tossing its head spiritedly. There was nothing sleepy or sluggish about it. The matador skipped in, and threw his hat into the crowd which yelled its approval. He made several successful *veronicas*, and the 'Oles' were swelling. The *picadores* entered the scene and did their bit. Then it was the turn of the matador again. There was a sudden hush, as the bull stopped dead in its tracks and starting pawing the sand furiously. It was then that someone cried out "It's Maria Beatriz, in the ring." The cry was taken up. "Maria Beatriz, Ole, Maria Beatriz, Ole." The whole audience was on its feet now, cheering as she planted her *banderillas* with aplomb. Again it was time for the *coup de grace*, and she wielded the sword hidden under the cape. The roar of the crowd became so deafening that no one heard the single shot which felled the bull just as Maria Beatriz thrust the sword into the neck of the animal. She was carried aloft by the other matadors, and the crowd became delirious as they jogged around the ring with her.

"Give her the ears and the tail, give her the ears and the tail," the crowd chanted. "Long live our Maria Beatriz."

Again there was a sudden hush as she approached the prostrate animal and sliced off its ears and tail.

"Maria Beatriz for President!" a voice bellowed into the hush. It was a cry which was taken up slowly but surely as she walked proudly towards the VIP spectator benches and looked up, searching for someone. Finally she spotted him in the first row and threw the bloodied ear up to him. It hit Maurizio squarely in the chest and he fell back, blood all over his beige linen suit and shirt front.

"Oh God, poor Maurizio; he won't have a thing left to wear at this rate," Mei-Ling murmured. "He's got a real talent for getting blood all over himself."

"What on earth do you mean?" Young Chang was clearly puzzled.

"I'll explain it to you soon. Let's go, I've seen enough gore for one day."

They fought their way past the cheering crowd and finally made it to the exit. Maurizio Capponcini was struggling to get out on the opposite side. He looked green under his tan and clearly disgusted with the whole affair. Mei-Ling walked up to him.

"Are you alright?"

"No, I feel rotten, but I'm grateful for your concern, Minnehaha." He held up the bloodied bull's ear gingerly between two fingers. "Would you care for a little gift? It'll make good soup, I expect, or chop suey."

"You know what that means, Maurizio. It is tantamount to a marriage proposal by Maria Beatriz. How would you like to become President Consort of

'Tequila'? I confess she looked rather splendid in the ring. There appears to be a growing popular movement which would support her if she made a bid for the Presidency. My God, you really do look ill, what you need is a good slug of brandy. Here." She groped in her bag and produced a small hip flask. He took it and drank.

"Ah...that's done me good. Better than your dire prediction about my future."

She laughed and said, "do you want us to drive you to the harbour?"

Maurizio shook his head. "No thanks, I'm fine now."

She turned to Young Chang who had hung behind. "You know Maurizio, of course, Deng?" Young Chang bowed formally. "I want you to be the first to know, Maurizio, that Deng and I are going to be married." Maurizio looked taken aback.

"That's rather sudden. I was under the distinct impression that you two didn't even like each other much."

"Oh, that was just our inscrutable Chinese kind of courtship," Mei-Ling smiled happily.

"I suppose your fiancé knows all about your line of work?"

Mei-Ling blinked at Maurizio furiously. "Naturally he knows I'm a diving instructor."

"Of course, how stupid of me. I assume that our night dive is still on?"

"Definitely; you need it for your dive master certificate. I have also scheduled you for the written exam tomorrow afternoon, four o'clock sharp." She looked at him meaningfully. "See you later at the Happening?"

Maurizio shook his head. "I've had enough happen to me today." He looked around for a rubbish bin.

When he had finally located one, he dropped the ear into it and wiped his hands on his handkerchief. "Oh, and all my sincere congratulations on your engagement," he called after them. The blood was starting to congeal on his stone-coloured linen suit and fine cotton shirt and he took the jacket off as he walked briskly towards the harbour. He reached his boat and jumped aboard. He found an empty plastic bag and started to take off the rest of his clothes, which he stuffed into the bag. He would order a whole new wardrobe when he returned to Italy, assuming he didn't end up wearing prison garb. The consul had agreed to make discreet inquiries about the state of the "Club Royale" affairs.

"Do you want to be arrested for indecent exposure, Mr. Capponcini? Why aren't you wearing any clothes?" The Harbourmaster, who had abandoned his post in order to see the last of the *corrida*, stopped in his tracks and looked at the naked man in the boat tied to the quay-side

"I'm throwing them away, they got soaked in blood," Maurizio answered.

"Murdered someone?"

"Not yet, but I'm sorely tempted to."

"You haven't been fighting a bull, have you?"

"No, my friend, it was just the ears which were bestowed on me."

"That is a great honour, worth getting bloody for. All the same, I would advise you to put something on or leave the dock area. We don't approve of public nudity on this island."

Maurizio nodded as he slipped the ropes off the bollard and turned on the engine. It was the end of an imperfect day and all he wanted was to return to 'Trade Winds'.

153

Chapter Six

Maurizio was nursing his second rum punch. He would no doubt have a third before eating his solitary dinner. It occurred to him that he was probably on the verge of becoming a depressed neurotic. He had swum for a long time after returning from the *corrida* and the water had soothed him for a little while. He watched the sun set and the sky turn bright pink, and then indigo. It was impossibly beautiful and he felt increasingly sad and abandoned. The only messages on his answer-phone had been from Maria Beatriz. The first announced that she was no longer going to sell her property on the beach. The second was that she was looking forward to seeing him at the Happening. He pulled a face at the thought of the trophy which had landed on his lap. He did not find Mei-Ling's little joke about the meaning of it all the least bit amusing. The telephone rang again but he had left the answer-phone on. He heard Mei-Ling asking for God's sake not to say anything about her mission in front of Young Chang. That she was counting on Maurizio's discretion, that she wished he would pick up the phone because she knew he was there.

"All right, Minnehaha, so I'm here, but I'm tired, depressed and lonely. And of course surprised. I didn't even know you fancied Young Chang the least bit."

"I've fancied him for some time, but he was engaged elsewhere."

"I hope you know what you're doing. He's so very, how shall I put it ..."

"Chinese?" She laughed softly. "I know what you mean, but he'll adapt to our American ways in time. Besides, don't forget I'm basically Chinese too."

"Your body is perhaps, but what about your soul?"

"I've stopped searching it."

"What about this double life you're leading? Will you be able to give it up?"

"Not instantly. We've got a job to finish, you and I. Why don't you come to the Happening and stop brooding all by yourself? It's quite an experience. You could come with us and have a ringside seat, courtesy of Old Crone."

"I've had my fill of ringside seats for one day, I assure you. Besides, I have nothing left to wear."

"Don't be so squeamish," she teased. "Just throw on your djelabbah and we'll pick you up at the dock, 10 p.m. sharp."

Maurizio hung up and continued sipping his rum punch. He felt violently homesick. The devil take them all; the whole damned island could sink. He would never miss it.

The Happening had been meticulously orchestrated by Old Crone. She had coached Sorciero relentlessly and now his moment was about to come. Shortly before the Happening was to begin, Old Crone gave Sorciero a good old-fashioned pep-talk.

"This is your night, Sorciero, don't waste it. You are going to astonish the whole of 'Tequila'." Sorciero nodded but looked dubious. "Your whole life could change if you listen to me. You know I've always given you good advice." Sorciero nodded again.

"Think of Maria Beatriz, Sorciero," she said gravely.

155

He raised his eyebrows. "You could marry the girl." Sorciero shook his head in disbelief.

"Me, marry the President's daughter?"

"The President is dead and long live the new President Maria Beatriz. That's what the people of this island are saying and that is what they want. The girl needs a husband, you need a wife. What better match could there be for either of you? Together you've got this island sewn up."

"But, Old Crone, she's going with this Italian Curria and then she threw the bull's ears into another Italian's lap. She likes only rich white men, I think. She would never look at me. I've no car or yacht or any of the things she likes."

"You're a good man, Sorciero, a handsome virile man." He looked astonished. "After tonight, you could hold the whole island in your thrall. After all, you are the great Sorciero, witch-doctor and medicine man. You are going to walk on hot coals and speak to your people in strange voices and tongues. You are their spiritual leader."

"What about the Archbishop? He won't like it. He keeps on telling everyone that I'm a charleston."

"A charlatan, my boy, a *charlatan* – not a charleston. No matter, forget the old goat. Think of your future. You could be receiving your clients in the pink marble villa." She paused, giving him time to digest her words. "Perhaps you don't fancy Maria Beatriz as a wife?"

"Of course I'd fancy her. She's some woman." Sorciero said reverently.

"Then this is will be your plan. Immediately after the dance you'll carry her off into the forest and show her what you can do. Pleasure her, Sorciero, in the way I will instruct you. Then she will be yours for ever. Now pay attention, because we're running out of time. First of all, don't forget to trample in the liquid which I have prepared for you before you walk on the coals. As for Maria Beatriz..." Old Crone continued to speak in her low but forceful voice, while Sorciero listened attentively, grinning now and then with anticipated pleasure. He did find it extraordinary that Old Crone was so well versed in matters of sex; the old woman didn't look as if she had had that much experience. Those Chinese obviously were great guys in the sack. Sorciero would never have thought of all the things Old Crone whispered to him about.

The clearing around Sorciero's hut was crammed with people, as was the road leading up to it. Rich and poor alike were thronging towards the place where the glowing coals had been set down for Sorciero to dance on. Most of the crowd was high on alcohol, and reefers were being passed around. Men and women had painted their faces in the tribal manner and were swaying in time to the steel band. Chinese lanterns were hanging on the trees and incense burners were perfuming the air. Old Crone was seated on her throne, decked out in her gold and scarlet mandarin's robe. She had a brazier in front of her and occasionally threw some crystals into the glowing coals which flared into a small fireworks. A rain of coloured glowing sparks illuminated her before falling to the ground. The young help-meet was ladling out Old Crone's special brew into coconut cups. The brew was more potent than usual and affected the drinkers rather more quickly. There was a good deal of kissing and fumbling in the bushes. A rumour had been skilfully put about that the new President would be chosen by the spirits and proclaimed by Sorciero, their mouth-piece. Everybody held the spirits and their prophecies in awe and the Del Rey brothers were each separately seen in earnest discussion with Sorciero who was seated on his throne. He cut a splendid figure in his feathered headdress which was securely tied around his head. His oiled body, which was dressed only in a loincloth, was well muscled and trim, and caught the eyes of many a maiden.

Maria Beatriz was still wearing her matador outfit. She stood by Old Crone, telling her about her triumph in the arena. Old Crone listened to her chatter impassively. Then she held up her hand.

"Maria Beatriz, you have truly shown courage today, not only at the *corrida*, but also at the Cathedral. I have news for you. The spirits have spoken to Sorciero. You," Old Crone pointed a forceful finger at her. "*You* have been chosen by the spirits to follow in your father's footsteps." Maria Beatriz gave a nervous giggle.

"My brothers would never allow it, Old Crone. They would probably banish me from the island or murder me first."

"Not if you had a good man by your side. Not an Italian gangster but one of your own people. It is high time you settled down and had children. What better place to have them than in the pink marble villa?"

"Who did you have in mind to father them?"

Old Crone stared into the brazier. "The spirits have spoken. None other but Sorciero, our witchdoctor, will do."

Maria Beatriz cut a grimace. "But he's a savage, Old Crone; he has no education and no conversation. Besides he's poor," she protested.

"Don't be fooled by his simple ways. The people respect him and he makes good money. He is healthy and a fine figure of a man. He'll make you fine strong babies. You take a good look at him tonight. I'm sure you'll see him in a different light." Old Crone smiled her most mysterious smile. "Drink this, Maria Beatriz, I have kept it for very special guests." She poured some liquid into two coconut cups. "A toast to our new President," Old Crone whispered.

The music became increasingly frenetic and Sorciero started to lead the dance through the trees, then all around the clearing, with everybody following him in an unbroken line. There was a sudden hush as he stopped in front of Old Crone's throne and threw hands full of crystals into the brazier. The flames shot up and a great shower of sparks fell down.

"Tell us, Sorciero, who's going to take Big Daddy's place?" a chorus arose from the people.

"Oh spirits illuminate me, illuminate my mind, give me the answer my people want to hear," Sorciero chanted and danced towards the glowing coals. His body was shaking with intense fervour and the feathers of his head-dress rippled furiously. He pranced over the hot coals chanting shrilly. He ripped off his loin cloth and dropped it onto the coals behind him. He started rubbing his penis into a mighty erection. The crowd gasped at the spectacle of Sorciero jerking his seed onto the hissing coals as he danced to the end of the fiery path.

"Maria Beatriz for President!" he roared. "She has been chosen by the spirits and by me." The crowd cheered wildly.

"He forgot to soak his feet in the liquid and yet walked over the coals without burning them. I do believe he's in a real trance," Old Crone murmured to Mei-Ling.

"Having an orgasm in public was not a bad bit of ad-libbing. I hope he can get it up again with Maria Beatriz though," She saw Sorciero swoop towards Maria Beatriz, pick up the struggling girl and carry her away into the woods.

"Stop beating me on the head like that, Maria Beatriz," Sorciero panted as he loped through the trees.

"Just listen to me, Sorciero, you're going in the wrong direction."

"I'm not going in any direction."

"That's what I thought. I don't want to be raped in the dirt like an animal. Turn around and run to the road. My camper's there and it's got a lovely bed in it. Soft and springy. Hurry up, now."

"I'm going as fast as I can. It would be quicker if I didn't have to carry you."

"Oh, alright, put me down then, and follow me."

"Are you sorry you joined us?" Mei-Ling asked Maurizio. "I thought it was quite a show, didn't you?"

"I'm not quite sure what it was, but it was certainly different. Sorciero seemed extremely well hung and our Maria Beatriz should be able to relegate her vibrator to her bottom drawer. I must conclude that blistered feet are a powerful aphrodisiac."

"Old Crone says that Sorciero didn't even have the tiniest blister. He made real magic tonight, she feels."

"Did you see the Del Rey brothers when Sorciero proclaimed the spirits' choice for President?"

Maurizio nodded. "They were mad as hornets, but do you think that they feel seriously threatened?"

"Definitely. Sorciero has grown into a real prophet tonight and nobody defies the spirits in this part of the world."

"Perhaps if I returned to Italy and masturbated in public they might elect me President, too. Maurizio Capponcini for President. Sounds good."

"Don't forget the burning coals, though. It's not legit otherwise."

Curria was in a huddle with the Del Rey brothers. It was obvious that they were engaged in an agitated discussion. Suddenly the Minister of Religious Affairs started to shed his clothes and shoes and danced towards the coals in an imitation of Sorciero.

"I'll show you idiots that this is all a sham," he

shouted. "You have all been taken in by a trick. Sorciero can no more dance on hot coals without burning his feet than fly to the moon. As for hearing the spirits call 'Maria Beatriz for President', we only have his word for it. We never heard a thing. I will do exactly as he did and prove to you that you have all been tricked." With that he jumped onto the coals with enormous confidence. There was an instant smell of burning flesh and his mouth fell open in a soundless scream.

"Bloody hell," he gasped. "I don't think I shall ever walk again."

Monday morning dawned with many an alka seltzer being consumed for breakfast. The Happening had left its mark on most of the freaked-out population. The streets were deserted, schools were closed, offices shut and shops boarded up. The Monday after the Happening had wisely been declared a public holiday by El Viejo years ago. It suited Mei-Ling that there were no curious onlookers about as she loaded her gear into the boat. She did it with particular care, handling the dive bags somewhat gingerly. She took the boat out of the harbour and soon swung around the spit and tied up at the 'Trade Winds' dock. She started up the steps. The alarm went off and Maurizio looked over the parapet.

"Can I come aboard?" she asked, "or are you coming down? I have some things to show you."

"I'm coming down. I also have something to show you," he said grimly. He came down the steps to meet her. He was carrying the large flashlight and had his trainers on. "Put on some shoes, we're going back in the tunnel."

"Have you found more stuff?"

"Sort of." He sounded noncommittal. "I thought I'd explore the cave and tunnel a bit more thoroughly

161

today. I was fairly confident that there would be nobody about."

Mei-Ling slipped on her espadrilles and followed him to the entrance of the cave. Maurizio picked up a spade he had left at the entrance.

"Have you been digging? Don't tell me you've found some buried treasure?" she asked curiously.

"Not really."

"Must you keep me in suspense?" He shrugged but remained silent. They moved forward, until Maurizio stopped at a crack in the passage wall. It was just large enough for them to squeeze through into a smallish chamber. He shone the torch on a partly dug out grave. The putrid remains of a body wrapped in a clear heavy duty plastic bag were lying in it. The rats had obviously been digging out the loose earth and gnawing at the thick plastic.

"Who the hell can this be?" Mei-Ling whispered.

"Certainly not a pirate of the 18th century," he said flatly.

"Someone Curria had to get rid of in a hurry?"

"I suspect that it is old Rosenberg, the previous owner of 'Trade Winds'. Curria must have thought that the old boy had seen something and knew too much. He did not have a family, so perhaps no one's missed him. Clemmie kept on saying that he had promised to keep in touch, but she never heard anything from him. Do you think we should dig him out?"

"He'd be better off covered up again, poor old man," she said. "I wouldn't touch a thing. Let's get out of here, there's nothing we can do about it anyway, except see that Curria gets what he deserves. You are just as much at risk as old Rosenberg was. They'll get rid of you as soon as they don't need you any more."

They stumbled out into the balmy sundrenched day with relief. Even so, Mei-Ling was shivering.

"Am I going to tell the police about this?" Maurizio asked.

"I'm not sure. They might think that you did it. We'll have to find irrefutable evidence that Curria is involved in the drug dealing, and that he alone has been using the cave. Without your consent and knowledge, of course."

"Of course. All these things are happening beneath my very nose, on my property, and I knew nothing about it; never suspected a thing. Who would believe that?"

"As long as the Chief of Police believes it, that's all that matters." She leaned into the boat and picked up the diving bags one by one. "Take them and store them in the boathouse. And go carefully please." He started to carry them to the boathouse.

"What's in them anyway?"

"The limpet mines. Remember?"

"I didn't take you seriously enough," he grumbled. "What about Young Chang? Does he know that you're fooling around with such dangerous stuff? Perhaps I should tell him. Perhaps he could prevent you from risking both our lives."

"You know he doesn't know." She looked at him pleadingly. "It'll all be over by tomorrow evening."

"I wish I could share your optimism, Minnehaha. Coming up for a drink?"

She nodded. "I think we should go over the whole thing again. By the way, guess what they are doing at the chemical factory?" She followed him up the steps carrying a waterproof document container.

"Making cocaine or some such thing?"

"Right, but there is something else as well. Remember the pills I picked up in the lab at the factory?"

"They looked like aspirin." he said.

"They are very like aspirin, but with a little bit of

hash thrown in to make them more interesting. Very beneficial for severe aches and pains."

"Rather like Old Crone's special brew. A little bit of it does you good. You'll have to put a stop to that, you know. Can't have a CIA agent with a drug-pushing mother-in-law." She pulled a face at him.

"Have you heard anything from Maria Beatriz?" she asked.

He shook his head. "Nothing, thank heaven; Sorciero appears to have replaced both Curria and me in her affections, thanks to Old Crone's clever bit of stage managing. Any news of the Minister for Religious Affairs?"

"He is allegedly nursing some third degree burns and is in a terrible rage. Old Crone was summoned to minister to the soles of his feet four times already."

Mei-Ling burst out laughing at the memory of Juan Pablo Del Rey's exhibition.

"The young are so cruel," Maurizio mused. "Have you no pity for the poor man? He's not all bad. He's being used by a clever and ruthless criminal. Just like I am being used." He opened the door to the icebox. "What'll you have?"

"A beer." Mei-Ling stretched out on the deck-bed. "Have you made any plans for the future?"

"I plan to stay alive. If I do live to see the day after tomorrow, I intend to go home and take the consequences, whatever they may be. I'll look for another site for my 'Club Royale', since Maria Beatriz has decided not to part with her property. I shall probably sell 'Trade Winds'. One thing I'm sure of. I'll never, never come back to 'Tequila'." He sounded bitter.

"Nonsense, you'll have to come back. I'm counting on you to be my witness at the wedding."

"Better a wedding than a funeral, I suppose."

"That depends on whose funeral it is," she said brightly.

"I won't argue with that." He smiled at her.

"But how can we be absolutely certain that Curria is going to go out on the sub to the mother vessel?"

"Because he always carries the in-and-outgoing cash and checks on the in-and-outgoing merchandise. He doesn't trust any one else with it. I've seen it happen again and again," Maurizio maintained.

"I wish I could devise something which will make it 100 percent." Mei-Ling had a worried little frown on her usually smooth forehead. "If he took the Minister of Religious Affairs along with him it would be even better. I don't believe that he's merely an innocent bystander. Get rid of them both."

"I doubt whether the government could afford two state funerals within the week," was Maurizio's comment. "Besides, you said that the Minister didn't like the sea. What would persuade him to go in the sub?"

"You've got a point there. Furthermore, I think he'll still be nursing his wounds. Let me think." Mei-Ling closed her eyes and waited for inspiration. "Fear, fear for his skin," she said suddenly. "I could start a rumour that an assassination attempt will be made on his life. I could get it leaked through the Consulate. Jason is sure that one of the lines is tapped."

Maurizio shook his head in wonderment. "I thought these things only happened in the movies."

"Movies are competing with us all the time trying to father ever more ingenious schemes. There is no end to our combined inventiveness."

Maurizio scratched his chin. "I don't always want to be the devil's advocate, but even if the Minister does get rattled, wouldn't it be easier for him to fly off the island rather than take a drug smuggler's sub?"

"Someone would have to suggest it to him; Old Crone perhaps. He's bound to have her in to look to his feet. And stop scratching your square, manly, unshaven chin. I can't stand the noise." She opened the document container and took out a booklet.

"This is a manual on limpet mines; how to handle them and how to use them."

Maurizio took the manual and looked at it with repugnance. "I take it that you've experimented with these toys before?"

"No, not really, but it looks quite straightforward to me. Here's what you're supposed to do." He bent his reluctant head next to hers and listened to her explanations as she went over the diagrams in the manual.

Maria Beatriz and Sorciero were lying in a bundle of tousled sheets sipping ice cold Tequila and chewing on slices of Hungarian salami. They had slept intermittently and made love copiously. Most of his war paint had rubbed off on the sheets and his feathered head-dress had lost a good many of its plumes, which were scattered over the bed and the floor.

"I wonder what time of day it is," Sorciero said.

"Why worry, you don't have to get back to mother, do you?"

He raised himself on his elbow. "Na, but I have an appointment with Old Crone Chang." He looked at the luminous dial of the alarm clock. "You're to come along with me, she said last night."

Maria Beatriz yawned, stretched and sat up. "It's only just past midday. What time's the appointment?"

"Five-thirty to six,"

Maria Beatriz put down her glass and pulled him down to her. "C'mon lover, we've got plenty of time to practise some more."

When they surfaced again it was four o'clock. Maria Beatriz stood under the shower and soaped herself. She beckoned him in and he obeyed reluctantly. He endured her attack on his body with the soap and shampoo, and shook himself like a dog when they emerged from the cubicle. She rubbed him dry with a large fluffy towel and sat him down on a stool.

"Listen, Sorciero, you're a fine man, but you've no sense of hygiene." She clucked her tongue. "What's your name anyway? I can't keep calling you Sorciero. You do have a Christian name, don't you?"

"Sam; they used to call me Sammie."

"OK, Sammie, it looks like we're going together from now on, you and me, and I want you to be the finest looking fellow on the island." She took his hands and looked at his fingernails.

"I'll give you a manicure and a pedicure. Just sit still." She pulled up another stool and sat in front of him. She unzipped her leather manicure case and took out the nail clippers. He pulled his hand away

"What are you afraid of?"

"I don't like them cut."

"You want it done under complete anaesthetic, or what? C'mon, don't be such a baby."

"No, it's *mala suerte* to cut a Sorciero's nails," he protested. "Especially the little finger nail."

"Bullshit. Give it here." She grabbed his resisting hand and clipped away at the nails in spite of his vociferous protests. She filed them and buffed them and admired her work. Then she took his feet on her lap and gave them the same treatment.

"We'll have to get you some clothes. You can't go and call on Old Crone in your skin."

"All the shops are closed today," he ventured.

"You'll have to wear some of mine." She looked through her wardrobe and took out a loose shirt and a pair of jeans.

"These ain't women's clothes," Sorciero muttered. "How's it that you've got men's wear in your cupboard?"

"None of your business," she replied saucily. She reeled under the slap he gave her naked buttocks.

"From now on it's my business. I've heard all about your lovers, and if I ever find you with another man, I'll kill you both. Swear to me that you will never go with another man again."

"That hurt, Sam," she yelled and pummelled his chest with her fists. "Don't you ever dare lay a finger on me again."

He touched her. "Not even like that?" he asked and touched her again, entangling his fingers in her abundant pubic hair, exploring her damp flesh. She bit into his shoulder with delight and he groaned with pain.

"Looks like we're going to have one of those very stormy relationships," Maria Beatriz murmured with relish. "How's about keeping Old Crone waiting for a little while? After all, this was all her idea."

In the early evening 'Tequila' arose again from its deep sleep. The citizens stirred in their homes and soon the streets were humming with the evening *paseo* which ran up Main Street towards the deep water harbour and back to Spanish Square where the bars and coffee shops had opened and the waiters had put out tables and chairs again. At seven o'clock there wasn't a seat to be had in the Old Sea Dog bar. Jason jumped up and waved to Mei-Ling. She waved her way through the crowd and greeted him with a kiss on the cheek.

"All set for the great adventure? Mind you don't blow yourself up." he said.

"Spare me the irony."

"Sorry, Mei-Ling, anxiety makes me facetious. What can I do to help?"

"Stand by with your boat to pick us up, as we agreed. We may not have enough air left to get back into the cove. I shall surface and let off a flare to indicate our position. Another thing; we thought, Maurizio and I, that it would be nice if the Minister of Religious Affairs would join his pal on the ride in the sub."

Jason looked dubious and said "Aren't you being a wee bit too ambitious? I don't see how you can stage-manage that."

"I can't, but *you* can. Tell someone on the tapped line that the Minister's life is in danger and that the CIA has warned you that an assassination attempt is imminent. That there most probably will be a bomb on any aircraft he's likely to board, on any yacht he thinks of escaping in. The only chance of a get-away is in some clandestine way. He's bound to think of Curria's sub, isn't he?"

"Sounds a bit far-fetched to me. Do you think that he'll swallow that?"

"I'll put Old Crone into the picture and she'll suggest it to him when she goes to minister to his feet. It's worth a try."

Jason Reed took off his glasses and cleaned them with a damp square. It was a routine he always went through when he was worried or playing for time.

"You'll rub a hole into those specs, Jason. Spit it out, whatever's worrying you." He looked at Mei-Ling, thinking that a delicate, fine boned and exotically pretty creature like her had no business playing cops and robbers. At first he had been selfishly pleased because the game had thrown them together often and he had found her combination of mental toughness and superficial physical frailty very attractive. He had been confident of getting her into bed sooner or later and his nose had been thoroughly put out of joint when she as good as announced her engagement to Young Chang by going to the *corrida* with him. Those damned inscrutable Orientals, they always stuck together in the end. He sighed sorrowfully and put his glasses back on.

"What's worrying me is that playing with explosives and defying Curria is bloody dangerous, and I wish I didn't care for you so much."

She quickly stroked his cheek. "You're very dear, Jason, and I appreciate your concern; everything will work out fine. Maurizio's a good diver and he's co-operating fully. Just say a Hail Mary for us and put the champagne on ice for our return."

"Has Capponcini had another visit from the local police?" Jason asked.

She shook her head. "Limbo Limone is well and truly in limbo and will soon be joined by his boss. Hopefully." She glanced at her watch. "I've an appointment with Old Crone. I want to brief her before she goes to the Minister for Religious Affairs."

"What about Young Chang; are you going to brief him as well?" Jason asked a little pointedly. "How much does he know about your activities?"

"He knows only what everyone else knows. That I'm a diving instructor."

"How are you going to keep that fairy tale up when you two get hitched? You are going to get married, I assume?"

"You assume right. I'll tender my resignation in due course. See you tomorrow night, Jason," she said cheerfully and left the table.

Old Crone Chang reclined on the daybed in the living-room. Her head lay on the traditional Chinese ceramic head-rest. It was an antique piece dating from the 12th century and was one of many priceless objets of Chinese pottery in her collection. Her eyes were closed and her facial muscles relaxed. She was resting in preparation for her late afternoon appointments.

170

The Happening had taken it out of her and she was weary. She heard the door open softly.

"Are you asleep, Mother?"

"If I was, I'm not any more now, my son," she answered a little testily. Young Chang decided to ignore the rebuke and pulled up a chair beside her. He looked cool and neat in his starched laundered Oxford shirt and white jeans. She opened her eyes and looked at him approvingly. He was about to fulfil all her expectations.

"Can we talk?" he asked. She nodded and closed her eyes again.

"Mei-Ling and I are going to get married," he said. She smiled and patted his hand lovingly.

"A very good and wise choice," she said. "I couldn't wish for a better daughter. She's intelligent, polite, educated, beautiful and virtuous."

"She's all of these things, Mother, but she's also stubborn and independent. She's not the stay-at-home type of girl I always imagined I would spend my life with."

Old Crone Chang chuckled softly. "You should thank the Lord for that. Think of how bored you would get with such a girl. Besides, just wait until you give her her first child. Things change, my son."

"There is something else, Mother. I don't like her diving with this Capponcini all the time. There's something going on there, but I can't figure out what it is."

"Stop worrying, Deng. Let her do what she's got to do. Don't let your possessive jealous nature take over and cloud your happiness. Let's start making arrangements for the wedding as soon as possible. Leave me now, Deng, I have to prepare for my evening session."

"Who are you expecting, Mother?"

"First Mei-Ling and then Maria Beatriz and Sorciero."

Young Chang's stern face broke into a smile. "You're an incorrigible matchmaker, Mother. I should have thought that Maria Beatriz and Sorciero are a strangely ill-assorted couple."

"Not as ill-assorted as you think, my son. Their union will prove to be quite powerful. There's no doubt in my mind that she's going to take over the office of President on the island."

"And you, Mother, are going to be her and Sorciero's unofficial chief adviser, I suppose." He couldn't disguise a little mocking smile. She lifted her head and held out her hand. Young Chang helped her sit up. He put her satin slippers on her small feet and she rose from the daybed.

"They could do worse than listen to my advice, and so could you. Go and receive your bride-to-be while I tidy myself up. We will take tea together and I will give her my wedding gift."

There was always an instant of shyness between them when they met during the day. What had been perfect and inevitable during the night, seemed to have taken place on another planet between two other people. She looked charmingly demure in her jonquil chungsam, her silky black hair tied back with the same colour ribbon. He could not fault her appearance nor her sudden loving smile and the crinkling of her eyes, as she said: "Well, aren't you going to ask me in?" His embarrassment became acute and she thought she detected a slight flush on his cheeks. He stood back and closed the door after them. She was suddenly in his arms, crushed against his chest.

"My God, Mei-Ling, you do the most wonderful, terrible things to me. I couldn't stop thinking of you all day. Couldn't stop wondering what you were doing all that time with that goddamned Capponcini."

"I also did something with Jason Reed," she teased.

"Don't provoke me, Mei-Ling," he pleaded. "You're making me suffer."

"You're suffering needlessly, Deng." She nuzzled the soft skin on his neck and felt his erection pressing against her body. "Let me go, I don't want to keep your mother waiting." He released her reluctantly and watched her enter his mother's inner sanctum. It was only half-an-hour later that he was summoned to take tea with them, and admire the carved imperial jade and diamond ear-drops that graced his fiancée's delicate lobes. They were the most precious pieces his mother had possessed, and her gift put the seal of approval and blessing on his union with Mei-Ling.

Maria Beatriz drove up in front of the Chang house with her usual panache. The gravel sprayed beneath the crunch of the wheels as she braked to a sudden stop. She looked at herself in the mirror and tightened the peacock blue satin turban around her head. She had on a matching bare mid-riff top and palazzo pyjamas. As always, there was an exotic style quite her own in her appearance. Sorciero looked unlike his usual self, a circumstance which made him uneasy. His feet were uncomfortably squeezed into a pair of loafers not quite his size. His dread-locks were held back at the nape of his neck with a black towelling band. Maria Beatriz eyed him approvingly and patted his knee.

"You're really a fine-looking man, Sammie. Let's go and show you off to Old Crone. She'll not recognize you."

"You're late, Maria Beatriz," Old Crone admonished her.

"Sorry, but we've been very busy,"

"I can see that." Old Crone smiled. "I'm proud of you, Sorciero, very proud. You're truly a bona fide witchdoctor now; and you've done it all by yourself. You're looking very…what do the youngsters say nowadays?…cool, my friend. I can see that Maria Beatriz has looked after you well." Maria Beatriz glowed with pleasure at Old Crone's praise. She set great store by Old Crone's opinion. "But, my dear," the latter continued, "his image should not be changed too rapidly. A witch doctor must look like a witch doctor when he's working."

Maria Beatriz took Sorciero's hand and grinned. "He's not working now, and I think he looks gorgeous." Old Crone nodded in agreement.

"We're going to stay together from now on. In fact, we plan to get married, don't we, Sammie?" Sorciero's head wagged in mute approval.

"It's almost an epidemic," said Old Crone. "My son, Young Chang, is also getting married. To Mei-Ling Chang. You know her I think. She's the dive teacher. She's a distant relative and such a beautiful girl. Sorciero, you must buy a nice ring for your fiancée. Young Chang will advise you." Old Crone poured out jasmine tea into almost transparent porcelain cups. "You must taste this tea; it has arrived quite recently straight from China. The cups of course, are Japanese. There is nothing more delicate than their porcelain." Maria Beatriz and Sorciero obediently sipped the brew. "Isn't it lucky, Sorciero, that you didn't spend all your money building a new house? Before the week is out, you and Maria Beatriz will move into the pink marble villa, mark my words. I advise you to get married immediately. The Archbishop should perform the ceremony without delay."

"Old Crone, stop putting all these ideas into our heads. My brothers will never allow it, but we're getting married just the same. I want a proper expensive wedding gown and Sammie needs a decent suit.

We could fly to Caracas and get kitted out and have a sort of honeymoon at the same time." Maria Beatriz sounded excited at the prospect of spending a vast sum on their wedding clothes. She was brought down to earth by Old Crone's stern protest.

"You're not going to Caracas or off island, my girl. That would be playing right into your brothers' hands. You can get your bridal outfit here, and it had better be modest and lady-like too. As for a honeymoon, it is usually commenced after the wedding ceremony. You have to practice a little more decorum, befitting your future position on this island. You heard Sorciero's prediction," Old Crone intoned solemnly.

"You, Maria Beatriz, are the chosen one, chosen to become President. Sorciero will be by your side, and I will be always be there for you both, to advise and counsel you, as long as you need me." They stared at the old lady and were enthralled by her words. "Get married before the week is out and go on to the streets, talk to your people. Tell them that you will look after the poor and needy, that there will be free education and health care for all, and that there will be no more poaching from the coffers of the government."

Maria Beatriz looked worried and doubtful. "That's all very nice, Old Crone, but how are we going to live without poaching from the coffers? That kind of thing's been going on for ever. It is customary, you know."

"It's up to you to change these customs. The office of the President is well remunerated and Sorciero must go on with his work. His influence on the people must be maintained." She lifted her hands. "Go now, I am tired. Do as I say and you'll never regret it."

Night had fallen and Old Crone stepped into her

bicycle rickshaw. She was carrying a basket filled with an assortment of salves and bandages. She had a couple of phials of potent painkillers in the basket as well. In a little paper bag were two of the pseudo aspirin pills manufactured in the new chemical factory. She looked forward to trying them on the Minister for Religious Affairs. It was only fair that he should be the guinea-pig for his own product. She was lost in thought as the boy cycled up the hill slowly, finding the ascent almost too hard for his scrawny young legs. The Minister for Religious Affairs lived in a villa overlooking the harbour. It was not quite as grand as El Viejo's pink marble edifice, but it was almost as luxurious, nestling behind the white-washed high walls. Beyond the strong steel gate was an avenue of flowering cacti and oleanders which led to the intricately carved double entrance doors of the house. The policeman on duty waved Old Crone's rickshaw through and the boy put on an end spurt and arrived breathless at the front doors. A servant stepped out and helped Old Crone out. She was dressed in a black chungsam, with decorous long sleeves and skirt. She stood erect and proud, her fine white-streaked hair neatly held up with a pair of jewelled hair pins.

"Please give my boy a cold drink; he prefers Coca-Cola," she said pleasantly. The servant bowed and made to take the basket from her. She shook her head and held the basket close to her side. "It's not heavy, thank you all the same. The Minister is expecting me, I think." Again the servant bowed and led the way through the large airy hall to the private apartments of the Minister. He was lying on a daybed, watching a video in the company of his wife. It wasn't often that he spent the evening at home with the family. He was usually out at some official dinner or unofficial entertainment where, for obvious reasons, wives were not welcome. He had an apartment in the town where his friend Claudio Curria often threw parties for him, enlivened by entertainers who were imported for the casino floorshow. All tastes were catered for on those occasions. Especially the Minister's. In truth he was not difficult to please. He liked women of any nationality, colour or creed, as long as they had big breasts, generous hips and very long hair. It mattered not to him if the legs were short or bandy, the nose long or broad, the eyes blue or brown. He wanted to rest his head between a large pair of boobs, hold an ample buttock with one hand, and wind long hair around his fingers and pull hard when he came. The agonizing scream which the hair pulling elicited from the chosen one brought on the culmination of the Minister's pleasure. Once, one of the girls, afraid of not being chosen for one of the night's entertainments because her hair hadn't reached the desired length, had bought a luxuriant curly red wig. It was not long before she attracted the attention of the Minister, was invited to a party and subsequently to the Minister's couch. When the wig came away in his hand, even the girl's outsize bosom could not make up for the scream she failed to utter; the scream which triggered his final fulfilment. She was dismissed without the usual hand-out.

Old Crone was well aware of the Minister's idiosyncrasies and had her own idea on how this fixation had come about. She had seen the Minister's eye rove over El Viejo's daughter Maria Dolores on the few occasions the latter had been present in public. Had he perhaps had a taste of forbidden fruit by way of Maria Dolores? There was no doubt about the expanse of her bosom, the breadth of her buttocks or the length of her hair. Old Crone almost felt sorry for the Minister when she looked at his tall, slender wife, with her boyish haircut. She had been a model of some repute in the USA and wore clothes exceedingly well. She had blinded him with her elegance, which, when abandoned for the marital bed, left nothing but a bag of skin and bones in his arms.

Civilities were exchanged and the wife left the room, allowing Old Crone to take care of the Minister's blistered feet. She removed the icepacks and smoothed fresh salve over the injuries. He winced and grimaced like a child, exhorting her to be gentle.

"It's much better, your Excellency, you'll be almost healed by tomorrow."

"Ah, ah," he groaned. "I don't believe it. I'll never be able to put my feet on the ground again,"

"Of course you will, and if you take my advice, as soon as possible. I have heard rumours." The Minister thrived on rumours and was insatiably inquisitive. Old Crone waited for him to take up his cue.

"Rumours? What rumours?" he said petulantly. "I suppose all the island is still laughing at me. How will it affect my chances of becoming President? That's what I would like to know." Old Crone reapplied the ice packs and set his feet back on the cushion. "Go on, Old Crone, tell me what the rumours are."

"It would be a good idea for you to leave the island for a short while. There is a plot afoot to remove you in order to make room for one of your brothers. Sorciero has heard that your very life is in danger." She sounded grave.

"One of my own brothers...take my life..." The Minister's mien reflected both fear and anger. "They wouldn't dare, their own flesh and blood...or would they? They've got the army, police and finances under their thumb." Tears of frustration gathered in his eyes. "What am I to do?"

His heavy frame seemed to shrink as he rolled himself up into a foetal position on the daybed. "What am I to do?" Old Crone fully expected him to start sucking his thumb.

"I know what I would do," she said softly. "I'd get off the island for a few days, and let your friend Curria's henchmen deal with the brothers, that's what I'd do. I would secretly leave the island, not using any of the public services or your own yacht or private plane which are bound to be prime targets. Your friend Curria would help with that as well, don't you think, your Excellency?" Having planted the seed of fear in his Excellency's breast and watered it with ideas of escape, Old Crone packed up her basket and quietly left the Minister's apartments. She never expected to be paid in cash for her services to the Del Rey family, preferring to call in the debt in other ways if the need arose. She climbed into the rickshaw and drew a light black cashmere shawl around her shoulders. The night had brought the freshening trade-wind and a few rain-clouds. She urged the boy on, hoping to reach her home before the tropical shower caught up with them.

The employee of the telephone company sought entry to the Minister for Religious Affairs residence. He usually reported to his master by telephone. Tonight however, what he had overheard on the tapped line of the US embassy brooked no delay, and needed complete discretion.

"It's late, Mon, you can't see the Minister now," the guard on duty at the gate said.

"Just tell the Minister that Jaime from the telephones is out here. It's very urgent, Mon, really." The guard took off his helmet and scratched his head; he consulted his watch again. It was gone 10 o'clock. He finally picked up the intercom phone and announced the late visitor. To his astonishment, the visitor was to be let in without delay. The visitor didn't stay long and the guard locked the gate after him and sat down in his hut. He looked towards the villa and saw that the lights were still on in the Minister's apartments and stayed on till well into the early hours of the morning.

Chapter Seven

There was no sign left of the rain which had cascaded
from the heavens in great tropical abundance during
the night. It had helped fill the water catchments, but
the earth was cracked and almost dry again. The flora
still needed watering and Maurizio was activating the
hose on the flower planters on the deck. The hibiscus,
the oleander and the passion fruit climbers were
beginning to droop visibly in the morning sun. It was
set fair for a spectacular day and Maurizio looked
about his property with more than a touch of nostal-
gia. Although he had decided to part with it, it was
still very close to his heart. He had looked around
each room. Together, he and Domitilla had modernized it with such excitement, not sparing any expense.
The rustic but elegant imported Italian tiles for the
bathrooms, the Florentine cotto for the floors and the
cane furniture with bright, sunny chintz upholstery,
all spoke of Domitilla's impeccable taste. Yellow,
apple-green and ultra-marine blue were the dominant
colours which were mixed and matched successfully,
mirroring the sea, the sky and the vegetation.
Domitilla had put all her skill into the redecoration of
their dream house. The hibiscus print had been
designed by her and exclusively produced for them. It
was so attractive that Maurizio had decided to use it
for the new 'Royale Club' on 'Tequila'. Now he was
preparing to abandon it all. He had told Domitilla that

he was returning to Italy for Easter, and for her not to come out to 'Tequila' with the children. He had booked his flight back to Milan on Good Friday and they were going to spend the holiday together in their apartment, as a family. Daria Ferrari could do what she liked with the 'Royale' file. He was no longer prepared to be blackmailed by her, or anyone else. Maurizio sat down in his study and looked over his papers. He studied the preliminary plans which their architect had sent them for the 'Royale Club' in 'Tequila'. Reluctantly he fed them into the shredder. There would be no 'Royale Club' on this island. He could kiss the thousands of dollars spent on bribes good-bye. A slow burning rage was starting to grow in him as he watched the shredder turn his dreams into confetti. A curse on Curria and his partners, he swore silently. They would be made to pay. They would be blown up into so many little pieces that no one would ever be able to put them together again. Maurizio hadn't known about the bloodthirsty streak imbedded in a secret corner of his innermost self. It was surfacing now and he was joyously anticipating the demise of Curria and Co. in a boiling sea, gory limbs severed and bobbing on the foaming bloodied surface. Sharks attacking in a feeding frenzy, tearing at the torsos with saw-like monstrous teeth, swallowing every last morsel within their sight, including the Gucci belts and loafers. There wouldn't even be a particle left by the ravenous scavengers. Oh, how sadistically satisfying a vision that was; it cheered him up considerably and calmed his fears about the actual implementation of Mei-Ling's scheme. He was able to contemplate the planting of limpet mines with more zeal than hitherto.

It took Maurizio several hours to sort out the rest of his confidential papers. He emptied the large safe and continued shredding, keeping only the really essential documents. It was almost noon by the time he had dealt with the last papers. He packed his briefcase and locked it in the safe. It was time for the swim he usually had at that hour. The water was sparkling in the cove, tempting him to dive in. He changed into his trunks and ran down the steps. He cut into the water cleanly and swam to the reef with long easy strokes. He lay on his back and squinted into the cloud-flecked sky. There was nothing quite like the feeling of the sea and the warmth of the sun on his body. It would be something he would miss in Europe, where the weather was often uncertain and the sea polluted. Yet he knew that it was time; time for him abandon the island and return to pick up his life, his marriage and the reigns of his business. The months spent on 'Tequila' were like an unreal episode in an unreal world of strange tropical flora, peopled with strange and exotic creatures. Extravagant humans with extravagant customs. His face creased into a grin and he laughed aloud as he recalled the Happening. He would miss seeing Maria Beatriz installed as the President of the island, with Sorciero as prince consort. She, at least, had her heart in the right place and might make a success of her reign. Once Curria was out of the way. Which he soon would be. Maurizio heard Clemmie shouting from the deck and waved at her. She was brandishing the red flag which meant an urgent telephone call. He returned to the dock and climbed out of the water. The phone was ringing in the boat-house and he hurried to pick it up.

"Capponcini speaking,"

"Just to remind you that there will be a delivery tonight. Keep the cove clear. No guests and no staff. Is that understood?"

"I don't need reminding, Curria."

"And no peeking, not by you or anyone."

"You'll be entirely on your own, I can assure you. I'm out to dinner and will spend the night in town."

"Already found yourself a new girl, now that your little China lass has got herself engaged?" Curria sniggered.

"Any objections?" Maurizio said laconically.

"Naw, you can fuck yourself to death as far as I'm concerned, but before you do, you'll have to tell about what happened to Limbo Limone. The police haven't got the slightest clue, but you, Capponcini, you're hiding something from me. I have a nose for such things."

"Yea, and like Pinocchio's, it's growing longer by the minute."

"Always cracking jokes, aren't we?" Curria couldn't keep the annoyance out of his voice.

"Speak for yourself," Maurizio answered. "Or were you using the royal 'we'?"

"Oh why don't you just go to hell, Capponcini? You'll be sorry when the police really start to pull your place apart. The Chief told me that he was not satisfied the trainers they took from you the other day were yours. They found a tiny smear of blood on the inside. They'll be going to check your blood, they are ... Science is a great thing. What do you say to that, Capponcini?"

"Was that a rhetorical question, or do you require an answer?"

The phone was crashed down by Curria and Maurizio hung up. He walked to the dive bags which were stored in the darkest corner of the boat house. A shiver ran down his back at the thought of having to transport them several miles under water to the target. He was amazed at the calm with which Mei-Ling was planning to blow up the sub and all its inmates. What amazed him even more was that he was prepared to go along with it. Perhaps he was only dreaming and would wake up from this nightmare.

The Minister for Religious Affairs had not slept a wink that night. After Jaime from the telephone company had made his report, the Minister's panic had risen to dangerous heights. He had moaned, wringing his hands, until his wife had pushed him out of the bedroom, complaining about his restless behaviour. It interfered with her beauty sleep. He had not divulged the reason for his agitation, preferring not to answer her pressing questions. He had hobbled into his study and had tried to find Curria, but had only got the answer phone. The Minister had left a mass of messages at intervals of fifteen minutes. It was only around three o'clock in the morning that he established contact and blurted out his fears to his business partner.

"You have to get me off the island, Curria, today."

"There should be two flights out during the day, one to Caracas and one to Costa Rica. Why don't you take one of those?" Curria sounded a bit curt. He had had a long day and was aching to go to bed.

"No, no, I want to go with you."

"But I'm not going anywhere. All I want is to go to bed. Can't we discuss this over lunch? By the way, we had good takings at the casino tonight," he had added, hoping it would calm the Minister.

"What do I care about that?" the Minister had yelled. "My life is more important than a few dollars, isn't it?" This didn't sound like the Minister's usual self. Curria had started to pay attention. "They are out to get me, Curria. They're going to try to assassinate me, so you'll have to help me get off the island. They are watching all the flights that leave, and all the yachts."

"Who, in heaven's name, and why?"

"My brothers and possibly my sister. They are conspiring against me, to prevent me from becoming President."

"Aw, balls, Minister, whatever gave you that idea?"

"It's not an idea, it's a fact. You have a shipment coming in later on today. I want your sub to evacuate me. And you will kill the enemy, before it kills me. I don't have to tell you how to do that."

"Sounds like you're starting a real war."

"When I was at the military academy, that's what they taught me; attack is the best method of defence."

"Yea, well, I'll take care of you. Let's discuss it at lunch, and don't forget to put on your full uniform, with medals, if you really want to start a war." Currja had yawned loudly. "Goodnight, Juan Pablo."

"You can spare me the sarcasm, Currja, and address me in the proper way," the Minister had said huffily and put an end to the conversation.

Mei-Ling had packed a picnic and was waiting for young Chang to drive her down to the harbour. Chang had a sailing boat moored there. It was a fine old wooden yacht, all mahogany and highly polished brass. He hadn't used it much during the past year, because Maria Clara was a bad sailor and had thrown up all over the saloon the very first time he had taken her out in the boat. It had dashed all his hopes for a romantic shipboard seduction and the smell had lingered on for several days. She had finally given herself to him in the flat he had rented at considerable expense for their trysts. Now he was looking forward to the sail with Mei-Ling. No chance of her fouling his precious new carpet. He was humming in tune with the radio as he drew up in front of her house. It was going to be another sunny, balmy day, and he felt good. He looked good too, she thought, as he vaulted over the door of the convertible, ran up the small path and rang the doorbell. Mei-Ling had been watching him from behind her louvred windows. His hair was ruffled by the breeze and his immaculately laundered shorts and shirt fitted perfectly. He had lost his usual solemnity and looked really relaxed. She could hear the music and saw him doing a joyous little dance, waiting for her to answer the bell. She took the cooler and opened the door. He picked her up and whirled her around.

"Shall we dance?" he asked.

"Why not?" she laughed. "We've never danced together before."

"No, we haven't; there's such a lot we've got to catch up with. How about a romantic dinner dance tonight? Candles, champagne, and Cha Cha Cha?"

"Sounds divine, but I'm working tonight. Can I have a raincheck?" She rubbed his cheek. "Don't look so angry, you know that I work nights sometimes."

"What are you doing? No, no, don't tell me, let me guess. You're going night diving with Capponcini?"

"Oh boy, you're really jealous, aren't you? But you're right, that's exactly what I'm doing." He put her down a little abruptly and looked at her.

"Fine, that's OK by me," he said quietly. "I'm coming along. I'd like to learn how to night dive."

"Oh darling, really. You've got to learn day diving first, but I'll teach you. You'll see how wonderful it is, deep under the water," she tried to console him.

"OK, so I'll sit in the boat and wait for you both."

"We'll see, darling." She stood on tip toe and tried to kiss him.

"We'll see alright, you little witch. Don't try and distract me with your pretty manoeuvres." He picked her up again and slammed the door with his foot. He sat her down in the car and stored the cooler on the back seat. He drove to the harbour and parked the car. They wandered to the dock hand-in-hand and stopped by the gangplank of the yacht. A wiry Tequilan was standing on the deck. He wore a bright yellow T-shirt with 'Maria Beatriz for President' printed on it.

"They haven't wasted any time, have they?" Young Chang commented in an aside to Mei-Ling. She nodded and waved a greeting to the deck-hand.

"Do you really mean that, Juanito? Maria Beatriz for President?" Young Chang asked.

"Well why not, Cap'n? Besides they'se handing out them shirts for free and I needed a new one. Pretty colours they have too." The sailor grinned. "And they gives me a dollar to wear it. Look at the other side, Cap'n," The sailor turned round. 'Maria Beatriz and Sorciero, our choice' was printed boldly on the back of the T-shirt. "With Sorciero giving her good advice, and all, it should work pretty good." Juanito blinked his eyes knowingly. "I got two more for you Cap'n, they'se in the cabin."

"Thanks, Juanito: take the cooler please and stow it. You can stay on shore today."

"You sure, Cap'n? I says there be a storm brewing, more like a hurricane, my signals tells me."

"Don't be daft, Juanito, who's ever heard of a hurricane in April? You must have misunderstood the signals. Just look at the sky, not a cloud in it."

The deck-hand shrugged and ran down the gangplank. "It's blowy though, Cap'n. Yous better listen to the weatherman again when you set sail," he said before he loped away towards the Harbour Tavern.

There was a considerable crowd gathering outside the Harbour Tavern and most of the people were wearing the coloured T-shirts. Old Crone had organized the distribution of the garments at the most important crossroads of the town. The initial batch had been given away in record time and the dollar accompanying it was being rapidly turned into alcohol. The Harbour Tavern, which normally opened its door at noon, had bent the rules and opened at ten, beating the Coffeepot Cafe to it. Beer and Tequila flowed freely as did the discussions about the forthcoming elections. For once there seemed to be a consensus of opinion and Maria Beatriz' candidature was welcomed with satisfaction. Her association with Sorciero drew the inevitable lewd comments, but they were delivered with affection rather than malice. The coupling of Sorciero and Maria Beatriz promised to be fruitful and beneficial for the island. Already the tide was turning in favour of the couple. Alcohol enhanced the optimistic forecasts even more. Those who had not yet received their T-shirt and dollar were hanging around the cross-roads waiting for the new batch to arrive. Toasts were drunk to the happy couple all over the island.

Alcohol flowed in the Minister for Religious Affairs' library as well, although there were no toasts being offered. Claudio Curria had been unceremoniously wakened and summoned to the villa and was now standing by the window with a pair of binoculars trained on to the dockside and the 'Harbour Tavern.' He whistled through his teeth, producing a shrill, grating sound.

"Stop that damned whistling, Curria, it's giving me a headache," the Minister for Religious Affairs groaned.

"I should have thought you had one already."

"So I do, and you're not making it any better. What are you looking at anyway?"

Curria gave him the binoculars. "They haven't wasted a minute, your sister and her new paramour. Putana...It's a clever move, those T-shirts and the dollar to spend. I wonder who thought of it? Certainly not that half-witted witchdoctor." He slapped his hands together. "I bet you a grand that it's that Chinese mummy, Old Crone. Say," Curria smiled wickedly, "you ought to be careful, Juan Pablo, 'bout letting her have the run of your place. She might well stick a knife into you."

"Don't be ridiculous, she's much too frail for any violence. Besides, she's the only one who can cure my third degree burns."

"Third degree burns my ass. Come and look at the Harbour Square. What are you going to do about that, huh?"

The Minister for Religious Affairs hobbled to the window and surveyed the scene. He shrugged his shoulders feebly and sighed.

"I know what I would do," Curria said calmly.

"Oh why don't you just shut up? Why is the whole world always telling me what they would do?"

"Probably because you ask them. As I was saying: I would call out the police and shut down the Tavern and any other places which have opened early. You know that it's against the law to serve alcohol before noon. Crack down on them I say, and confiscate their takings. I would also confiscate any more T-shirts and burn them in the square. Put the fear of God into those local bastards, that's what I'd do."

"You'd better watch your tongue, Curria." The Minister glowered at Curria.

"There's no need to take on so, Juan Pablo. I'm just calling a spade a spade," Curria sniggered. "You've only yourself to blame for all this, covering yourself with ridicule in front of the whole population. Dancing on burning coals, indeed, like a bloody savage, dabbling in witchcraft…" Curria's scorn was almost palpable.

"You're underestimating Sorciero, Curria. He has found his magic powers and you don't know anything about that, do you?" There was a mixture of fear and respect in the Minister's tone of voice. "He will put a spell on all of us and destroy us. You must get him before he gets us."

Curria patted his hip. It was there he kept his snub-nosed revolver. "I should like to see Sorciero pit his magic against my little friend here." He pulled out the gun and aimed at the Minister.

"Put that damned thing away, Curria, I don't like firearms."

Curria held it firmly pointed. "The military academy wasn't quite your scene then?" he laughed. "You really should have your visitors searched, Juan Pablo, before letting them into your inner chamber. How do you know that I won't do you in, huh?" he continued baiting the Minister. The latter glared at his tormentor with something akin to loathing. Curria's outfit was as vulgar and expensive as usual. He wore a pair of tightfitting magenta coloured designer jeans and a multicoloured Missoni silk shirt to match. His feet were shod in snake skin booties with built up heels which were as shiny and black as the hair which was slicked back over his head. The Minister had his suspicions about the authenticity of the hair colour. It looked as if it might well run in the wash. Today Curria was sporting a gypsy hoop earring studded with tiny diamonds. He fancied that it gave him a vaguely piratical, romantic look. The Minister turned his back on him and stared out of the window.

"I want to see some action, Curria, not your damned posturing," he muttered. "You get me off the island tonight and tidy up after me."

Curria shook his head ruefully. "I can't promise that my partners will agree to having a passenger. Even if they do agree, it's going to cost you, Juan Pablo." The Minister thrust his hands into his dressing gown pockets. His broad nostrils flared angrily.

"And so what else is new? I've always paid for the favours. Through the nose," he snorted.

Curria slipped his gun back and smiled. "Your nose is big enough to take it. Don't get mad at me, Juan Pablo. I'll do my best. Got to run now; got to get myself a T-shirt and a dollar to spend. And don't forget about lunch at the club. It's your turn to buy. Ciao." The Minister waved his hands. "I'm not leaving the house today, so there'll be no chow at the club. Just get me off the island, Curria, otherwise I shall call in your casino licence."

Curria's smile faded into an icy grimace. "Don't threaten me, Juan Pablo, don't even think of it. Be glad that I'm here, ready to save your fat ass." He slammed the door behind him so violently that little particles of paint were dislodged from it, and fluttered on to the floor like a shower of dandruff. The Minister swore vilely and poured himself another brandy. He needed to calm down; work off this terrible anxiety which had kept him awake all night. He swallowed a double dose of the tablets that Old Crone had left behind. He needed some distraction. He needed a woman with big boobs to rest his head on. But could he trust an outsider at this moment in time? His frustration grew as he limped up and down. There was only one solution to his problem. He called his wife on the intercom.

"Put on your wig and strap on the falsies, I need to fuck," he bellowed into the telephone.

Old Crone Chang had her rickshaw waiting at the side-entrance of the T-shirt factory. The photo-print machine was working continuously, churning out the shirts with the bold print. A girl was stapling a small clear plastic bag containing a dollar coin on to the hem of each shirt. Old Crone had brought another bag of coins from the bank. She had picked up the last of the change from the local branch. She had nodded in approval as she had travelled down Main Street in her rickshaw. Almost everyone on the street was wearing a printed shirt and the campaign seemed to have been an unmitigated success. Now the last batch was ready to be taken out into the streets and distributed. There was a sudden noisy commotion outside the workshop, and the sound of shattered glass. A couple of hooded youths, brandishing clubs and flambeaux had forced entry and taken possession of the T-shirts. They heaped them up on the floor and set them afire. They were screaming with wild laughter as the flames rose high and the shirts started to burn. The smell was awful and smoke filled the workshop. The terrified workers fled into the street, gasping for air. The thugs disappeared as suddenly as they had come and an explosion lifted the roof off the workshop. Flames leapt up into the sky as the workers watched the wooden parts of the structure burn and crumble.

Old Crone got into her rickshaw and ordered the boy to head for the Minister for Religious Affairs residence. It was time to change the dressing on his feet. She was sorry for the T-shirt manufacturer, but it was somehow gratifying that the opposition had been cornered into resorting to such desperate measures. She would tell the Minister of the fire and watch his reaction. She never doubted that Curria's men were behind that act of arson. The wind was blowing cinders and ash across the street, and the fire-engine honked stridently as it raced towards the stricken workshop. The fire was about to spread to the next building and people had left the premises and were

193

yelling at the firemen to get a move on. Old Crone tapped the boy on the shoulder and urged him to hurry. She didn't particularly want to be seen in that part of town. She squinted into the sky at the gathering cloud and the gusting wind. It was not typical 'Tequila' weather for that time of year. It seemed as if a tropical storm was brewing although the weather forecast had not mentioned it, but then the reliability of the weather forecast was questionable in her view. Old Crone had had her fill of drenched silk gowns and mussed hair through the fault of the meteorological office. The meteorologists obviously were not sitting at the right hand of God. Old Crone never ventured out without adequate protection against the occasional turbulence. She slipped on a clear plastic mac and drew the hood over her head as the first drops fell. The wind subsided and it was suffocatingly hot and humid. The downpour was violent and the rickshaw boy tried to take cover under a shop awning. The water rushed down the open sewers, carrying a variety of curious flotsam and jetsam with it. Eventually a patch of blue sky appeared and the wind picked up again, chasing the clouds away. The rickshaw boy manoeuvred the vehicle back onto the road and pedalled towards the harbour. The wrought iron gates of the Minister's property swung open for them and Old Crone stepped down lightly when they had reached the front doors.

"Take me to his Excellency," Old Crone said to the manservant who stood in the doorway. He looked at her and shook his head.

"You gotta wait, Old Crone. The Minister, he busy."

"It's alright, I won't interfere with his affairs of state. I just came to change the dressing. Go and tell him that I'm waiting."

The manservant grinned. "Take a seat, Old Crone,

he will call when he be ready. This affair of state don't last very long unless he has a nap afterwards, so take a seat until he through." Old Crone looked sternly at him and raised herself up to her entire height. She still barely reached his shoulder.

"Stop sniggering, you impudent fellow, and see to it that my rickshaw boy gets his usual Coca-Cola." With that she chose the Louis Quinze chair covered in gold brocade and sat well back, letting her short legs dangle two inches off the marble floor. She studied her tiny feet, which were encased in the classical black cloth Chinese shoes, and wiggled her toes. It was typical of the Minister to have himself a small orgy instead of looking to his safety and to his political future. She wondered which of the whores he had summoned to the villa, because it was common knowledge that he didn't really fancy his wife anymore. Hadn't done so for ages. It came as something of a surprise to Old Crone when the female who exited from the room and hurried through the hall was none other than the Minister's wife, disguised in a luxuriant red mane which almost reached her buttocks. Her flesh-coloured silk top clung to a truly impressive chest with gigantic protuberant nipples. She raised her hand in greeting to Old Crone and rolled her eyes in mock despair.

"I almost didn't recognize you, my dear," Old Crone said.

"That's the whole idea. What do you think of them?" She prodded her chest with her finger. "His Excellency is a boobs fetishist. Boobs and long red hair. Do you think I should have a good implant done in Miami instead of wearing this?" She lifted the silk top and revealed an outsize moulded foam bosom attached to a harness which she wore like a brassiere.

Old Crone looked doubtful. "You know implants

can be harmful. You could develop an infection. I would have a word with Sorciero if I were you, and get him to cast a spell on the Minister. It'll cost you a fraction and be much less painful than an operation."

The Minister's wife snorted. "I don't believe in all this mumbo jumbo, Old Crone. You can fool some of the people all the time, and all the people some of the time, and heck, I don't know how the rest of it goes, but you sure can't fool me with witchcraft."

Old Crone smiled beatifically. "It's like the traditional Jewish chicken soup, my dear," she murmured. "It may not do you any good, but it can't harm you either, so why don't you give it a try? I could make an appointment for you."

The Minister's wife pulled her chemise down again. "I'll think about it, Old Crone. I gotta run and put my bosom in the wash. His Excellency came all over my chest."

Old Crone gently patted the sores on the Minister's feet. They were healing nicely, and she was pleased with the salve she had concocted in her kitchen.

"It's a miracle Old Crone," he repeated himself. "I hardly have any pain and I feel as if I were floating on top of the world. Have you got any more of these tablets?"

"Oh yes, Your Excellency, but you mustn't exceed the dose."

"What make are they; what are they called?"

"I don't think it's got a name yet but I have heard that they might call it 'Kick'. It's a kind of aspirin with a difference, which they have developed here, in the new chemical factory."

"Quite a difference I should say, with a *major* kick." The minister beamed. "I wasn't aware that our factory was producing such excellent medication. I took some just a little while ago, and already I feel, how shall I put it, so vigorous." He lowered his voice to a whisper. "I even made love to my wife."

"Oh very good, Sir, an excellent thing to do."

The Minister's mien darkened, however, and he looked closely at Old Crone. "I'm still very worried about the rumours that are being spread about, that my sister and Sorciero are planning a 'coup'. What do you say to that? What have you heard in the town, Old Crone? And furthermore, who is responsible for those damned T-shirts?"

"Nobody knows, Your Excellency, they just suddenly appeared on the streets this morning. But – set your mind at rest, I have heard that the workshop which printed them has gone out of business. It appears that there was a fire. I could see the flames as I came through the town. They say that it is burned down to the ground."

"So Curria's done his job. Serves them right," the Minister pronounced vindictively. "You should tell Sorciero not to make more of a fool of himself than he already is. He'll listen to you. He shouldn't meddle in politics. The fellow has no education or refinement."

Old Crone lowered her eyes. "Show me one person who will tell Sorciero anything after the performance at the Happening. He doesn't need education or refinement. He's got real magic."

"Magic? Magic is for the hoi polloi, not for us. There is no magic," the Minister said stoutly, although there was just a hint of hesitancy in this statement.

"If you say so, Your Excellency." Old Crone started to put back her salves and potions into the basket.

"Well, is there?" the Minister asked anxiously.

"You saw for yourself, Excellency. What more can I say?"

"Lots, you old witch, but I have no time now to listen

to your idle gossip. Leave me, I have important things to see to. My secretary will deal with your account."

Old Crone shook her head. "Oh no, Your Excellency, don't even mention it. It is an honour for me." She bowed several times. It was a ritual they always went through. It was understood that the Minister would offer, noblesse oblige, and that Old Crone would, for the same reason, refuse payment for her services.

On the other side of the island the Minister for Education, Trade and Development sat in conference with his brother, Juan Pedro, the Minister for the Environment. They had formed an uneasy alliance in the face of their sister's bid for the Presidency. They feared the competition coming from Juan Pablo's corner less. After all, he didn't have Sorciero on his side. Juan Pedro and Juan Batista had decided to share the power, allotting the positions of President and Prime Minister to themselves respectively. They were as yet unaware of the T-shirt and dollar campaign which had delighted the denizens of the island since the early morning. It was Curria who came to call with the offending garment draped over his arm, which showed them how far the situation had deteriorated.

"That's too much. She's gone too far. We should put them both under house arrest until the election is over," the Minister for the Environment said.

"May I remind you that she hasn't even got a house. She's living in that damned camper. Sorciero has moved in with her, and half the population is besieging the vehicle waiting for more miracles. Every time they show their faces a great cheer goes up." Curria flung the shirt to the ground. "House arrest is a feeble way of dealing with the problem you are facing."

"What else can we do? Slap them into jail for creating a disturbance of the peace perhaps?" the Minister for Education, Trade and Development suggested. His brother shook his head.

"It would be better to ship them off to Venezuela, before they have time to consolidate their advantage."

"Do you think that they would go of their own free will?" Juan Batista asked hopefully. "Perhaps we could offer an incentive?" He was the simplest of the three brothers and not given to violence. Curria looked at him with disgust.

"Fuck the incentive," Curria said brutally. "Just say the word and my men will take care of them. It's the only way. A clean tidy job. What do you say?"

Juan Pedro looked at his brother questioningly, but Juan Batista shuddered visibly and made a a negative grimace.

"Juan Pablo has agreed, so why don't you?" Curria asked, a touch belligerently.

Juan Pedro reared up from his leather armchair. "So, he has agreed to a spot of murder, has he? I suppose you would 'take care' of us too, but perhaps he didn't offer you enough for the job." He nudged his brother sharply in the ribs. "Say something, you dim-wit, don't you see what's being plotted behind our backs?" Juan Batista looked aggrieved and retreated, escaping the offending elbow of his sibling.

"That hurt, Juan Pedro; why must you always become so physical? Besides, you always call me names in front of strangers. It's not fair."

The Minister for the Environment sighed loudly. "Oh just stop whining Batistinio, now is not the time for silly recriminations. There are important decisions to be taken."

Curria had witnessed this brotherly bickering before. Juan Pedro usually got his way. He was born the runt of the litter, small boned and slight, but he had a mean temper and the tenacity of a terrier. He

199

completely dominated Juan Batista, who was a fine figure of a man, a gentle giant who was generally content to follow his brother's lead.

"I agree, Pedrinio, I agree, but there's to be no bloodshed. Let's just ship them off like Maria Dolores."

"Do you, or don't you, want to become President, Batistinio? Do you or don't you want me to become Prime Minister?"

"Of course I want all that."

"So why don't you go and review the presidential body-guard or something, and leave the rest to me?" The Minister for the Environment propelled his brother towards the door. "And not a word to anyone, do you understand? And especially not to Maria Jolanda, silly bitch."

"But she's my wife," Juan Batista protested.

"She's also the biggest blabber-mouth on the island. Just trust me Batistinio, and all will be well." He closed the door behind the Minister of Education, Trade and Development, and returned to face Curria who was busy combing back his hair.

"So, let's get down to business, Curria. What's the deal?"

"I'm open to offers, so let's hear yours."

Claudio Curria was sitting in his office at the casino. It was way past his lunch time. Except for the meeting with Maria Beatriz, it had been a most profitable and interesting morning and his rumbling stomach had been put on hold while he was stashing his wad of notes into the safe. Now, bent over his plate of pasta at last, he reflected on the morning's events. After having come to an agreement with the Minister for the Environment, Curria had scoured the island for the white camper, which he had finally located under a large group of acacia trees at the edge of the sand

200

dunes on Maria Beatriz' beach property. There were at least a dozen Tequilans crowded around it, all wearing the offending T-shirt. They had put their dollar to good use. Empty beer cans littered the area. They were squatting under the trees and had started to fry the local spicy sausages on a makeshift barbecue. Curria had inhaled the scent of scorched meat and garlic, and it was then that his stomach had started to rumble powerfully. They had stared at him, waiting to see what his next move would be. Curria had got out of his car and started to approach the vehicle. The men had immediately formed a human barrier around it.

"What's going on here?" Curria had asked.

"We's the President's bodyguards. Who's you?"

Curria had laughed derisively. "She ain't the President yet," he had said.

"But she going to be, Mon. She sure going to be."

Curria had decided to humour the fellow. "OK by me. Take me to your leader. I must speak to her."

The spokesman had shaken his head. "She's napping. Come back later."

"We'll soon see about that," Curria had muttered and gone back to his car and leant on the hooter. He had had a double siren installed and the racket was deafening. It had brought Maria Beatriz to the door. She was resplendent in a brocaded dressing gown the sight of which had drawn a large, collective sigh of admiration from her bodyguards.

"Tell these fellahs that it's alright for me to come and have a chat with you," Curria had called out.

She had laughed loudly. "Fancy you being intimidated, Claudio Curria. You know, Claudio, Sorciero told me you would be coming around to visit. He saw it when he threw the bones. Said you'd be coming with some kind of proposition."

"And my crystal ball tells me that you're both going to like it," Curria had said amiably and had started to skirt around the bodyguards.

"Stop, Claudio. Your crystal ball told you wrong. Sorciero said the proposition was no good and not to let you in."

"You sound like Snow-White; Who do you think I am, the evil Queen come to poison you?" Curria growled.

"Yea, that's it, except you're no Queen," she had giggled.

He had cursed under his breath, "You'll be sorry you didn't listen to me, Maria Beatriz. Tell that silly witch-doctor of yours that it's just not good enough to hop around on hot coals when you're going to have to be dealing with a major crisis. You'll need my assistance."

Maria Beatriz had tossed her head and laughed at him. "Oh, Claudio, stop trying to be so helpful. Go sell your assistance to some other fellah, we don't need it. Scram now, you're disturbing us." She closed the door of the camper firmly.

Curria sat in his car and glowered at the bodyguards who were still standing in closed ranks around the camper.

"You're damned right that I'm going to sell my assistance to some other fellahs. I've already done so, you stupid cow. I'd have given you your chance, but you don't want it," he had muttered and revved up the engine. "That's sealed your fate alright."

He was into his main course, still trying to digest Maria Beatriz' snub. It had given him a stomach ache and he was wondering whether he wasn't growing an ulcer. Things were not going quite the way he had imagined; on the other hand things were not going too

202

badly. He had decided to promise all the heirs his help and play them off one against the other, sitting it out until one of them won. Whoever it was, was sure to think that he, Claudio Curria, had been instrumental in procuring victory for the victor. He would take credit for it anyhow. He sloshed the wine around in the glass, sniffing and tasting it, mimicking the connoisseurs he had seen performing the same gestures. It was an anonymous, potent red, laced with cheap Algerian and sold as vintage Chianti in the elegant casino restaurant. It bore a fancy label designed for Curria's winery. He was the importer of all the Italian produce on the island, be it Parma hams, Tuscan olive oil or wines and spirits. He mopped up the sauce with a crusty piece of schiacciata and chewed on it. A sharp twinge in his belly made him wince. He stabbed at the table bell impatiently holding his finger on it. Grillo Griletti was not as quick off the mark as Limbo Limone had been. He was willing enough but Curria missed Limone. Curria had been too busy to think any more about the inexplicable disappearance of his henchman. Now he was reminded of it again as Griletti ambled unhurriedly into the office.

"Have you turned up anything on Limbo?"

"Na, Boss, nothin." Grillo scratched at a scab on his lobe. He had had to remove his gold stud because of an infection in his pierced ear.

"Stop picking at your ear. It looks disgusting,"

"OK, Boss, but it's itching something awful," Griletti complained.

"Have you been around all the bars and brothels?"

"Sure, Boss, but he's been missing for nearly a week. He can't be fucking a whore for a whole week, or be on a binge for that long, can he?"

"Yea, you're right. It's long even for Limbo."

"You know what I think, boss?"

"C'mon, surprise me." Curria yawned loudly.

"Are you sure there's no moola missin'? I think he's done a bunk, that's what he done. With a pile of money."

Curria smiled. "You're thinking shit, Grillo, as usual. He hasn't left the island. No trace at the airport of his leaving. Even a shithead like you knows that every passenger's registered. You've checked the passenger lists every day."

Grillo Griletti bridled at the insult. "Course I knows that, Boss. Even the *dead* body was registered last week."

"What dead body?" Curria lifted his head and his nostrils trembled like a rabbit's. "What dead body?"

"The US Consulate shipped out a stiff las' week."

"Where was it shipped to, Grillo? Did you find that out?"

"Yea, boss. To Washington DC. He must have been some VIP. Couldn't find out what the name was."

Curria chewed hard at his lip. "I never heard of any VIP croaking on the island. I wonder who it could have been? Where did it happen, some hotel? Chief Pereira must know about that."

Griletti studied the crust he had finally eased off his lobe. He stealthily popped the scab in to his mouth.

"I saw that, *porco*. You make me sick. Get the hell out of here, and bring the car around. I'm going to pay a visit to Chief Pereira."

"But, Boss, it's siesta time."

"Yea, you make me tired and I sure could use some rest, but the devil never sleeps, Grillo, remember that. No siestas for him."

Chapter Eight

The day continued as strangely as it had begun. An ominous, heavy blanket of cloud had overcast the island now. It was completely wind-still and sound-less. The birds were mute and had settled into the trees for what they took to be their bedtime. The heat was oppressive and the islanders had retired into their houses. The stallholders had packed up their mer-chandise and the bars and cafes were deserted. The streets had emptied of the carousers who had spent their last dollar and were now sleeping off their alcoholic excesses.

Boats, which had gone out for the day, were return-ing into harbour although it was only early afternoon. One of the last yachts to come in was Young Chang's. He had drawn in his sails a long while ago and was thankful that he had a powerful engine and extra fuel. The lull had caught them quite far out to sea and they were glad to be safely berthed.

"I've never felt like that at sea before," Chang said.

Mei-Ling nodded. "Whatever happened to the breeze and that gorgeous day? I was afraid we might have to row back."

"The weather report sounds completely normal, and yet there's something strange in the air. Or rather, there's no air at all. I think we're going to have the mother of all storms before long." He looked at her thoughtfully. "Do you agree?"

"It'll blow over before evening, I expect," she said casually. "Can I lure you to my place for a cup of tea?"

"That is an offer I cannot refuse. I'll take you out to dinner as well."

She shook her head gently. "You know that I'm working tonight. Please don't let us argue about that again."

"No argument," he assured her. "You're not diving in this weather."

"Don't dictate to me, Deng."

"Why can't you understand that I'm concerned for you?"

"I understand, but there's no need. It's not the same under the water."

"I'll believe that when I see it." He opened the car door for her. "I'll be waiting for you to come back and God help you if you're going to be late. I'll have the whole of the coast guard looking for you." She stood on tiptoe and kissed him. "Get in now, and let's have that tea and sympathy," he murmured. He drove through the empty streets and stopped in front of her cottage.

"Place is like a ghost town," he said.

"D'you think that we're the only two people left on the planet?" she asked.

"You've been watching too many episodes of the 'X Files'."

"Why didn't you comment on the strange movement of the patch of water when we were out at sea? This sort of uncanny bubbling of waves. I knew that you were concerned by it."

"You seemed not to notice so I didn't wish to alarm you. I never had encountered that phenomenon before."

They entered the house and Mei-Ling took the cooler into the kitchen. She put the kettle on and laid out the tea tray.

"May I phone my mother, darling?" he called from the sitting-room. "I think she might be worrying about us."

"Of course, I'll only be a minute. I want to have a quick wash and slip into something more comfortable."

Mei-Ling took off her shorts and halter and stood under the shower. She rinsed her hair and wrapped it into a towel. She heard a ringing sound and called out to Chang. "My answer-phone is on. Put it on audio please."

After three rings Maurizio Capponcini's voice came over caressingly. "My dear little Minnehaha, I can't wait for this evening's night dive. See you, and don't forget to bring the champagne."

Mei-Ling hurried into the sitting-room and was confronted by a pale Chang.

"So, Mister Capponcini can't wait for his night dive and the champagne? I wonder what the two of you might be celebrating?" There was no mistaking his frosty tone.

"He's just kidding around, Deng. He always does that. There's nothing between us, I swear it."

"I truly find that hard to swallow. I can't believe this is happening to me; that you're actually two-timing me." He made for the door.

"Why do you believe it then? You know it's not true." She stared at him angrily but he didn't turn around. "You have offended me," she said, "and unless you are willing to apologize, I would rather you went."

The door slammed behind Young Chang and Mei-Ling shook her head in despair. He would be too proud to admit he was wrong and lose face. Old Chinese habits were hard to break. Old Crone would have to mediate between them. Mei-Ling picked up the phone and dialled. Maurizio answered almost instantly.

"Hallo there, what's new?"

"My fiancé has just walked out on me because of the damned silly message you left on the answer-phone."

"So you've had your first lover's tiff? I'm sorry, Mei-Ling." He sounded contrite. "Didn't he realize I was just kidding?"

"No, he didn't. He's a very jealous man, and he's particularly jealous of you."

"So, perhaps you're better off without him. You might both look Chinese, but you don't both think Chinese."

"You don't know *how* I think, Maurizio, and I'm upset."

"Perhaps we should call off tonight anyway?" He sounded hopeful.

"Not a chance. Only if the sub's cancelled. Is it?" she asked.

"I've not heard anything, but it might well be. There's been some talk on the radio about strange movements in the ocean some miles off the coast. Did you notice anything out there today?" She hesitated. "Well, cat got your tongue, Minnehaha?"

"There were some odd swells; nothing to get excited about, if you ask me," she answered reluctantly.

"No escape then?"

"No chickening out. See you as planned, Maurizio."

He stood in front of the bathroom mirror and shaved. He had always had a strong growth of beard and it cast the proverbial five o'clock shadow. In truth, he felt a bit of a fool shaving for the evening. Most of it would be spent under water in a wet suit and a mask, so who cared about a bit of stubble? Habit was powerful, though, and he scraped away at his face as if he were getting ready to go to Buckingham Palace. Perhaps he might even meet his Maker before the night was out. It was a thought which made him feel cold and uncomfortable. He imagined that he had still a lot of living and loving to do and he was by no means ready to attempt the descent to Lucifer's kingdom. His misgivings about Mei-Ling's plan were increasing rapidly as the hour of their meeting drew closer. She had concocted a kind of James Bond scenario and had made it sound plausible. Now the scheme seemed utterly mad. He splashed some ice cold water on his face and rubbed some moisturizing cream into his cheeks and neck. He studied his hair and decided he would have a haircut as soon as he was back in Milan. It seemed to him that it had turned greyer on his temples. It was still thick and springy though. He would probably turn white overnight if he survived the next 12 hours. He thumbed his nose at the reflection of Maurizio Capponcini in the mirror. "*Che sara, sara, caro mio,*" he said to his mirror image, and turned off the bathroom light. He put on a pair of slacks, a fine lisle knitted shirt and espadrilles. He slung a pullover across his shoulders and picked up his wallet. He locked up the house and left the deck-lights on. He went down the steps to the boat house. Gingerly he carried the two dive-bags across to his launch and loaded them aboard.

He took the launch out of the bay, careful not to rock the boat too much. There was a bit of a swell and he switched his powerful searchlights on. The short ride to Little Cove was uneventful and he met no other boats. He was relieved to tie up the launch at the dive buoy. He turned off his searchlights and settled down to wait for Mei-Ling. He uncorked a VSOP Cognac and took a drink out of the bottle. The liquid burned a fiery path down his throat and spread a pleasant warmth into his body. He heard a boat sweep past and recognized the elegant shape of Curria's yacht. There were lights on in the saloon and music drifted across the water. He felt a constriction in the region of his heart. He took another drink out of the bottle. It would be ironic if he were to have a heart attack here in the darkness of Little Cove all by himself, and he wished Mei-Ling would hurry up and join him. He peered at the luminous dial of his Swatch. It was almost time.

Her small craft chugged into Little Cove and she tied up next to him at the buoy. She crossed into his boat and he saw the flash of her white even teeth.

"You're almost late," he complained.

"Not so," she replied. "What d'you have in that bottle?"

"Cognac. You wouldn't like it."

"Let me have a bit, it's not all that warm tonight."

"You feeling the chill as well? I thought it was only my nerves getting the better of me," he mouthed and passed the bottle along. "Were you able to see who got on Curria's boat?"

"Yup, it was the Minister for Religious Affairs and Griletti. Just as we had hoped." She tilted the bottle again. "I could get used to this stuff," she murmured.

"You should be ashamed of yourself, drinking alcohol before a dive. Remember all the advice you give your pupils." He took the cognac away from her, corked it and stowed it under the seat. "We'll finish it when we return."

"Sure, that's what we'll do. Better get your gear on, Maurizio. I'll check the equipment."

He went below and struggled into his wet suit. When he came up she had already slipped on her BC, bottles and fins. She let herself fall over the side and adjusted her mask and regulator as she bobbed on the water. He lowered two underwater scooters which were tied to the boat with rope. Then he handed her the two sealed plastic bags which were held up by small buoys. It was his turn to get his gear on and let

210

himself fall into the water. He took his knife and cut the ropes holding the scooters. She grabbed hers and handed him one of the plastic bags. With her teeth she removed the stopper of the buoys which held the plastic bags afloat and started her descent. He followed her example and dived after her until they were nearly on the sandy bottom. They had flashlights clipped to their masks and made the OK signs to each other. He clamped one plastic bag on to the front of each scooter and she started off, consulting her compass as she made for the *passe* in Little Cove. He followed her, praying that she knew where she was going because he felt totally at sea. One day he would laugh about his little joke, he hoped.

Normally he would have enjoyed churning through the water on the scooter. He had practised it with Mei-Ling on several occasions. Tonight however, all he could think of were the plastic bags tied to the scooters, and imagining how lethal their contents were. He couldn't convince himself that their air would last them long enough to get to their target and back to home base, although she had assured him that their bottles would be adequate. He knew that to hold his breath would burst his lungs, yet he only controlled his respiration with difficulty. To lose her in the darkness of this vast ocean filled him with panic – panic that could be fatal. She turned to look at him and he made the OK sign, although he had never felt less OK in all his life. They skirted some rocks and she stopped her scooter and pointed up. He could see the dark shadows of two keels gently swinging to and fro. They were close to the "Trade Winds" dock and without a doubt they were peering up at Curria's launch and the mini-sub. They saw the screw of the mini-sub start up and the vessel submerge slowly. Mei-Ling started to fin above the sub and found something to latch on to. She beckoned him to come and join her. They were carried away by the sub as it gathered speed and headed out to sea. The mother ship was anchored somewhere out there just beyond the 12 mile limit, waiting for its baby to come home. The water which had been dark and clear, gradually got murky. Maurizio rubbed the glass of his mask but visibility got progressively worse. The ocean started to boil around them, throwing the sub from side to side violently. Mei-Ling let go of the bar and held out her hand to him. Maurizio clutched it and they were catapulted through the water, losing both scooters and their cargo. A thunderous, growling roar sounded in their ears and they were swept upward, swirling through a wild, churned-up angry sea. Maurizio felt the bottles unhook from his BC and tear the regulator out of his mouth. He knew that he had taken his last breath of compressed air. A violent explosion threw rocks, sand and debris on them and after a short fruitless struggle, he stopped fighting the overwhelming desire to close his eyes, and lost consciousness.

Chapter Nine

There was an eerie glow in the low cavern which was lit up by the powerful torch. A myriad of stalactites hung down from the ceiling, twists of reedy crystals reflecting the torchlight. A deep pool of water, dark aquamarine, lay still and mysterious. Now and then a droplet fell from a stalactite and ruffled the water, creating ever increasing rings which reached the sandy shore and died. He lay motionless on his side, water dribbling out of the side of his mouth. She turned him onto his back and put her mouth to his again, giving and expelling air. Suddenly he started to thrash around, moaning and gasping for air.

"I can't breathe," he cried and clutched at his throat. "Let me buddy-breathe, Mei-Ling... Where are you... I'm going to die, going to die, going to die..."

"You're not going to die for a long time yet, you're much too handsome and attractive to do that to me. Just don't panic and open your eyes."

He obeyed the gentle order and raised his eyelids. His eyes were dark with untold fear and horror.

"Where am I?" he whispered and gazed at the woman who bent over him.

"I knew you'd say that," she answered, "but at least you didn't ask me who I was."

"Oh, I know who you are. You must be the little mermaid who's rescued the prince from drowning by giving him a lovely kiss." He closed his eyes again.

She laughed and rubbed his cheek. "I may not be a mermaid, but you're a prince alright. At least you haven't lost your sense of humour." She splashed some water over his face and unzipped his wet-suit. "And it was no kiss, it was just a bit of buddy-breathing."

"It seemed uncommonly like a kiss to me." He tried a grin. "Perhaps I'm dead, and this is what heaven's like. Funny, I always imagined it to be a very light and shiny place way up high, in a limitless sky. Nothing like this watery tomb." He tried to sit up and coughed violently. "I'm going to be sick," he muttered. She held his head as he heaved. He fell back with a groan. "My head's spinning."

"You've got quite a big bruise on your head. Probably you're slightly concussed. Just rest for a little while," she said.

He touched his head and felt the bump under his hair. He winced as his fingers probed around it. "It feels as if I've grown a second head. Will I ever look normal again?" he asked.

"You might lose your hair, but that's all," she remarked.

"Such comforting words, my dear. Anything else I've lost or might lose?"

She shook her head. "I've checked, it's all there and you've no broken bones thank the Lord. We must be thankful for that."

"Are you alright?" he queried.

She stretched her legs and winced. "I thought you'd never ask. I took a crack on my ankle and lost a fin. Apart from that," she shrugged, "I'm very tired and I think we should try and have a sleep. I'm going switch off the torch to save the battery."

"I don't like staying in the dark with a bump on my head."

"I'll hold your hand and tell you a story."

"Don't please, your stories are too terrifying, but I'll accept the offer of the hand." He reached out and she grasped his hand firmly and snuggled down beside him. "Mei-Ling, if we're not in heaven then where are we?" he asked tentatively after a little while. "How did we get here ...?"

"I'm not sure as to how we got here, but we're in a cavern not too far from the sea, because the water is salt and undrinkable, worse luck. The good news is that where water comes in, it must go out again, and we'll find an exit to this prison. In the meantime try and have a nap. Close your eyes and count sheep or something." She switched off the flashlight and closed her eyes. She waited for his breath to come evenly and deeply, telling her that he had fallen asleep. Then she too let herself doze for a while. It was important that they should regain some of their strength.

She couldn't reckon how long it was before she felt the water rise and lap around their bodies. She made a grab for the torch and got it just in time. She switched it on and saw that the water in the pool was rising fairly fast and starting to cover the sandy banks. The sound of rushing water became audible and she shook Maurizio and got him to sit up.

"Are you still feeling sick?" she asked anxiously.

"It's not as bad as before. What's going on?"

"I think it's the tide coming in."

"So there's an entry in to this dark heaven, is there?"

"Just as I thought, it would seem."

"For the sea definitely, but what about us?"

"I don't know, Maurizio, that's the honest truth. It depends on how high the water will rise and how far the exit is." She couldn't help the slight catch in her voice and he put his arms around her.

"Dear little Minnehaha, you don't always have to keep a stiff upper lip, you know. It's quite alright to scream and cry now and then," he tried to comfort her. "If we go into the pool we might feel from where the water is coming in. Shall we investigate?" she nodded her agreement and they glided into the water.

It was no longer calm and little waves were forming. The sand banks around the pool had already disappeared and the water splashed against the rocks of the cavern. They swam towards the middle of the pool and trod water. It was quite deep. Their feet no longer touched bottom. Mei-Ling held the torch aloft. He took it from her.

"My arms are longer," he said. "Do you feel anything?" he continued.

"Yes, I feel scared."

"What an admission from a seasoned CIA agent. Feel anything else? I seem to notice a swell of water coming from this side, here." He pointed to the left.

"Me too, definitely. There must be some channel there. I'll go and investigate." She took a deep breath and nosed down. He saw the dark shadow of her body disappear and waited. The water rose steadily and he tried to steer clear of the stalactites. She broke out of the water beside him, panting.

"I thought you'd found the way out and left me here," he said reproachfully.

"I might have done, because it's there. It's too hard to swim against the current though. We'll have to wait until the tide stops coming in and then use the ebb." She clung to him. "We'll make it, Maurizio."

He smiled crookedly. "I wish I had your optimism, dear girl. I also wish we had the bottle of cognac with us, that would help keep my spirits up."

"We should try and keep dry." She looked around. "Shine the torch into the corner there. Do you see that ledge, maybe we can crawl onto it? Hopefully the water won't reach to there." They hoisted themselves on to the narrow ledge and sat there, their heads touching the rocky ceiling. When the water started to wash over the ledge and reached their waists they looked at each other. If the tide didn't stop very soon they would drown. It was time to take a decision.

"I'll go first, Maurizio."

"No, we can afford to wait another couple of minutes. Besides, let me go first. I've still got both my fins. If the passage is wide enough, we'll go side by side, and you'll hang on to me. If not, try and get above me and hang onto my belt. We'll have more power that way."

"If you say so," she answered. "God be with you, Maurizio Capponcini, I am glad to have met you."

"Hey, this isn't the moment to get sentimental on me. It'll be a piece of cake, you'll see," he said with more confidence than he felt. He looked at the water intently. It looked as if the upward flow had suddenly stopped. "See," he said triumphantly, "I was right, the tide's peaked. Now let's just have a little more patience until the ebb starts."

They slid off the edge, took a deep breath and started their descent. She pointed to the dark patch at the side of the pool and he swam towards it. The slowly receding tide carried them along as they finned furiously through the narrow passage. She had moved above him and hung on to his belt. They slowly exhaled air as they had been taught to do, hoping to see the light at the end of the tunnel before their lungs burst. And light there was. A bright patch above the water as they broke surface in another cavern. This time there was a ray of sunshine piercing through a funnel in the rocky ceiling. They trod water and panted, smiling foolishly at each other, nodding their heads. They could hear the waves of the sea breaking against cliffs and knew that they had a good chance now.

"Shall we climb the funnel, or look for the tunnel?" she asked.

"Now you're talking in verse..." he said in mock admiration. She splashed him.

"Stop your snide remarks and just answer me."

"I'm for climbing the funnel," he said. "I don't like the sound of that rough sea." She nodded in approval and swam to the edge. "What about our fins? We might need them later."

"Let's stick them in our suits." They squeezed the fins into the front of their suits and started to ascend. It was a laborious climb and Maurizio had to haul Mei-Ling up most of the way. When they finally reached the end and were safely out in the open, Maurizio crossed himself. She looked at him, strangely amused.

"Yes, I know, it's taken me a long time to find religion,' he muttered.

"You can say thank you for me as well, whilst you're about it," she said reverently.

They sat by the edge of the funnel and took stock of their surroundings. Maurizio shielded his eyes from the morning sun and swivelled his head from side to side. They were, or so it appeared to him, sitting on a small rocky protuberance on an otherwise rather flat partly sandy atoll which couldn't have been more than two hundred metres square. There wasn't any vegetation of any kind growing visibly anywhere, but a cloud of greedy white seagulls was busy picking out dead or dying fish from the crevasses in the boulders. The smell of rotting fish was unmistakable and the screeching of the gulls almost deafening. The sea around the atoll was fairly rough and bringing up seaweed and more fish. There were great banks of fog and heavy cloud, in the distance. Maurizio scanned the far horizon but couldn't make out a coastline. They looked at each other in dismay. Could Tequila have been totally submerged, like the fabled city Atlantis? It was a depressing, terrible thought.

"Let me ask you, Mr. Capponcini, which would be your ten favourite compact discs you would take with you if you were to be marooned on a desert island?"

"Mmmm...My very first choice, without question, would be 'Show me the Way to Go Home.' What would yours be Miss Chang?"

"It would have to be, 'I'll Take Manhattan,' stirred not shaken, of course."

"Naturally, it's the only way to drink it. My second choice would certainly be 'We have no bananas today'. How long do you think we can go on playing this game, Minnehaha?"

"Until we run out of appropriate titles, Mr. Capponcini."

"I've run out, Miss Chang. If we don't find some water to drink, Mei-Ling, we'll be in serious trouble."

"Well, let's go and investigate this island of ours and see whether it can deliver anything beside rotting fish." She stood up and stretched. She unzipped her wetsuit, slipped out of it and laid it over the rocks to dry. Maurizio followed her example. He looked through the zipper pockets of his suit and triumphantly drew out a tube of sugarless mint sweets. "We'll keep those for dessert," he said.

"Bend down and let me look at that bruise." He obeyed and bowed. "Still feeling queasy?"

"Only now and then, when I get a whiff of that fish. Let's have a look at your ankle, now." She held out her leg and he examined the scratches in her skin. They looked angry and swollen.

"Nothing's broken," she said. "I can hobble."

They started to walk, stepping gingerly across the rough rocks, shooing the gulls away as they went. Little pools of water were in the crevasses of the boulders and small fish were struggling to escape the gulls' beaks.

"Looks as if that would be the only edible thing here, so prepare yourself."

He looked disgusted. "I suppose you like raw fish, like sushi."

"It's delicious, healthy, available and for free."

"You must be the most practical girl in the world, Mei-Ling. I suppose you would have some seaweed for garnish." He shuddered.

"Don't give up hope, Maurizio, we might yet find tinned spaghetti or something," she tried to console him.

He laughed. "Gimme 'or something', then." He stopped and pointed to a larger pool in the middle of the atoll. It seemed to bubble in the distance. "D'you think it could be a fresh water spring?"

"I don't know," she shrugged her shoulders. "Is there a slight haze above it, like steam perhaps?"

"Perhaps it's a hot spring. Hurry up girl, and let's taste it. I'm dying of thirst."

They increased their pace and were almost there, when he lifted up his nose, nostrils trembling. "It's not dead fish this time, but it's equally unpleasant. Look at the colour of this water." He knelt down and stuck a finger in the pool. "It's coal black and sticky. Smells like tar. Can't drink that anyhow."

"No, but once it's refined you can put it in your gasoline tank," she grinned. "Never seen crude before?" He shook his head. "Do you know what that means? That you are actually standing at the edge of an enormous natural oil well. We'll be millionaires, just like the Arabs, like Mr. Gulbenkian before them," she jubilated.

He sat down heavily and took his head in his hands. "We're sitting in the middle of nowhere without any food or water, without shelter, without the slightest hope of being rescued, my head aches, and you're yelling about oil wells. Just tell me what this all means? Where the hell are we, where is 'Tequila', where's the sub and the mother vessel, and where are the mines? Did they explode? What in God's name happened down there?"

She laid her hand on his shoulder. "The mines didn't explode, certainly not then. We would have been torn to pieces if they had. I think that we've experienced an earthquake and this is a new atoll, emerged from the seabed. We were lucky to be swept into the cavern." She felt his forehead. "I think you're running a fever. Better come back to the rocks, we'll find a bit of shade there."

"I thought that perhaps our mines had exploded for some reason. I never thought of an earthquake. What happened to the sub, I wonder, and the mother vessel? Do you think they might have sunk?

"With all hands on board? That would truly be a sign from God."

He smiled. "Without us having to do the dirty work. Wouldn't that be nice? I could die quietly of thirst and starvation, but with a clear conscience. No killing." He let himself be led back and lay down. He closed his eyes and sighed. Mei-Ling hung one of the wetsuits across two boulders which gave a bit of shade. She squinted at the sky and saw several clouds. It was going to rain shortly, a few drops at least, as it always did in the Caribbean. She dug out a hole and lined it with the second wet suit. It would give them some rain water to drink. He opened his eyes slightly and watched her busying herself.

"Proper little girl scout, aren't you?" he teased.

221

"Now you're going to rub two pieces of wood together and start a fire."

"Wrong, my friend, I'm going to take a walk and do a bit of beach-combing. Who knows what the tide's brought in."

"A bottle of some kind, make it be a bottle," he wished fervently.

She walked along the beach balancing her fin on her head. It gave her some protection from the sun. She estimated that it was early afternoon now, according to the position of the sun. She had lost her wristwatch in the turmoil of what she was convinced was an earthquake. Mei-Ling thought back to the strange weather of the previous day. The patchy turbulence of the ocean...it had been heralding the earthquake. Of that she was sure. They could not be all that far from 'Tequila', but if they could not signal, it might be days before they were rescued. A small atoll was easily overlooked, or not seen at all. It was lucky that the boulders were there to provide a modicum of shade and shelter. Mei-Ling was worried about the fever Maurizio seemed to have developed and the water situation was precarious, even if they could manage to retain some rainwater in their makeshift catchment. She walked along the shore but found nothing of significance. There were some conches which had been deposited by the tide, and great balls of seaweed, to which small shrimp were clinging. All good food, she mused, if one was able to cook them. Her mouth started to water, and she clutched at her belly. When she had walked around the atoll, she sat down on the sand and stared out to sea. She had noticed that the sand was almost black on one side of the atoll denoting volcanic activity. The water was receding little by little and she waded a little way in. It was quite shallow on that side but there was a slight undertow and the water was cloudy with roughed up rubble and gritty sand.

It was inevitable that she would stub her toe hard on the crate which was partly embedded in the sand. At first she cursed and held on to her bleeding toe. Then, eagerly, she tugged at the crate and tried to dig it out of its niche. She managed to dislodge it and dragged it out of the sea. It was an ordinary wooden crate and had "San Pellegrino" stencilled all over it. She started to laugh and cry and clapped her hands together. She took the diving knife out of her fin and furiously tried break open the crate. She prayed silently that at least some of the bottles might be intact. The wood splintered away finally and she surveyed her treasure. Four broken bottles and two whole ones. She let out a whoop of joy and stumbled through the sand with her treasure.

"Maurizio, wake up, Maurizio," she said gently. "Look what I've found and brought you." She held a bottle aloft. He opened his eyes and shaded them from the bright light. He saw the bottle and grinned.

"Let me guess... I know what it is, a bottle of Dom Perignon," he murmured.

"No, my friend, something much, much better, a bottle of Veuve Pellegrino mineral water. Here, drink as much as you can of it. I have another bottle." He put it to his mouth and swallowed greedily, then held it out to her.

"I've already had my share. Perhaps I can tempt Monsieur with bit of fresh, grilled shrimp?"

"I wish... A book of matches hasn't been washed ashore, has it?" She shook her head regretfully.

"Even if it had, there's nothing to burn, except perhaps the sea weed, once it's been dried."

"How were you proposing to grill the shrimp?"

"I thought of letting the shards of the bottles lie in

the sun until they grow burning hot, and then just pop the shrimp on them." He looked dubious.

"I suppose it's worth a try, but now I'm so hungry I would even eat them raw."

"Good," she said approvingly, "that means that you're feeling better."

"I guess, and look – it's starting to rain." He held out his hand and felt a few drops. Suddenly it poured, and they stood in the rain and washed their bodies, faces and hair as best they could. They scooped the rainwater out of their catchment and drank it. When the sky cleared, she showed him the handful of shrimp she had freed from the seaweed. She shared them out between them.

"Eat," she commanded him. "Think of all those untold millions of Japanese who do this every day, and think it's the greatest delicacy in the world."

"I dunno...I might prefer live monkey brains," he said.

"That's disgusting," she cried. "Don't put me off my food." She chewed on her shrimp spitting out the carapace. "Well, what do you think?"

He shuddered. "Please, please don't make me think about what we're eating, but now that you're asking, a touch of garlic and olive oil would work wonders."

"I meant, do you think that there are other survivors swimming about in the ocean somewhere?"

He nodded seriously. "I'm sure that Curria is having a game of pinochle with the shark. I'll bet he's cheated them out off their nine lots of spare teeth. Now for some dessert," he continued and held out the tube of sugarless mints.

"Oh what a treat, thank you, Sir." she sucked on the little round sweet.

"Do you think that 'Tequila' has disappeared into the sea, just like Atlantis?"

"If you believe in legends then it could be possible, but I don't suppose that an island the size of 'Tequila' could vanish, just like that. There may have been extensive damage, though. Have you noticed that the gulls have gone? It's getting late. They probably have flown back to 'Tequila', or some other island. Oh, would we had wings to fly."

"Where would you fly to, Maurizio?"

"I'd fly to my kids and my beloved Domitilla, who is waiting with open arms for me to return. And you, where would you fly to?"

"I'm not sure. Chang and I had this fight, you know, and maybe he won't wait for me with open arms. And all because of your silly message on the answer-phone."

"Blame me, if you must," Maurizio sighed, "but your Chang is the least trusting person I know. Anyhow, Old Crone will talk some sense into him and you'll patch it up. Believe me, he'll come around."

"You do realize that they probably think we're both dead, drowned while diving. A simple accident, an act of God." She felt her tears well up and she brushed them away from her cheeks. "They may not even be looking for us." She gave a strangled little sob and threw herself onto his breast. He cradled her gently.

"My poor abandoned Mei-Ling; they've already arranged for our memorial service, Young Chang is disporting himself with the Tourist Guide, and you not even cold in your watery grave yet," he mur-mured.

She tore herself away. "I should have guessed I'd get no sympathy from you. I should have let you drown."

"Maybe that would have been kinder. At least I wouldn't have to die of thirst, starvation and expo-sure." He managed a slight chuckle. "Come, Mei-Ling, I was only trying to stop your tears. Come and lie down beside me; let's keep each other warm and go to sleep. It's the only sensible thing to do." Wordlessly she snuggled up against him again and closed her eyes, but sleep wouldn't come. Her shoulders burned and her skin hurt from the scratchy sand. She stood up very quietly.

"Stop fidgeting, woman, and get some rest."

"I can't, the sand's too rough. I'm going to put my wetsuit on."

"You're worrying, I can tell, but you've forgotten Jason Reed. He knew of your mission. The navy will send out a search party for you."

"Stop treating me like a child, Maurizio, I know our situation is as good as hopeless."

"Don't talk nonsense; as long as we have rain water, and providentially, mineral water, we can survive long enough for the search party to find us. Besides, heaven knows what else will get washed up on these shores. Have you put your wet suit on?" He peered at her in the darkness as she struggled with it.

"Come and lie down now," he said again, "we must rest as much as we can. You'll feel much better after a good night's sleep." She sighed and lay down beside him and reached for his hand.

"I shan't be able to sleep a wink, I know," she said and yawned. He held her hand fast until she breathed quietly and evenly. He lay with his eyes open and stared into the night. He didn't feel in the least confident that they would be rescued off this atoll and he hoped that he would be able to keep up this pretence for Mei-Ling's sake. Then, mercifully, he too fell asleep.

Chapter Ten

The earthquake which shook 'Tequila' and the neighbouring islands was measured seven on the Richter scale. The epicentre was out at sea and a giant tidal wave crashed onto the north shore. When it receded, it left destruction in its wake. Shattered homes, drowned animals, dead men. In the town some buildings had tumbled down, trapping the citizens under the rubble. Considering the severity of the tremor, there was, however, relatively little loss of life, and the population was out again in the morning, helping the police force and firemen in their efforts to clear the worst of the damage. The electricity had failed but there were some generators which were working. Luckily the museum, the handsome cathedral, most of the new hotels and Government buildings had weathered the earthquake reasonably well. After the initial panic, the people had coped with the catastrophe. It was, after all, no worse than some of the hurricanes which swept over the island every so often. They had developed a certain philosophical acceptance of the so-called acts of God which rained upon them. They continued to go to services and praise the Lord and implore his mercy. This was a time when the churches were full, and Sorciero's magic had to work overtime.

The American Consul sat at his desk and stared at

227

its polished surface. He felt far from calm but retained his composure in front of the Chief of Police, who sat in the visitor's chair. Twenty-four hours had gone by since the earthquake had shaken 'Tequila' out of its sleep and still there was no sign of life from Mei-Ling Chang or Maurizio Capponcini. The Chief of Police had come to report that Miss Chang's dinghy had been located in Little Bay, lifted by the waters and teetering on the rocks. There was no one at Mr. Capponcini's house either. The boat man had managed to take his dinghy in and checked the premises.

"So I take it Chief, there's been no further news at all?"

"No Sir. I've also checked with Old Crone, I mean Mrs Chang. Neither she nor Young Chang have had word from Miss Chang."

Jason drummed the usual rhythm with his fingers on the desk. The air-conditioning had packed up and he was sweating, as much from the oppressive heat as from the anxiety he felt. He left unsightly fingerprints all over the shiny top.

"I'm extremely worried, Chief, as you can imagine. Miss Chang is an American Citizen, and I will have to report to her family." The Chief nodded seriously.

"I hear that Mr. Curria is also missing. He too is an American Citizen. So more worry for you, Sir."

"More worry alive than dead, that gentleman," Jason Reed muttered sourly. He looked at the Chief sternly. "He is a gangster, Chief, a drug-pusher, a thoroughly disreputable character."

The Chief looked suitably surprised. "You don't mean it, Sir; surely our Minister for Religious Affairs would not take such a person for a friend and partner?"

"I wouldn't care to say, Chief." Jason scrutinized him. "I have heard that the Minister was leaving the

228

island yesterday on a business trip. Are all the other Members of the Government safe? And Miss Maria Beatriz, I trust the future first lady didn't come to any harm?"

The Chief grinned broadly, showing a row of healthy white teeth. "Oh, no worries Sir, all dem Del Reys – except for the Minister for Religious Affairs – are accounted for, and Miz Maria Beatriz spent the night in the Presidential villa with Sorciero. Nothing could ever happen to Miz Maria Beatriz now that Sorciero is looking after her." The Chief stood up and straightened his uniform. "If you will excuse me Sir, I have things to attend to."

"Well, let me know if anything turns up. I shall spend the night here."

The Chief saluted and left Jason to his dark thoughts.

Jason called the marine to bring in some storm lanterns. The Consulate had a good generator, but Jason decided to turn it off to save fuel. He intended to spend the night on the couch in his office. The marine brought in the storm lanterns and said that a Mrs. Chang was outside and desired to be received by the Consul. Jason was surprised but agreed to see the old lady. Old Crone appeared in the doorway, struggling to hold on to her large basket which the marine was trying to relieve her of.

"What are you doing, Corporal?"

"It's regulation, Sir, I have to search everything that's brought into the Consulate. C'mon lady, let go."

"Let her come in Corporal, Mrs. Chang will not hurt anyone. Just tell him what you've got in there, Mrs. Chang." Old Crone smiled sweetly at the Marine.

"It's just a small token of my respect; some Peking duck cooked just right for the Consul to have for his dinner."

"How very thoughtful, Mrs. Chang. I do believe that I could manage to eat something, but only of course if you'll join me." Old Crone bowed and smiled. "That'll be all Corporal. Go and get something to eat yourself if you can."

Old Crone moved gracefully towards the desk and put down her basket. "May I set it up on your desk, Mr. Reed?"

"Be my guest, Mrs. Chang."

She swiftly took out a white damask cloth and spread it over the desk. Then she brought out two plates covered in foil which she set out on either side of the desk. She took out some small china cups and filled them with jasmine tea from a thermos flask. Finally she unwrapped two pairs of delicately carved ivory chopsticks. She removed the aluminium foil and a cloud of steam wafted across bearing the most wonderful aromas.

"Let us eat, Mr. Reed, before it gets cold."

Something like a companionable silence settled between them, interrupted only by the occasional flattering comment on the food by Jason Reed. When they had polished off every morsel and were sipping on the jasmine tea, Old Crone opened the conversation.

"Mr. Reed, have you any news of my daughter-in-law to be? My son is worried sick and doesn't know who to turn to."

Jason put on his best innocent look: "Dear Lady, why do you ask me? I have not the slightest idea where Miss Chang could be. All I know is that she went diving with Mr. Capponcini last night. Has she not returned home?"

"No, she has not," Old Crone said softly. "Did you really expect her to come out of this adventure safely?"

"I don't know that I had anything to expect. I agree that she may have had an accident because of the earthquake, but that is hardly my fault, Mrs. Chang."

Old Crone set down her teacup firmly. "I'm not talking about the earthquake, Mr. Reed. I am really more concerned about the limpet mines which they were to plant on Mr. Curria's drug boat." Jason's tea got into his windpipe and he spluttered and coughed hard. He held the fine linen napkin over his mouth and wondered what to answer.

"Mrs. Chang, what are you talking about?" he finally said, trying to sound outraged.

"Mei-Ling took me into her confidence because she was apprehensive and wanted me to be aware of the situation. I am very alarmed, Sir, as you can imagine. I am very fond of Mei-Ling. The perfect daughter-in-law ... My son Chang was so happy. Are you sure there is nothing that you can tell? Young Chang knows nothing of this; he would have prevented her from going if he had known. I had to promise not to reveal her secret to anyone, least of all my son."

"So she's blown her cover," he said sadly, "not very professional."

"Is that so important now? She couldn't have gone on with that job after her wedding anyway," Old Crone said softly.

Jason nodded and blew his nose. "You're right I suppose, Mrs. Chang. Unfortunately, I was not withholding any news from you. I haven't heard anything at all. I keep on hoping that some news will come in, and will sit here all night, waiting."

"Are you at least going to send a search party out to look for them?"

"I've asked for an American coast guard vessel from Puerto Rico and we'll use the helicopter at first light. Until then we can just hope and pray."

"Mr. Curria and the Minister?" Old Crone asked.

"So you know about that too? No, they have not surfaced either so far as I know." He stared at the old Chinese lady who sat demurely on the chair. "I don't suppose there is much on this island that you don't know about."

She smiled enigmatically. He continued to stare at her but she did not drop her eyes.

"I too know quite a lot of things," he said finally. "That you use the pills and powders produced by the new chemical factory in the draughts you sell to your clients. It improves Sorciero's magic no doubt."

"It makes unhappy people a bit happier."

"You're breaking the law, Mrs. Chang; in America you would find yourself under arrest for drug pushing. I told Mei-Ling that you should desist from continuing these practices." Jason Reed got up from his chair and walked to the window.

"I'm a citizen of 'Tequila' and what happens in America does not concern me. Besides, I should like to see who would arrest Sorciero." She smiled kindly at Jason's back. "However, in view of the fact that my beloved daughter-in-law to be has asked me to desist, I will do it to please her. Besides, Sorciero does not need any help anymore. He can make magic without the assistance of drugs."

Jonathan snorted loudly and turned around. "I really cannot believe in this hocus pocus. Why don't we ask him what's become of Mei-Ling and Capponcini? Let us put him to the test, Mrs. Chang, what do you say to that?" He laughed, took off his glasses and polished them.

"You shouldn't scoff, Mr. Reed, magic is a serious business. Ask any witchdoctor." She rose from her chair and tripped around the desk, picking up the crockery and stowing it away in her basket. When she had packed it all away and polished the desk, she looked up at him. "Whenever you're ready Mr. Reed. Sorciero is waiting for us at his cabin. He knew that you would want to consult him. He said to tell you that there would be no fee, no payment."

Jason put his glasses on again. "How very civil of him," he snapped. "And what if I don't want to go, my good woman?"

"You would be very foolish indeed, my good man," Old Crone answered tartly. For an instant she lost her customary inscrutability. "You don't really deserve it, but I'll let you ride with me in my rickshaw."

Old Crone's rickshaw made good progress. The lad was careful not ride over the worst potholes. He couldn't entirely avoid the cracks the earthquake had caused and soon they were on the track leading to Sorciero's cabin. A storm lantern was hanging outside the door, and the girl who took the appointments was trying to keep order among the people who were pushing to get in. They let Old Crone and Jason Reed pass through and enter. Sorciero was crouched over the embers of a fire. He had put on his working finery and painted his face. Maria Beatriz was kneeling beside him. She had wrapped a shimmering emerald green sarong around herself and had wound a turban around her head, made of the same silk. Together they were an awesome sight and the people outside gasped in unison as they caught a glimpse of them through the open door.

"Close the door, Old Crone, the draft might kill the fire completely," Sorciero greeted them. "Welcome Mr. Reed, take a seat." He pointed to the damp mats which were spread around the fire. "It's difficult to keep the fire going, all the wood has got soaked."

Jason looked at the mats and shook his head. "I'll stand if you don't mind." He bowed slightly to Maria Beatriz. "Miss Del Rey, I am glad to see you're safe."

"Thank you Mr. Reed. I'm fine, but my camper has

been washed away." Her eyes glistened with a few tears. "I did love my camper."

"Don't fuss about that, woman," Sorciero said, "the government will buy you a new one when you become President." He looked at Old Crone. "Won't they?"

"I don't know, Sorciero, it all depends." She sat down on her raised chair. "The island has suffered considerable damage and the government will have to take care of that. So you would be both ill advised to spend money on luxuries. You have a home in the villa and can use a government car." She cocked her head. "On the other hand, I suppose that some international organisation will step in with funds for reconstruction. What do you think Mr. Reed?"

"More than likely, Mrs. Chang, but then who are we to guess what will happen? It is surely Sorciero's business to look into the future? And he could start by telling us what's happened to Mei-Ling and Capponcini."

"I will try, Mun, I will try." Sorciero sat back on his haunches and started to chant loudly, mumbling incomprehensible words. Old Crone dipped into her bag and brought out a fistful of crystals which she threw into the embers. A spray of green fire leapt up and gave off a strange scent, acrid yet with a hint of sweetness. Jason pursed his lips and looked at Old Crone. "Do you really expect me to take this seriously?"

"Quite seriously; yes, Mr. Reed," Old Crone whispered. She put her finger on her lips. "He's about to go into a trance. No more talking, it disturbs him. Maria Beatriz, tell the people outside to remain quiet otherwise the magic will go away. Tell them also that their turn will come to ask questions." Maria Beatriz tiptoed to the cabin door and went outside. A hush fell as the crowd settled down to wait.

Sorciero's head had begun to swivel and the chant got faster and faster. He stopped suddenly and sat with his mouth wide open, seemingly not breathing. His eyes were glazed and unseeing. Old Crone spoke to him quietly.

"Are you ready to answer our questions, Sorciero?"

He nodded and closed his eyes.

"Can you see Mei-Ling, my daughter-in-law to be, and the Italian, Maurizio Capponcini?"

Slowly Sorciero picked up a stick and started to draw in the dirt floor. He scratched away laboriously like a first-grader. Then he put down the stick and stared at his handy-work.

"They live, oh yes they live," he muttered.

"Where?" Jason asked impatiently.

"Why there, Mun, there." Sorciero pointed at the writing on the ground and Jason and Old Crone knelt down to look at it. Jason examined it perfunctorily and got up abruptly.

"This looks like complete drivel to me; just a mess of numbers and letters," he said loudly. Old Crone again held her fingers to her lips and continued studying the marks on the dirt floor.

"You are much too impatient, Mr Reed," she admonished him then. "I think that they are latitude and longitude numbers and letters. I would ask our local coast guard to investigate, but they lost the ship. Will you please send your coast guards, when they arrive? It may not be too late."

"My dear Mrs. Chang, you don't really think that I'm going to send out the U.S. Coast Guard on such a wild goose chase!"

"What have they got to lose but a little bit of fuel?" Old Crone implored. "Don't you care about recovering your agent? You might at least take note of the numbers and letters, Mr. Reed."

"I won't have anything to do with this gibberish," he answered.

"Indulge an old woman's whim, then. You won't regret it. I will write it down for you, and you can check with the Harbourmaster whether I'm right about the meaning of Sorciero's message." Old Crone rapidly copied the numbers and letters and gave them to Jason Reed. "Go now, Sir, hurry. I will remain here."

Jason reluctantly took the piece of paper and left the cabin. Dark, silent faces turned towards him as he wound his way through the crowd. The sun was about to rise and the birds had started their morning concert. He was stopped by the Minister for Religious Affairs' wife, who was elbowing her way towards him.

"Mr. Reed," she called, "Mr. Reed, what gives? Do you think Sorciero can tell me what's happened to my husband?"

"The fellow's in a trance and they are holding some sort of seance in there, so it depends how gullible you are. See?" He waved his piece of paper in the air. "I've got my message, for what it's worth." The Minister's wife waved back and pushed through the crowd to the cabin. The people made way for her and she entered the cabin. She nodded to Maria Beatriz and Old Crone.

"Can I ask my question?" the Minister's wife whispered. Old Crone nodded silently.

"Sorciero, can you tell me what has happened to my husband, the Minister for Religious Affairs? He left the island with Mr. Curria."

Sorciero blinked twice, started to shake and bared his teeth. "Curria, Curria," he hissed. "A snake, in our garden of Eden. Stoned to death, stoned to death, stoned to death ..."

"OK, we all know Curria was into drugs, but what happened to the Minister?"

Sorciero's eyes started to glow and he rocked back and forth on his heels.

236

"Stoned to death, all of them stoned to death by the rocks...the ocean is very angry..." Sorciero jumped up and threw his arms about and made swooshing noises. "The ship is sinking, the explosion..." He howled as if in pain, hiding his face in his hands and rocking back and forth.

"Explosion?" the Minister's wife whispered. "I suppose he means earthquake."

Old Crone nodded sagely. "You should leave now, your Excellency, you've had your answer. My sincerest condolences on the demise of your husband."

"Thank you, thank you for your concern, but can I really take this as gospel?"

"I'm sure you can," Old Crone murmured.

"Oh dear, what am I going to do now?" The Minister's wife sounded perturbed rather than distressed.

"You won't need to have a breast implant."

"That at least is a blessed relief."

Jason Reed got into the jeep which his driver had brought to the side of the road where the dirt track led to Sorciero's cabin. Jason sat in the passenger seat silently and held a flashlight over the scrap of paper which Old Crone had given him. The sky began to lighten into a luminescent blue. There were just a couple of little clouds being wafted across the heavens by a mild breeze. No one would have guessed at the earthquake and the rushing waters which had so nearly devastated the island less than forty-eight hours ago.

"Where to, Sir?" The driver interrupted his thoughts.

"Let's go and find the Harbourmaster, what have I got to lose?"

"I don't know, Sir, but it's barely dawn and he'll still be asleep."

"We'll just have to wake him up then. Drive on."

A somewhat dishevelled, unshaven man opened the door cursing at the disturbance. "What the hell you want, Mun, at this hour?" he squinted at the unexpected visitor.

"I am the United States Consul, Harbourmaster Bellow; my name is Reed, we have met before."

"Never at this ungodly hour, Sir. What do you want?"

"I do apologize for this early visit, but I have something of the utmost importance to show you. How good are you on navigation?"

The Harbourmaster groaned. "Rotten, until I've had my morning coffee. Come in then, Mr. Reed, and take a seat while I tidy myself up. You can go to the kitchen, and put the kettle on the gas in the meantime. You'll find cups and saucers, coffee, sugar and milk on the tray on the counter."

It was still quite dark in the house, there being no electricity coming from the mains. Bellow shone his torch onto the generator and threw the switch. The machine was an antiquated Honda model and it coughed and sputtered loudly, reluctant to come out of its hibernation. Finally it settled into a kind of rhythm and the Harbourmaster turned on the lights in his office. He beckoned Jason into the room and sat him down in the visitor's chair. He thrust some old periodicals into Jason's hand and disappeared into his bathroom. The kettle started to whistle and Jason hurried to the kitchen to turn the gas off. He spooned some coffee into the cups and added the boiled water. He hunted around until he found a tin of biscuits which he added to the tray.

"That smells good," the Harbourmaster cried. "Bring it in, please, will you?"

He had put on a pair of jeans and a polo shirt and was already sitting at his desk. "Now what is it you wanted me to look at?"

Jason put the tray down on the desk and took a crumpled piece of paper out of his pocket. He smoothed it out and laid it in front of Bellow. The Harbourmaster picked up a cup and added the sugar and powdered milk to it. He stirred it thoughtfully, then sipped the coffee.

"That's better," he sighed and put the cup down. "Now let's see what we have here." He picked up his instruments and started a calculation.

"Is it really longitude and latitude?" Jason asked.

The Harbourmaster nodded and went on with his calculations. "So you want to know where this is, Sir?"

"It's not just gibberish?"

"No, it seems to make sense. It is not quite twelve miles due south of 'Tequila'. Is that any help to you?"

"I'll be damned." Jason bent over the man's shoulder. "Show me where that is on the charts."

The Harbourmaster spread a chart over the desk and pointed to a group of islands.

"You see, this is 'Tequila', and about twelve miles due south would take you to a spot right here." He stabbed at the chart with his finger. "And right here there is nothing, no land, not even a rock within a radius of 160 degrees," the Harbourmaster said decisively. "Can't tell you any more than that, Mun."

"Could you mark it visibly on the chart and let me borrow it for a couple of hours?" Bellow looked dubious. "It's government property, I really shouldn't."

"It may be a matter of life and death, Sir," Jason pleaded.

"I'll photocopy it for you if my machine hasn't packed up." Bellow went to the machine and put the chart on. He activated the photocopier and it purred quietly. "I think it still works, Mr. Reed," he said.

"Look – it's not at all bad, just a wee bit smudged." He pulled off the copy and handed it to Jason. "There you go, Mun, and good luck, for what it's worth." He accompanied Jason to the door. "What are you going to do with it?" he asked curiously.

"Take the coast guard vessel as soon as it arrives from Puerto Rico and investigate the spot. It should be docking very soon."

"Why don't you wait here for it, have another cup of coffee? I'll go and have a shower if you don't mind. It's not worth going back to bed now."

"Thank you for the offer, but I have a few things to deal with at the Consulate."

Jason Reed returned to the Consulate. He felt tired and dirty, and badly needed a change of clothes. He smelled of sweat and the stubble on his chin and cheeks gave him a disreputable mien. He had had a small bathroom installed at his office. It was simple but usually efficient. He longed to get under the shower and called to the Marine to switch on the generator. He bundled his dirty clothes into a plastic bag and put it away in a drawer of the filing cabinet. He usually kept some fresh underwear, a T-shirt and a pair of slacks in reserve at the office. With a sigh of anticipation he turned on the hot water tap. After the initial gush there was only a slight trickle coming from the shower head. He cursed and wiped himself off with a wet cloth. There wasn't enough hot water to shave with. He would have to use his electric razor, if the batteries hadn't run too low. He wondered why there was no water. The generator was powerful enough to activate the pump. Jason pulled on his fresh clothes and put the electric razor to the test. To his astonishment it took off and cruised up and down his face, leaving it smooth and free of stubble. He splashed some aftershave on, brushed his hair and cleaned his glasses. He was now ready to take on the rest of what promised to be another ghastly day, and sat down at his desk. He turned on the intercom and asked for the Marine to come in.

"Why don't we have any water, Marine? Is the pump out of order?"

"No Sir, it's the catchment. The earthquake cracked the cement and most of the water's run out. We're trying to patch it up, Sir."

"Has my secretary come in?"

"No, Sir, she sent in a message not to expect her today."

"The Harbourmaster is going to radio us as soon as the coast guard arrives. Send a driver down to Sorciero's place and ask Old Crone, Sorciero, and Miz Maria Beatriz to go to the harbour. I shall meet them there and pick up Young Chang on the way. Tell them I want them all to come on the coast guard boat with me."

"Yes, Sir." The Marine saluted. "Sir, the Italian Consul is outside and wants a word with you, Sir."

"Show him in, please."

The Italian Consul was considered a fine looking figure of a man. He managed to appear sleek and immaculate even after the events of the last couple of days. He greeted Jason with a firm handshake and sat down. Andrea Sandrini was close to retirement and was contemplating taking up residence permanently on the island. The climate and the company suited him. He was a widower who had found comfort and solace on the island. He had struck up a relationship with a French widow who owned the best fashion boutique in town. The fly in his ointment was Curria's circle of thugs who were a destructive and corrupting influence in this little paradise. Sandrini had met the Capponcinis in Milan and was delighted when the posting to 'Tequila' had come through. The Capponcinis had raved about the beauty of the island and had discussed their intention of building another Club Royale there. Sandrini had been their houseguest at 'Trade Winds' for a few weeks, until he had found a small beach villa to buy. Now he sat in front of Jason Reed and seemed quite agitated.

"Sorry to bother you, Jason, but I thought that you might have some news; I would have telephoned, but your line's still down."

"Yours is working already?" Jason sounded a bit miffed.

"Well, you know, the consulate is right next door to Government House, so I persuaded them to do ours at the same time as they did theirs."

"I don't know when they'll put ours on again, it's very frustrating." He cracked his knuckles. "I don't know what kind of news you expect to hear from me when I'm almost totally cut off from the world."

"It's about Maurizio Capponcini. He told me he was going to do a night-dive with Mei-Ling Chang, and I've heard nothing from him for almost 48 hours. Young Chang, who took the phone call at Mei-Ling's, is totally frantic because she's missing. I thought that perhaps, given the circumstances, you might be able to tell me."

"What circumstances, Andrea?"

"You know what I mean, we're colleagues, after all. You see I've got this message," Andrea Sandrini held up a piece of paper, "from Domitilla, that she and the children will be on the very next flight that comes in. Whenever that might be...there is also some other good news for him."

Jason nodded and polished his spectacles. "I don't have any really reliable news, but as soon as the coast guards arrive from San Juan, I'm going out to sea with them to look. You could come along if you wished."

Sandrini agreed. "I'll be at the Consulate. Pick me up on the way to the harbour? That would be great." He hurried out and bumped into Old Crone who was waiting in the reception hall with a small group of people. Maria Beatriz was still wrapped in the emerald green silk, but Sorciero had changed into a pair of jeans and a brightly coloured Hawaiian shirt. Young Chang looked ghastly pale and had lost some of his habitual crispness. The Minister's wife seemed quite unperturbed and was primping her short hair in front of the antique mirror which hung in the hall. She smoothed down the silk jersey dress over her boyish figure and smiled at her reflection. It was, after all, a '*jour de fête*' for her. She had been quite convinced for some little time that it was a far, far better thing to lose the Minister than to find him. She hoped that that might never happen, not alive anyway.

"Good morning, Mesdames," Andrea Sandrini bowed to old Crone, the Minister's wife and Maria Beatriz. "Sorciero, that's a splendid shirt you're wearing."

Sorciero beamed, showing his strong white teeth. "Yea, Maria Beatriz bought it for me at your woman's boutique."

The Consul cleared his throat in some embarrassment. He had not realized that his liaison was public knowledge.

"Hum, yes, she does have excellent taste..." he said hastily. "You all coming to call on Mr. Reed?"

Old Crone bowed her head twice and said, "we are waiting for the U.S. Coast Guard to arrive, Sir, and then we all expect Mr. Reed to let us accompany him."

"We shall be quite a search-party then, because I'm also coming along. Perhaps I should wait here with you? It'll save time."

A marine came through the reception hall and knocked at the Consul's door. He opened it and they heard him say that the Harbourmaster had radioed that the Coast Guard was docking and that the Consul should hurry down right away. After some protestation, Jason Reed agreed to take the delegation, as he called them, along on the ship. Young Chang and Old Crone got into her rickshaw, while Sorciero, Maria Beatriz and Andrea Sandrini and the Minister's wife climbed into the jeep with Jason Reed. It didn't take them long to reach the dockyard. It was time again to test Sorciero's magic and powers of prediction, and it was with a frisson of anticipation that they all boarded the vessel.

Chapter Eleven

Maurizio woke from his troubled sleep and moved slightly to disengage himself from Mei-Ling, who had flung her arm over his chest. He heard the wings of the gulls beating in the air above and their shrill screeches as they circled overhead. He crawled out of the protective shelter of the rocks and gazed at the brightening sky. The sun was a burning red orb on the horizon, tinting the heavens – and the sea – gold and pink. It would be another brilliant day and Maurizio was dreading it. His head still throbbed as he started to crawl painfully towards their catchment. There was a little bit of water left in it and he scooped it up in his palm and drank it. It hardly slaked the terrible thirst which parched his throat and mouth. He resisted the temptation to drink out of the bottle. Every drop of water had to be conserved. He longed to go to the edge of the sea and bathe in the cool water. It took him longer than he had anticipated and he was exhausted by the time he reached the shore. He stripped off his shorts and waded into the shallows, lay down on his back and floated with his eyes closed. He looked calm and contented but his mind was in a turmoil. He had no idea how to relieve their situation and, no matter how hard he tried, no feasible solution presented itself. They couldn't make smoke signals and the 'message in the bottle' bit only succeeded in boys' adventure stories. His stomach started to rumble and he had visions of crusty fresh bread and sweet butter. His tastes were simple really, he thought to himself. Good country fare and a Chianti wine. He heard something splash beside him and started up. He opened his eyes and saw Mei-Ling angrily staring down at him. Her thick black hair was matted and her eyes were red with weeping.

"Don't you do that again, ever," she sobbed.

"What's happened? For God's sake, what's happened? Are you alright?"

"I woke up and you weren't there, that's what happened; and I got scared."

"You, scared, Minnehaha? I don't believe it," he smiled at her ironically.

"And take that silly grin off your face," she snapped. "C'mon, get out of the water and let's find something to eat."

"I can't get out, I've nothing on. I left my shorts on the shore."

It was her turn to grin: "Oh, have we got an attack of modesty all of a sudden?" She turned her back on him. "It's OK, I won't look." He snorted, waded to the shore and grabbed his shorts. He struggled into them and almost lost his balance. The cool water had soothed the headache but his eyes still felt dry and gritty. Mei-Ling came to him and took his hand. They started to paddle along the shore keeping a lookout for anything that might have been washed up by the waves.

They saw the body at exactly the same instant and stopped, their feet rooted to the sand. The water was gently flowing over the corpse, revealing the half-clad form as the waves receded, then spilt over it again with inevitable regularity. It lay face down, mouth and nose buried in the sand, arms spread out, and it was patently clear that there couldn't possibly be life left in it. The tattered trousers, the shortish black hair and the width of the shoulders pronounced it to be a man. They started to move forwards again very slowly, curious to see who it was, yet unwilling to come close enough to identify the new arrival.

"Who do you think it is?" she whispered.

"Damned if I know … and why are you whispering? He can't hear you."

"It could be Curria. Go and turn him around," she said.

"It's certainly not the Minister, the colour's wrong. Why don't you help turn him around? I'm not doing it by myself." They came a little bit closer and saw that the left hand had been severed from the wrist and was missing. It was not a pretty sight and Mei-Ling shuddered and hid her face against Maurizio's chest.

"It's Curria alright, I recognize the ear-stud," he said. "It looks as if he's been in a shark attack. There are chunks torn out of his back too."

"It could have been from an explosion." She lifted her head and took another look at the body. "Let's turn him around, just to make sure." They bent down and turned the corpse over. "I think I'm going to be sick," she cried and ran a few steps, heaving and retching. Maurizio laid the body face down as they had found it. He felt nauseous, weak and helpless. He moved away and sat down, putting his head between his knees as he had been taught to do.

"We can't just leave him there," he heard her say. "And don't faint on me, for God's sake." She pulled his head up and slapped his cheeks gently. "Please Maurizio, don't." He moaned softly and rocked back and forth. He felt a bottle pressed against his mouth. "Swallow that, Maurizio." He drank some water and the nausea faded.

"What do you propose to do with him?" he uttered at last. "Give him a Christian burial?"

247

"We must cover him with sand, at least, so that the gulls won't get him."

"I agree, it might give them indigestion." He got up groggily. "Give me a hand and let's pull him further on to the shore." They dragged the corpse by the shoulders until it was completely out of the water and several metres inland where the sand was powdery and dry. They started to scoop sand out with their cupped hands and pour it over the body. It ran away as quickly as they scooped it on.

"This is getting us nowhere. We've got to dig a trench and then fill it in."

"I don't know whether I have the strength," she complained. "Not now. Let's move along, perhaps something more useful's been deposited on the shore."

"You've talked me into it," he said and started to walk away.

"Hey, wait for me," she cried and limped after him. He slowed his pace and looked back at her.

"Does your leg hurt?"

"A little," she answered.

"I'll carry you piggyback." He knelt down and she climbed onto his shoulders.

"Why, you're as light as a feather, Miss Chang. Take a good look around; perhaps you can see something from your perch which I can't." He did a slow pirouette and she shielded her eyes against the sun with her hand. She shook her head despondently.

"Apart from the oil slick, I can't see a thing...but walk on, I've not given up hope. Where there's St Pellegrino, there might be spaghetti or tinned tomatoes."

"Can't wait to have a taste of that delicacy. Raw pasta and an unopenable tin of tomatoes. Yumm, Yummy." He walked on, kicking up sand, scanning the shallows.

"Why don't you try standing on my shoulders — perhaps you can see something on the horizon?"

"Just because you've heard of the Chinese circuses doesn't mean that I can do a balancing act."

"You can do it; I'll hold onto you. Try, you can do it," he encouraged her. Mei-Ling hoisted herself up and teetered on his shoulder, while he steadied her with his hands. She concentrated on the horizon but there was a heat haze on the water and visibility was a little blurred. Yet it seemed to her that there was a speck moving out at sea. She shut her eyes tightly, then opened them again. The speck, she thought, had slightly changed position, yet she couldn't be sure that it was not just a mirage brought about by wishful thinking. Again, she closed her eyes, and opened them after a few seconds. She laughed out loud and started to wave an arm about so wildly that she lost her footing and landed on the sand.

"You could have broken your back, you silly girl," Maurizio chided her. "This is no time to get hysterical," he continued as she went on laughing and crying and waving her arms about.

"There's a boat, there's a boat out there!" she finally managed to blurt out.

"Yes, my dear, there must quite a number of them," he said soothingly and helped her up. She jumped up and down waving her arms, screaming "We're here, we're here!" She turned to him. "Help me up again, Maurizio, they might see us that way."

"Is this a joke, Mei-Ling? It's in very bad taste if I may say so," he said huffily.

"No, you great obtuse idiot, there's someone out there, and they're closing in at quite a speed."

"Pirates, perhaps," he muttered derisively as she dug her heels into his shoulders.

"No, my dear Maurizio, it's the Marines..." she yelled

as the far away throbbing of an engine finally reached their ears. Mei-Ling had stripped off the top of the white cotton bikini she usually wore under her wetsuit and twirled it like a flag. They heard a shot, and a rocket flew into the sky, leaving a coloured trail behind it.

"They've seen us, Maurizio, they've really seen us. I can't believe it, what a stroke of luck. Let me down, let me down." She stood beside him now still waving her white bikini top. He started forward into the shallows dragging her behind him, shouting with her. They could see the vessel quite clearly now. It had stopped and was throwing out the anchor. People were getting into the dinghy, which then made for the shore. Mei-Ling and Maurizio had stopped waving. They clung together, weak, exhausted and tearful, waiting for the rescuers who had literally appeared out of the blue.

"I think you'd better put your bikini top on again, Minnehaha. I wouldn't want the US Coast Guard to get the wrong idea."

"Don't be so old-fashioned, Maurizio, these sailors have seen boobs before."

"I think that there's more than one sailor aboard. I wonder who all these people can be?" he said as the dinghy approached. "I do believe that Maria Beatriz is on board, and Sorciero."

"Good Lord," Mei-Ling cried. "It's Young Chang standing up, rocking the boat, and Old Crone hanging on to his legs." She hurriedly put on her bikini top and turned to Maurizio. "How do I look?" she asked anxiously.

"Decent, my dear," he sounded relieved. "But your make-up's a bit smudged and your hair's a proper bird's nest." She pinched his bottom hard and he winced.

"That's not a very nice thing for a young lady of quality, and a bride to be at that, to do to a strange man. It might give him ideas."

She ignored that remark and said, "I think Jason Reed's there and some other woman. It could be the Minister's wife."

The dinghy was almost at the shore and the sailor pulled in the outboard and jumped out into the shallows. He dragged the dinghy up the sandy bank, helped by Jason Reed and Young Chang. There was an orgy of embracing and laughing, tearful reconciliation and promises of undying love. Old Crone Chang, who never went anywhere without her basket, took out some sandwiches and a bottle of brandy.

"You must be starving, you poor people," she said.

They all looked at her in amazement. "You brought food and drink, without even being sure that we would find someone?" Jason Reed asked.

"Contrary to you, Sir, I have faith in Sorciero's magic." she answered.

Maria Beatriz and Sorciero were looking at the atoll in wonderment. The coast guards had informed them that the islet was within the national limit which entitled 'Tequila' to claim it as its territory. Maria Beatriz had taken a little Tequilan flag from the ship's collection and planted it in the sand.

"This is a great moment for us Tequilans. What shall we call our new island, Sammy?"

Sorciero thought for a bit and then said, "'Lucky Island', that's what it feels like to me. What do you think, Old Crone?"

"Speaking as a Chinese, I think it is a very appropriate name. It's saved my dear daughter-in-law to be."

"Coming to explore our Lucky Island, Sammy? Maybe we could build a house here, for holidays."

Sorciero shook his head. "Not here, Maria Beatriz, there's no water."

She looked at him in amazement. "How do you know for certain?"

"I ain't a Sorciero for nothin', my pretty," he smirked. "I feel water, and there ain't none here." He closed his eyes and concentrated. "I feel something else though, bubblin' away."

"Not another earthquake?" Maria Beatriz shrieked in panic. "I'm out of here, folks. One is quite enough for me."

"No, don't run away, it's something good. Just follow me," Sorciero said, and led the way into the sand dunes.

"Oh my poor love," Young Chang murmured, his usual reserve cast aside. He held a trembling Mei-Ling in his arms and she cried quietly into his shoulder.

"You must have gone through hell, and to think that I let you go on these night dives. That I didn't put my foot down." He sounded masterful and tender at the same time. "I won't let it happen again, I'll keep you safe with me, always." She nodded and let herself be comforted. There would be time to argue the point later.

Jason Reed handed a shirt to Maurizio, who put it on, glad to cover his burning shoulders. Then Maurizio bit into one of Old Crone's sandwiches and munched contentedly. It was oozing mayonnaise and chopped ham, and he thought that it was the best thing he had ever tasted.

"What happened?" Jason asked him.

"I haven't the vaguest notion...well that's not strictly true. I suspect that we were right in the epicentre of the earthquake and never had the chance to put those mines in position. I got thrown about, lost my bottles, lost Mei-Ling, and lost consciousness. When I regained my senses, I was in an underground cavern and Mei-Ling was giving me mouth to mouth."

"Better not let Young Chang hear about the mouth to mouth bit. He's got an infernally jealous disposition."

"Do you want to hear the rest?" Maurizio asked, taking another giant bite out of his sandwich, chewing furiously. "We found an underwater passage and swam through to another cavern which had an exit below those rocks, there." He pointed to the highest part of the islet. "This little piece of land must have been pushed up by the quake, and we were lucky to be stranded here."

"What did you do for water?"

"We collected rainwater, and — believe it or not — a case of mineral water was washed up. There were only two bottles left intact, but it seemed miraculous to us."

"Anything else washed up?" Jason asked.

Maurizio glanced at him. "Yea, Curria joined the party."

Jason Reed whistled softly and looked around. "Where is he now? There's no place to hide here."

"We tried to bury him in the sand but gave up after a while. No good digging a grave without a shovel."

"So he's dead?"

"As a door nail. The ship must have been damaged and sunk by the earthquake. I suppose there are going to be other items washed ashore in due course?"

"What about the Minister? What'll I tell her?" Jason Reed pointed to the Minister's wife who was in animated conversation with the Italian Consul.

Maurizio shrugged his shoulders. "He might still turn up somewhere."

Maria Beatriz and Sorciero were shouting and waving at the landing party. They had obviously found something which merited everyone's attention. The party started to trudge through the dune to where Maria Beatriz and Sorciero had started a kind of war dance around a dark patch.

"They've gone demented," the Italian Consul said.

"There's water there," Old Crone cried as she tripped after them in her little black satin slippers.

"Oh no, Ma'am," Maurizio said, "not water, just a little oil well. Can you smell the vapours steaming off it?"

"Sure I can smell it," Jason said, "I wondered what it was." He slapped his knee and laughed. "I'll claim it for the USA ."

"Not a chance, Jason, it's quite definitely Tequilan territory."

They were now all gathered around the bubbling pool of thick, dark liquid and stared at it in awe.

"Is it really, really, oil?" Maria Beatriz whispered.

Jason bent down and dipped his finger in it, tentatively. He rubbed his fingers together, then sniffed them. "No doubt about it, Miz Del Rey," he pronounced.

"What did I tell you, my pretty? I felt there was something good on this here island," Sorciero said.

"Do you know what that means, Sammy?" Maria Beatriz jubilated. "'Tequila' will be rich, we'll build schools and hospitals and skyscrapers ..."

"No skyscrapers, Maria Beatriz, please. You could scrap the Casino and the illegal drugs manufacturing, now that your gross national income will grow to huge proportions," Jason Reed said.

They continued to watch the bubbles which would turn the economy of 'Tequila' around. The Minister's wife dipped her red lacquered toe into the greasy matter.

"It's all very well for some, but what about me? Does that mean that my widow's pension will be increased?"

"We don't even know that the Minister's dead, Ma'm. Isn't it a little early to talk of widow's pensions?" Maria Beatriz sounded aggrieved.

"Nope, he's a goner alright," the Minister's wife crowed, "and don't pretend that you're grieving for your dear brother. It improves your chances of becoming President, doesn't it? Sorciero got the message, that's good enough for me." She looked at Sorciero, who had bent down and picked up a piece of paper which had been dropped by one of the party.

"Got any messages for anybody else, Sorciero?"

"Oh yes, a good message for Mr. Cappucino." He closed his eyes and everybody hushed so as not to disturb his concentration. He spread his arms and cried loudly, "Your woman be coming with your kids, maybe already tomorrow, and there's been a general amnesty for exchange control offences. That's de message."

Maurizio took a step toward him and grabbed hold of his arm. "How did you get that message? Did you read it in the stars?" His voice trembled with excitement. A huge grin broke over Sorciero's face. He handed the piece of paper to Maurizio.

"Nah, Mun, I read it in de fax ... here it is."